Her body tingled with excitement as she realized what she wanted. A kiss—*his* kiss.

She came alive under his touch.

"Have you ever been kissed?" he asked.

"Certainly." Several men had pulled her away from the dancing to steal a kiss.

His words brushed her lips. "What did you think of it?"

"I rather found the dancing more invigorating."

He chuckled. "Did they kiss you like this?"

He dipped to brush his lips gently to hers.

She nodded, thinking he had rather a better hang of it than the others.

"I thought so. That's not how I want to kiss you."

Her body trembled like a plucked violin string as she waited for him to come to her.

"Do you want me to kiss you, Lena?"

A lady would never say yes.

"Yes."

* * *

The Trapper
Harlequin Historical #768—September 2005

Praise for Jenna Kernan

Turner's Woman
"…makes for tip-top reading."
—*Romantic Times*

Winter Woman
"…presents a fascinating portrait of the early days of the West and the extraordinary men and woman who traveled and settled in the area…. Kernan has a knack for writing a solid western with likable characters."
—*Romantic Times*

"*Winter Woman* is an exciting, no holds barred story with unforgettable characters. Ms Kernan's first novel is a winner!"
—*Rendezvous*

"With this strong debut, Jenna Kernan puts her name on the list of writers to watch for and *Winter Woman* may just be the start of a long career."
—*TheRomanceReader.com*

THE TRAPPER

Jenna Kernan

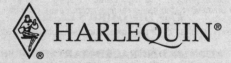

HARLEQUIN®

TORONTO • NEW YORK • LONDON
AMSTERDAM • PARIS • SYDNEY • HAMBURG
STOCKHOLM • ATHENS • TOKYO • MILAN • MADRID
PRAGUE • WARSAW • BUDAPEST • AUCKLAND

ISBN 0-373-29368-2

THE TRAPPER

Copyright © 2005 by Jeannette H. Monaco

This edition published by arrangement with Harlequin Books S.A.

® and TM are trademarks of the publisher. Trademarks indicated with ® are registered in the United States Patent and Trademark Office, the Canadian Trade Marks Office and in other countries.

www.eHarlequin.com

Printed in U.S.A.

Please address questions and book requests to:
Harlequin Reader Service
U.S.: 3010 Walden Ave., P.O. Box 1325, Buffalo, NY 14269
Canadian: P.O. Box 609, Fort Erie, Ont. L2A 5X3

For my mother, who taught me the power of love
and the importance of a good book.

Chapter 1

Fort Union, Missouri River, 1840

"I hate to be the harbinger of bad news, Mr. Price, but the leader of the expedition died of cholera in New Orleans."

Troy Price furrowed his brow, bracing as the first mate of the steamer *Yellow Stone* drew a breath and continued.

"Their ship put them ashore when the first man grew ill. I understand they died quite quickly," said Fairchild.

His party of New York scientists never even made it to St. Louis. So much for his first attempt at guiding easterners. He touched the light pouch that held his dwindling funds. No beaver, no party and no money.

"Thank ye, kindly." He turned to leave the deck of the steamer, *Yellow Stone*, knowing the army had already hired its scouts for the season. Damn.

"Captain Price?"

He paused.

"They aren't all dead. One survived and is still anxious to proceed."

A tiny seedling of hope sprouted. "Where is he?"

Fairchild reddened and then coughed like something was stuck in his craw.

"Maybe you best spit it out."

"Yes, just so. If you'll come with me, I'll introduce you."

Troy followed the man as he strode to the gangplank.

He could not help but notice the woman.

She looked like a green parrot standing amidst a flock of mud hens. The whole world seemed brown by comparison. All about her, on the Missouri River, men unloaded the steamer moving like drones to the direction of the queen bee.

Troy took in the velvet skirts trailing in the river mud. The top half of her dress fit her like a snake's skin, making it impossible to ignore the full swell of her feminine curves contrasted by an impossibly narrow waist. A jolt of awareness hit his gut and burned like good whiskey. Oh, no, he told himself. No white woman, never again. Still his eye followed her, unable to pull free.

Perched on her head was a useless hat that did not even shade her nose from the sun. Her coppery hair was all done up in a style that sent curls dancing about her face when she moved. The ripple of desire quickened his heart rate as his eyes tracked her like prey.

Trailing Fairchild, his attention remained upon her. As he drew near, he studied the woman for some flaw. In his experience, God rarely graced one person with a face to match such a body. But this time He sure made an exception. Those eyes stopped him, bright as a robin's egg and dark-rimmed. Slight smudges beneath her eyes told of sleepless nights and made her seem real. She was younger than he expected from the riches she wore. Freckles dusted her straight nose.

But it was her lower lip that fascinated him. Just beneath and to the left clung a tiny mole.

His escort paused before the object of his fascination. She so distracted him that it took several moments for understanding to sink into his muddled brain. His insides clenched as the rational part of his mind kicked in.

"Now wait just a minute," he said.

Fairchild ignored him, sweeping his hand toward the woman. "Miss Eleanor Hart, may I present Captain Troy Price."

A tiny line formed between her eyebrows.

"Your guide, madam."

Their gazes met. She gaped at him. He did not know what she expected, but clearly he was not it. He tried to push his disappointment aside as her lovely eyes found him lacking. He scowled, gathering his shredded pride.

"O-oh my," she stammered at last.

He had to give her credit. She recovered first, plastering the smile back on her face.

Troy turned to Fairchild. "This is a mistake. I'm leading a party of scientists and artists."

"Miss Hart is the only remaining member of your party. A rather important member who funded this expedition. You must take especially good care of her. She is the daughter of John Hart."

The man said that like he ought to know her pa. His blank expression caused Fairchild to add, "Of Hart Shipping?"

Troy shook his head.

"He's only one of the wealthiest men in America. A giant."

Troy turned from Fairchild to gaze upon this bright butterfly before him. She could not possibly imagine the hardships of traveling upriver. Even if she were prepared, he couldn't guard her without her company of men to help with the task. He ground his teeth together as he admitted the last and truest reason he could not take her.

She was not only white, but from a world of privilege, as different from him as dove from raven. The woman stirred him up from thirty paces and the feelings only got worse with each step in her direction. So he'd best close his gaping mouth and send her packing.

"I don't care who her father is, I'm not toting a lone white woman up the Yellowstone."

The woman spoke to their go-between as if she could not hear him. "This is Mr. Price, my Indian scout?"

Troy lowered his chin as Fairchild nodded.

"I see," she said. "Then I am most happy to meet you, Mr. Price, and I can assure you that you need not be concerned."

The woman had some sense at least to recognize the impossibility of moving upriver alone.

"Glad to hear it," said Troy.

"Because," she added, "I have brought my own mount, you see, and she is quite capable of, how did you put it? 'Toting me' wherever you lead."

Her uppity tone reminded him of how most whites spoke to the Cherokee back in Georgia, condescending and superior. His insides hardened. Apparently her beauty was only on the outside. That made this next part easier.

He did not repeat his mistakes. He would not be tangling with this one. He drew a breath, preparing to cast her off before she had a chance to do the same to him. "What are you doing here?"

"I believe our objectives have been explained to you. If not, I have a copy of the letter you received." She fumbled for a small cloth bag dangling from her wrist.

"You should have turned back at New Orleans when your men all died of sickness."

He noted the lowering of her chin, like a buffalo preparing to charge. "I am *not* turning back."

"I can't help you."

She drew papers from her bag. Her fingers trembled as she unfolded the pages, but when she spoke her tone stayed level. Her voice and body sent opposite signals. Which was the truth, was she frightened or fearless?

"I have here a contract signed by Troy Joseph Price, scout, in which he agrees to lead an expedition west to the Yellowstone Valley departing in July of 1840 from Fort Union and returning in September of said year for the sum of fifty dollars per week. Is this your signature?"

Troy glanced at the even letters and thought of his mother, his first teacher who insisted he learn to read and write both English and Cherokee. She had known he would need both to survive in the white man's world.

"It is."

"Then you already have agreed to take me up the Yellowstone and I am prepared to pay you the agreed upon sum, though your task should be much easier with only one client."

Troy snorted. "Don't be so sure."

Fairchild cleared his throat. "I have duties to attend to. Best of luck on your journey, Miss Hart."

The fellow actually bent to kiss her hand and she let him. Troy imagined kissing her yarn, half gloves would not be too thrilling, though her mouth was tempting enough. The man gave Troy a quick salute and made a hasty retreat up the gangplank. Troy turned back to her. Taking her upriver would be pure torture. She hired him as a competent guide. He'd start acting like it by not leading her into danger.

"I agreed to lead a party of men."

"That's not exactly true. See here, I am listed by name E. Hart, artist." She pointed a slim pink finger from the half gloves showing a carefully manicured nail buffed to a high shine. He made a fist to hide the dirt he knew lay beneath his nails and shifted uncomfortably. She made him feel as dirty as a wallowing hog.

"You tricked me, listing yourself like a man."

She had the decency to drop her gaze for a moment. When she glanced back, she looked as determined as ever. "If you fail to comply with the terms of our agreement, I will sue for damages."

He laughed.

"What are you going take from me, my horse? I got four dollars in my pocket and you can have them right now if you just turn round and get back on that steamer where you belong."

Her cheeks reddened, but she did not give in. He admired

her grit as she drew herself up for a fight. Her change in posture made her bosom swell, and his throat went dry, rendering him speechless. "Such a suit will besmirch your reputation, for who would hire an unreliable guide?"

He folded his arms in refusal and glared.

"I should think leading one person would be quite less trouble."

He laughed. "We have a difference of opinion on how much trouble a woman can be."

She scowled. "Then this is about money. You seek to take advantage of me. Very well, Mr. Price, I shall offer an additional ten dollars to the agreed upon sum per week."

"Not everything is about money, Princess. I ain't for sale."

"Not about money." She gave a dry laugh. "Don't be silly."

He stared at the mole beneath her lip and he forgot what he was saying. She lifted a brow as if vexed and he gathered his shattered wits. He tried reason.

"This is a dangerous route. Without the men to help guard the camp and stand watch, it's impossible. I agreed to lead a party, not shepherd a lone woman. Why don't you head back to your folks before you get us both killed?"

"I can stand watch. I know how to shoot."

He eyed her suspiciously. Having met other Easterners and seen the puny guns they carried, he suspected she hadn't the faintest idea what lay ahead. "What kind of shooting you done?"

"Clay pigeons."

He slapped himself on the forehead. "Target shooting?"

"I'm quite the crack shot." She beamed with pride.

"Here the critters run at you with fangs bared."

He turned away to pace in the mud. His moccasins made a sucking sound as he headed back to her. For his own sanity he must convince her to go home. "You ain't prepared for the Yellowstone. Few men are—a woman…" He shook his head. "Turn back."

She set her jaw and her nostrils flared. For a moment he

thought she would cry. When she spoke, the determination rang clear in her voice.

"I see you are not a man who keeps his word."

That blow landed hard. Unlike many white men of his experience, who signed agreements only to break them, his word was all-important. Until this moment, he'd never come across a situation where he had to go back on it. But she tricked him.

"This is a mistake," he said using a tone that had sent many men scurrying. "You go upriver, you'll live to regret it."

She did not flinch and he admired her for it.

"If you will not take me, then I shall find a guide more agreeable. I am certain for the right price there shall be no shortage of applicants."

A man would be a fool to take her, but for money, men would be foolish. Possible candidates ran through his mind and he cringed.

"Miss Hart, is your family willing to let you go running off with a man you don't know?"

Her cheeks glowed. "That is none of your affair."

He had his answer. They were against it. "What about your reputation? Your pa consent to having you live with a half-breed Cherokee scout for a month? How about we send word downriver and wait for his reply?"

"Your reputation is impeccable. You rescued that missionary woman from the wagon train and did not sully her honor. I'm sure you will treat me with the same respect."

"First, that weren't me, it was Thomas Nash and second, he had to marry that gal after their time together." He let that sink in and then added, "And I'm not the marrying type."

A realization dawned. When they first met she'd called him her Indian scout. That was the title of one of those damned dime novels.

"You read the stories, didn't you?" he asked.

She nodded and he slapped his hat against his leg.

"Damn it. Those are tall tales. I'm not the man in those yarns."

She regarded him with wide blue eyes that were as alluring as the call of a whip-poor-will. She swallowed back her apprehension and he watched the movement of her slender throat. He moved closer, unable to prevent himself from drawing near.

"But you are a man of honor."

"But still a man."

He leaned in, close enough to kiss her and inhaled her scent. His heart raced and he champed at the bit in his desire to touch her skin. Why didn't she move away? Did she want him to kiss her?

"Will you protect me?"

From everything but myself, he thought.

"You don't know one damned thing about me. How can you trust your life to a stranger?"

"If you don't take me I shall choose another."

"Ain't no man fit to be alone with you, including me." He knew the men here. They were rough and deadly. Anyone who had an opportunity elsewhere had already scat. "The men here are wild as wolves."

"Then my fate will be on your conscience."

He drew back. Sweat broke out on his brow. He already carried the death of one woman on his conscience. He could not afford another. His heart turned to ice as he realized he was already responsible for her.

"Please, Mr. Price, I must go upriver."

Her eyes begged him and he felt his resolve slipping. He'd only known the woman a few minutes and already she was wrapping him 'round her finger. He stifled the urge to throw her over his shoulder and carry her back on board the steamer.

"Why's this so important?"

"Have you ever needed to prove yourself, Mr. Price? To show the world that you are more than what they see? I am more and only need a chance to establish it."

That yearning struck a strong chord in his own life. His eyes rounded at her words. But what nonsense was this?

"You've got everything in the world waiting for you back east."

"You say that I know nothing about you. I could say the same. You do not know what awaits me."

"Something worth running from, I imagine."

"And you'd be correct in that assumption."

Now she was staring at *his* mouth. He felt himself growing hard under her consideration. If she could lather him up with only a glance, what might a touch do? He held his breath, trying to rein in his lust. If he didn't do something else quick he'd kiss her right here on the dock. His rescue came from a loud thump beside him.

He stared at the retreating porter and then down at the strangest looking saddle he'd ever laid eyes on. It rested on a crate. One stirrup was missing, but there were two on the other side, though one was all shriveled up and there was a horn where it shouldn't be.

"What the hell is that?"

"My saddle."

"How do you sit in it?"

She pressed her lips together, momentarily concealing her full mouth. "It's a sidesaddle. You sit sideways with one leg over the horn."

Troy pushed his hat back on his head and stared at the strange contrivance. "You can't ride over mountains and across rivers on that. You need a proper saddle."

"That is the only proper saddle for a lady. I'll have you know I've jumped a five-foot fence in that saddle and also won numerous awards for dressage."

"For what?"

"Dressage. It's an exact form of horsemanship. Very difficult."

"More difficult than outrunning a grizzly downhill?"

She arched a coppery brow. "I should doubt it."

"You set off in that silly saddle and you're stuck with it. I ain't buying you another."

"Does that mean you'll take me?"

"I ain't decided yet. What's all this?" He waved at the piles of boxes.

"Most are the belongings of the others." Her head sank and he did see a tear now.

Must have been hard watching them die. Cholera was a bad death. Stole a man's dignity. Although you didn't need to watch a death to have it break your heart. He thought of his family and his chest ached.

"I'm at a loss as to what to do with it."

"Leave it on the steamer and then climb on after it."

She drew herself up, rising only an inch so she just reached his shoulder. "I see. Well, if you will not help me, then kindly stand aside."

His mind urged him to turn away and leave this foolish woman on the docks. Perhaps if he left she would give up. But she seemed stubborn and spoiled enough to try another guide. Then her fate would be on his conscience. He paused in a rare moment of indecision. His heart ached with sorrow.

"Please turn back," he whispered.

"No."

Their gazes locked and he read her determination. An idea came to him, a possibility that gave him a way to keep her safe and still avoid dragging this woman to the Black Hills. She had no notion what life on the trail would demand. Explaining did no good, so he'd let her have a taste. If he just took her out for a few days, she'd give up. He'd bet his bottom dollar, which he was dangerously close to, that she'd quit inside a week. She'd beg him to bring her back to St. Louis and he would be happy to comply.

He studied her beautiful face. The only question was could he keep his hands off her until she quit? He mustered his resolve.

"Then I will be your guide, Miss Hart."

He nearly laughed at the suspicion reflecting in her eyes. "Why the turnabout, Mr. Price?"

"Like you said, I signed them papers. So, I'll take you as far as you'd like, but I don't expect traveling wild will be to your liking."

"I disagree. I should say it will be the experience of a lifetime."

He grinned imagining her riding all day in that saddle. "Surely it will be that."

The clatter of nervous hooves brought Troy spinning around. A small white horse danced on the end of a silken lead line afraid to cross the planking. The handler faced the beast and tugged ineffectively on the rope.

"What kind of an idiot brought a white horse out here?"

Eleanor Hart stepped up beside him. "This idiot."

Chapter 2

Miss Eleanor Hart faced the scout with chin raised, belying the quivering bowl of jelly that seemed to have replaced her stomach. Only years of rigorous training on deportment, coupled with the structural assistance of her corset, kept her upright before him. Her mother would be mortified to see all her elocution lessons represented so poorly. No man besides her stern, judgmental father had ever caused her to stammer and none had caused her breath to catch. But this one terrified and fascinated in equal measures.

He studied her horse now, giving Eleanor a moment to study him.

Troy Price. The man the dime novels described as compact and low to the ground. Wily as a fox—a noble representative of the dusky people of the forest. Her memory flashed to the black-and-white etchings of the famous Indian scout from her coveted collection of books. This man was not dusky or compact, leaving her unsure if she should feel disappointed or elated.

Low to the ground? He towered over her and was striking enough to stop traffic on Fourteenth Street. His skin was tanned the color of ground cinnamon, not red at all. His gray eyes surprised her greatly, as she expected deep brown. His hair was dark but showed a distinct wave. Didn't all Indians have straight black hair?

She studied his profile searching for the hawkish nose of an Indian and found the elegant tapered one instead. He glanced her way and again her stomach fluttered. It must be nerves. She was just excited to finally meet the legend. That was surely why her heart pounded and her throat went dry.

The porter cleared his throat.

"Oh, I'm so sorry," she said and accepted the lead line from the man.

Scheherazade nickered and Eleanor rubbed the horse's nose. Mud splattered her horse's silver-white legs, but there was no helping it. Yesterday's downpour had drenched the prairie. The violence of the jagged, tearing streaks of light and the explosive thunder here in the West frightened Eleanor nearly witless.

She glanced at the scout once more. When he stood so close a moment ago, she thought she'd faint from the sheer excitement of his presence. He made her all mixed-up inside.

Did he know how handsome he was?

He studied her horse.

"Looks like a damned pony."

She sighed. It seemed this expedition was destined to be a fight from start to finish. She had thought nothing could prove more difficult than convincing her father. Even the pledge of his dear and trusted friend, Mr. Thornton, who had assured him that she would remain at the fort and do nothing more dangerous than lift a paintbrush, had failed to move him. Her scout's refusal had come as a shock, as had his final acceptance, which had only come when she had threatened to seek another guide. What had changed his mind? Pride, likely. Men set a great store by their pride.

What would her father say if he knew she was now without escort, maid or lady's companion?

She trembled to think of the row. Her father was a shouter,

only in private of course, but his voice could shake the crystals on the chandeliers when he got on a tear. But he was not here to dictate. For the first time in her life, she was free.

Her father would arrive in September to collect his daughter and to trophy hunt. Until then, she made the decisions.

The trapper waited, making no attempt to assist her as she struggled in the infernal mud in her ruined shoes. This man urged her to turn back as well.

Having read all his adventures, she expected someone more gallant. According to *Troy Price, Mountain Man,* when defending Miss Massy Alstine and her daughters, he had shouted at the eleven attacking savages, "Shoot me if you dare, but you shall not sully these righteous women save through me."

Wasn't she a damsel in distress?

He did not speak at all as the man in the stories. Still, he was the most famous of all the mountain men. Dear Mr. Thornton, God rest him, set him in high regard, after she brought Price to his attention. She cast a sideways glance at her scout.

Clad entirely in buckskin, he wore a savage string of jagged fangs about his neck. Mud covered his leggings and spattered his back. His wide hat now shadowed his rugged features. At a time when most men wore beards, Mr. Price's cheeks were strangely bare of even the bushy sideburns now so fashionable. Perhaps Indians did not grow beards.

She leaned in to study his cheek, detecting some stubble, and he stared at her, brows lowering over his gray eyes, before he stepped back.

Why did he so dislike white horses? They were all the rage. Her father had gone to considerable expense to send the Arabian mare along, much to her relief. The thought of riding a strange mount after so many years of training with Scheherazade had caused her considerable distress.

Price laid a large hand upon her horse's neck and stroked.

Eleanor's stomach twitched in a most unexpected fashion and she could not seem to draw her gaze away from his dark fingers meshed in her mount's white coat.

"What kind of horse is it?"

"She's Arabian."

He made no response and his expression remained unchanged.

She tried again. "From Egypt."

Her hand came to rest upon the horse's withers.

"She fast?"

"Oh, exceedingly."

"Good, 'cause I imagine every Indian from here to the Pacific will be itching to steal that horse."

She glanced at the finely bred mare. It never occurred to her that someone would try to forcibly take her horse. "I thought such a crime was punishable by death."

"Who's gonna hang 'em—you?" He shook his head in obvious disgust.

Clearly he had no confidence in either her or her mount. But she would prove him wrong on both counts.

"We will be alone out there. Do you understand? No law, no hotels. Just you and me and thousands of thieving Indians, bad-tempered buffalo and vicious bears. We have to defend ourselves, feed ourselves and protect what is ours, or I should say, I have to."

Apprehension stirred 'round and 'round within her like a spoon in a teacup. She had never been anywhere in her life where help of all kinds was not within immediate call. She had maids and tutors, physicians and dressmakers. Could she do this?

She weighed her fears against her desire to be a part of John James Audubon's new undertaking. To have her paintings included in *The Quadrupeds of North America* would be such a feather in her cap and the opportunity had already cost her dearly. She pushed aside thoughts of the promise she gave to her father to secure his consent. The chance to be recognized as a noteworthy painter was worth any price.

For the better part of a year she had prepared herself for this journey. She rode daily before departure and trained in fencing and marksmanship, not to mention the trips to the country where she stayed with only one maid in her father's hunting lodge and learned to start a fire using a tinderbox.

She tied her mare to the metal handle of a large crate containing Mr. Tull's bell jars for collecting live botanical specimens. When she lifted her gaze from her horse to Mr. Price, she found him aiming another frown in her direction. Did the man have any other expression?

"Still going?" he asked.

"I remain resolute."

"That mean yes?"

She gave a quick nod.

"What is so all-fired important about drawing pictures of a few critters?"

Her hand pressed to her breast and she drew a gasp. "Have you not seen Audubon's *American Ornithological Biography*?"

"Who?"

"James Audubon, the most important painter and naturalist of our generation."

"Never met him."

"Well, you shall. He is coming west next year. Through my father's connection to his engraver, Mr. Robert Havell, I have secured Mr. Audubon's agreement to consider my work for his next collection. After this venture, I will have the opportunity to present my best paintings. If they are top drawer, I feel certain I will win him over."

"How does your pa know Havell?"

"He only owns the publishing house in which Mr. Havell is employed."

"And this other feller Audubon needs Havell to make his book?"

"Havell is the finest engraver in London. He couldn't do without him."

"Then I'd say you could paint just about anything you like. No reason to leave Fort Union."

Eleanor drew herself up in indignation. "I will have you know, Sir, that I will win this commission on my own merit."

He laughed in her face. Her cheeks heated and she knew they flamed with her embarrassment. How dare he?

"You never done a thing in your whole life on merit, Miss Hart, and you and I both know it."

Unshed tears stung her eyes, but she stood toe-to-toe with him, as pride and shame warred within her. It was obvious to even this stranger that without her family's influence, she was nothing. Somehow she managed to force the words past the lump in her throat.

"What you say is quite true, Mr. Price. Every opportunity I have had was given to me by virtue of my birth and nothing is expected of me save that I produce an 'heir and a spare.' But I want to produce paintings and I want them judged on their own worth."

He nodded his reluctant acceptance of this. How she admired him, this independent man who came and went as he wished. Free as a bird, he was. Did he appreciate the rareness of such a gift?

A wiry little porter dropped another crate before them.

"These all yours?" Vexation returned to his voice.

"They are."

"You do realize there ain't no steamers from here out? We have to haul this folderol across the prairie by mule."

"These packages are not trifles, Mr. Price. I have carefully planned each aspect of this journey and included only the bare essentials."

A second porter deposited a yellow hatbox before them and Price's brow lifted as if to say. "Oh really?"

He folded his arms across his chest. "You can keep only what fits on two mules. I'll have another for my gear."

"That's impossible."

"Then we don't go."

"Mr. Price, I can buy us all the mules we need." She extended her reticule and gave a shake. The distinctive sound of the coins jangled.

He hissed at her. "Put that away. Do you want someone to slit your throat for that bag?"

Her hand drew to her collar. "Would they?"

He flashed her a look of pure exasperation. "Men here are out of work. They're desperate. Then you dance in here with bags of money, expensive gear, a damned white horse no bigger than a pony and no man to protect you. Why don't you hang a sign round your neck that says, 'Rob me'?"

"I'm sorry."

"Don't make my job harder than it is."

"I only wanted you to know that I can afford to buy additional mounts, hire servants and cooks."

"With Daddy's money." His hard look pierced her like an arrow. "That what you call your own merit—hiring servants to cater to you?"

"Well, we have to have servants."

He laughed.

"Look around you. Men here are trappers, hunters and traders. We don't have servants."

"What about a lady's maid?"

"You're the only lady here."

Her stomach hardened to a little knot. Her next word came out in a whisper. "Only?"

He nodded his head.

"You beginning to see what you stepped into? This is a wild place and yet the most civilized spot you'll find unless you turn around and head downriver."

She fisted her hands. "No."

"Well then. I can only guard, feed and care for five animals."

She studied her things with a sinking feeling, knowing she would lose more than half the lot. "Are you certain this is necessary?"

"Only if you still want to go."

"What about hiring other men?"

He glanced downriver. "The good ones are already gone. I don't fancy the others, not if I want to sleep at night."

She glanced about the riverbank with a different eye and saw men idle and predatory. One particularly filthy fellow grinned at her, showing rotting front teeth. He lifted his chin and he drew his index finger beneath his jaw like a blade. Then blew her a kiss. A flash of terror struck her in the stomach like a blow. The whalebone in her corset suddenly seemed overly tight, as her breathing grew erratic. Spots danced before her and she knew she must sit.

Her fan waved as she tried vainly to recover herself.

"Great God, almighty. You fixing to faint?"

She could only nod as the ground tipped.

His fingers encircled her waist and he swore. "What the devil is this?"

Colors blurred and dimmed. She blinked her eyes and focused on the sky. In what seemed only an instant, she somehow came to lie upon her back. Wisps of clouds drifted along like boats on a blue river.

The scout loomed over her, blotting out the sun. She startled, then stared at his handsome face. Mr. Gallagher, one of the party members, had been an expert in physiognomy. What would he have said about this man's temperament and character based on his physical features? His long wavy hair revealed nothing, but she longed to see if the strands felt as silky soft as they appeared. He had a well-built jaw, that told of strength of character.

"And a Roman nose means determination," she said.

"You awake?" he asked.

Was his cheek smooth to the touch? She reached up and stroked his face. He jerked back as if burned. His gray eyes bored into hers and he dragged his hat from his head, waving it before her face. The fresh air smelled faintly of wood smoke and revived her to the point that she realized she lay flat on her back in the river mud with her head in his lap.

"My dress!" She lurched forward and saw her sleeves coated with the grime. Oh, and no maid to clean them. "I must find a laundress."

He laughed. "You're still out of your head."

He gripped her arm until she regained her equilibrium. Then she noted that every button on the front of her gown was undone and her corset strings were sliced.

She gaped at her chemise dipping dangerously low over her bosom and then at him. He squatted before her with a look of puzzlement upon his face.

"You—you cad!"

Shoving with all her might, she managed to push him to his hindquarter and had a moment's satisfaction as she scrambled to her feet.

"How dare you undress me in public?"

"In public?" He stood, rising tall before her.

Mud coated his leggings from his waist to his strange hide slippers. She tugged to close her dress, but as he had released her corset she could no longer fasten the middle buttons.

"Oh, my goodness. See what you've done?"

"You couldn't breathe. That thing was cutting off your air."

"Of course. How else could a lady fit into her dresses?"

He rubbed his forehead as if he suddenly had a headache. "Sew 'em so they fit."

"These do fit." She scrambled in her trunk and drew out a scarf, wrapping it about the opening at her waist.

"I look perfectly ridiculous, thanks to you."

She wobbled as she closed the box.

"Them trapping's ridiculous all on their own. You didn't need no help from me."

"How dare you?" Eleanor spun to face him and slipped in the mire at her feet.

His hand gripped her elbow. The heat of his touch traveled up her arm and down her spine as he leaned close.

"You'd be amazed at what I've dared."

Frightened that this contact brought such unexpected emotions, she shook him off.

"Don't touch me."

His hand slid away but he remained close. "Only reason you ain't wearing a mud hat right now is because I caught you."

Her face heated as guilt flashed through her. He'd done what he could to help, extreme though his ministrations were. In his rough way, he had restored her to full health only to have her spit at him like a wet kitten.

"Is it fair to say you are unfamiliar with the company of women?"

"The way you mean it, I guess so."

She didn't understand his comment.

"I thank you for your assistance."

He pushed back his hat and stared. At last he spoke. "Welcome."

"Perhaps we should try once more. I will allow you to dispose of the property of the others as you see fit and sort my belongings as well. But I must have my drawing equipment."

He nodded. "Deal."

"And you must agree not to cut away my clothing. It is simply not done."

"You weren't breathing right."

"I shall loosen my corset strings. Agreed?"

"I'd do it again."

She studied his nose. Perhaps instead of determination, the equine slant meant stubbornness. What of those full lips? They were too beautiful for a man, as were his thick black eyelashes. With his hat pushed back she noted the mahogany shine of his hair. Her fingers itched for her watercolor brushes.

"You have lovely hair."

He blinked at her. "You sure you're all right?"

"Certainly. How do we proceed?"

"You walk on over to the fort and get a room."

"That sounds like an acceptable arrangement. Will you be staying at the fort?"

"I sleep outdoors."

"If you need a lodging, I can provide for you."

A flush spread up his neck and she recognized too late that she had inadvertently insulted him again.

"Let's get this straight. I provide for you, not t'other way 'round."

"Of course."

He shook his head. She waited for him to extend his arm but he only stared at her as if expecting her to faint again.

"Will you escort me?"

"I will if you want all your gear took."

She leaned forward. "You mean we should not leave it unattended?"

"You're a real quick study."

Uncertainty curled within her, but she would not let it show. The vile men still lurked about the dock and she could not seem to leave the protection of her surly guide. She summoned up her flagging courage and nodded.

"Ahh. Well then, I shall endeavor to obtain lodgings for myself. It should be none too difficult." She lifted her purse and he grabbed her wrist. She felt the restrained strength of his grip clear down to her toes as her arm hung suspended in the air. She could not move. His iron hold caused not the slightest discomfort, like a well-trained pointer gripping his prey without piercing the skin. Her father called that having a "soft mouth."

She glanced up. This man had a soft mouth in the literal

sense and she found herself staring boldly up at him again. Wherever were her manners?

"Don't jangle those coins. Good God, didn't your folks teach you nothing?"

"Anything."

"What?"

"Didn't they teach me anything?"

"That's what I just asked you."

She sighed. "I have to pay for the room."

"No, you don't. I do. Folks take one look at you and charge double."

He released her wrist. Her skin tingled where his warmth still lingered. She rubbed the spot to regain her equilibrium.

"Then shall I pay you?"

"Later. And stick that purse someplace safe."

"Where?"

"I don't know, beneath your skirts or inside that armor plating you wear."

"That is not armor. This particular corset is whalebone."

He looked horrified. "Whale?"

"The very best," she assured him.

"Tarnation. Why would you strap bones around your middle?"

She smiled at his lack of refinement. "To give a woman the proper shape."

Now he smiled. "I've seen you without it and there ain't nothing wrong with your shape."

"Mr. Price!"

Her guide grasped her elbow. "Enough talk. Let's go."

Chapter 3

Eleanor faced her first go at independence with clacking teeth. Now that she actually stood on her own two feet, she found her knees wobbled as she approached the gates of the Fort Union. A few moments ago her guide had sent her on ahead with only a young porter as escort. The dirty fellow trudged along behind her, inspiring not the slightest confidence.

All about her, men came and went and she did, indeed, appear to be the only white woman within miles. Never in her life had she felt more out of place. Even standing in her mud-caked attire, she was badly overdressed. She followed the porter to the office where he left her to stand in the mud like a street urchin. Finally he emerged and then guided her across the courtyard.

Here, she came upon her first Indian. There was Mr. Price, of course, but he did not dress the part, nor did he share the features of this dark-skinned savage. The man before her wore only a loincloth and his bronze skin gleamed over sinew and muscles in the late July heat.

She had seen Indians along the shore from the safety of the steamer, of course, but now one walked past her and stared boldly. Her fingers itched to grab her brushes but self-preservation intervened and she instead grabbed the gaping collar of her ruined dress in an effort to draw it completely closed.

"What tribe are these Indians?" she asked the porter.

"All tribes. They come here to trade."

"Don't they fight?"

"On occasion. Mostly they wait until they are clear of the walls or they aren't welcomed back."

"Could you arrange for an Indian to sit for me? I am a painter."

There, she had said it as if it were true. If only she were. She could be, if given half a chance.

The porter did not question her, but nodded.

"That's no trouble, miss."

He left her at the door with no key. She discovered the facilities did include a sturdy bolt within, at least. Alone inside the primitive room, she waited as her belongings arrived, carried by men who merely dropped their loads and departed. She took a moment to repair her hair and remove the mud from her skin before attempting to change her clothing. She struggled to near exhaustion with her corset achieving less than satisfactory results. Twisting like a contortionist, she managed to fasten a row of hook and eyes at her side. Since she had lost her maid in New Orleans, she could no longer manage the dresses that closed in the back.

Reassembled at last, she recovered her painting equipment.

Unfettered by social responsibilities for the first time in memory, she anxiously began her life as an artist. A boy brought the first model.

As the day was bright and mild, she set her easel in the yard before her room, thus casting her subject and her work in full light.

The child said the Indian's name was Wind Dancer and he expected only a penny for his time. The man spoke some English and was a member of a tribe called Sioux.

He stood dressed in a buckskin shirt, leggings, a loincloth and beaded leather slippers. The area between his loins and the tops of his leggings was quite naked, revealing a well-muscled hip. This was the nearest she'd yet come to a nude study and excitement at the prospect made her hand tremble. Her graphite pencil flew across the page.

In a few minutes she completed several preliminary sketches. As was her habit, she dropped these pages from the easel, letting them lie about her feet on the compacted earth. She posed him for several more quick renditions. He stood very still, impressing her with his strength and control.

Her one concern was the man's habit of staring directly at her. His stern expression and piercing gaze rattled her quite more than she cared to admit. She had read James Fenimore Cooper, but rather thought these Indians were not of the same mold.

Three of the sketches lay at her feet as she brushed her hand over her current work, smudging the line to create a shadow. At last a gentle breeze touched her neck, cooling her.

"I'm finished now, Mr. Wind Dancer. If you know any other Indians who are willing to sit quietly for a time, I would appreciate you referring them."

The breeze lifted one drawing from the pile. The page seemed to dance across the distance separating them and stopped just upon the man's right foot.

He stooped gracefully, gathered the errant drawing and studied her work.

"I'm especially interested in Chiefs in full regalia. Head-dresses, feathers, your finest clothing. You understand?"

He nodded. "Yes."

She stood, leaving the last drawing on her easel, and then retrieved a penny from her reticule. "Here you are."

He lifted the drawing. "I take."

It wasn't very good, just a quick sketch to warm up. In fact she did not like the result. "I'd prefer not. That one, well, it's lacking."

"I take."

He seemed determined.

"Very well, then. Thank you." She extended the coin but he held up his palm in refusal.

Wind Dancer turned to go, pausing at Troy's approach. Her guide strode toward them scowling darkly.

The man lifted his hand and Price did the same. What followed was a series of odd gestured exchanges that seemed like conversation between the two men. Finally the Indian left, his new drawing rolled and thrust in his belt.

"You know that man is a war council leader for Charging Buffalo?" asked her guide.

"I did not." Nor did she know what a war council was or who Charging Buffalo might be, but she rather thought she'd exposed enough ignorance to him already. An adage sprang to mind. Better to remain silent and be thought a fool, than to speak and remove all doubt.

Troy moved to the easel and studied her work. She resisted the urge to throw a handkerchief over the drawing. Instead she hovered with clenched hands knowing that his opinion should not matter, but waited eagerly for it all the same.

When he turned his gaze to her, he seemed astonished. He looked back at her painting and then to her again. Disbelief changed to an expression she thought might be respect. That gave her pause, having never been looked at by a man in that way. With indulgence—surely. Amusement? Often. But respect—no, this was something new.

"Looks just like him."

She basked in his approval. "Thank you."

"Know what this is?" He pointed to her rendition of the circle of painted leather decorated with long strands of animal hair held in the man's left hand.

"I assume it is some kind of musical instrument related to a drum."

"Well, you assume wrong. That there is the man's medicine shield."

"A shield—of leather? That wouldn't even stop a stone."

"The Sioux set great store by their shield and the medicine bundle in the center. They believe that bundle and symbols on their shield protect them from their enemies."

"That's not medicine, it's some primitive superstition."

His eyes twinkled. "Ever wear a cross for protection?"

She stiffened. "That is completely different."

"Wouldn't stop a stone." He smiled at her then, pointed at her painting. "See this here is hair?"

Fascinating, the knowledge he held. She leaned in to study her own drawing.

"Buffalo?"

His smile was wicked. "I'd say more likely Crow."

"Crows? The accoutrements were definitely not feathers."

"Not the bird, the tribe. That's hair from their enemies, killed in battle, a most powerful medicine."

He stood waiting, his expression placid until understanding dawned. Her knees went first. He clutched her elbow and guided her to the chair. Her rump hit hard as she fought down a wave of nausea. She recalled the disks of leather, no bigger than a silver dollar, and the long black hair that hung from each. She had assumed it was buffalo and thought the decor very charming in a rustic way.

"Scalps?" she whispered.

He nodded. "So, I'd say you best be more careful about who you paint."

She nodded. "Yes. I'll be more careful."

"You hungry?"

Eleanor realized that she had not eaten since this morning on the steamer. She glanced at the sky, surprised to find that she'd spent the entire afternoon sketching. Her work always made her lose all track of time. The queasiness dissolved as the walls of her stomach rumpled together demanding sustenance.

"Famished," she admitted.

He took her to a crude little lodge in the center of the fort that seemed to be some kind of storage room on one side and tavern on the other. Stacks of furs and kegs of beer filled tables and lined the walls. The reek of stale beer mingled with tobacco as she searched the haze. Opposite the goods, several long tables stood on a dirt floor. It was for the tables that her guide steered.

"We certainly aren't going to eat here," she said, catching her breath at the stench of unwashed bodies.

"Why not?"

"Why it's dirty and smells abominable. I wouldn't dare eat here for fear of being poisoned. Please take me somewhere else."

"Glad to, Princess. Nearest place is just downriver in St. Louis."

She folded her arms across her bosom in a posture her mother absolutely loathed, saying it showed the world her stubborn nature.

"This is the only eatery in Fort Union?" Her voice challenged, suspecting a trick.

"Only grub here comes out of the kitchen behind this room."

"What about the steamer?"

"Unloaded and on its way back to St. Louis without you."

She took in the sweeping realization that she was stuck in this miserable little fort and swayed on her feet.

He grasped her elbow, guiding her to a bench, and plunked her down on the seat with enough force to make her teeth rattle.

Then he left her, returning with a plate of beans adorned with a grizzled piece of bacon fat and a chipped tin cup filled with black coffee. For utensils he brought only a wooden spoon.

An odd sense of unreality crashed through her mind. How could men possibly live in such primitive conditions?

"Change your mind, Princess?"

He sounded so sure of her surrender. The glint in his eye confirmed her supposition.

She sat up straight at the challenge in his voice and accepted the utensil. She lifted a spoonful, opened her lips, closed her eyes and swallowed, certain she would be sick. The beans tasted of molasses and she found the smoky flavor odd, but not unpleasant. Still, what might so many beans do to her digestion? She reached for the coffee.

"Cream and sugar?" she asked hopefully.

His grin never wavered. "Fresh out."

She sighed and lifted the scalding brew. She recognized the meal as the test it was. More disturbing than the food was the company. As they ate, the room slowly filled with men. They hovered by the doors and on the benches along the walls watching. Their intent, predatory gazes lifted the small hairs on her neck.

She glanced from the observers back to her guide.

"They won't bother you none." His quiet voice exuded a confidence she found contagious.

She met his steady gaze and knew that despite his attempts to frighten her, he would allow no real harm. That realization gave her peace that lasted only until they left the tavern or whatever one called such a place.

He guided her by the elbow in a loose grip that allowed the illusion of freedom while maintaining control.

"I have to buy supplies tomorrow."

"Certainly, how much money do you need?"

"Did you bring mules?"

"Why, no. Only my horse and saddle."

He scratched beneath his hat. "Mules is dear. You got a rifle?"

"Yes."

"Mules is fifteen dollars each. I got one, but you need two. Pack saddles will run another five. For the rest, ten dollars ought to cover it. That's forty-five dollars all told." He sat back and smiled as she took in the figure as if expecting the sum would send her back to New York.

She delivered *three* twenty-dollar gold pieces to his hand.

"If you need more, please ask. I have plenty."

He stared down at coins glinting in the last remaining rays of sun. She did not understand the dark expression that blackened his features.

"What's wrong?"

"They look new."

She smiled. "Gold always looks new. That is part of its allure."

He fisted the coins as if he meant to squeeze them to death, before he regained control of her elbow.

"My father says they are digging it up by the fistful in Georgia. Isn't that wonderful? Gold—just popping from the ground like dahlias."

He scowled. "Is that all you care about—gold?"

"Well, it does make life easier."

"Not for those who owned the land. Besides, life ain't supposed to be easy. You want easy? You should have stayed home."

She nodded. "I see your point. All the comforts make life less immediate, is that it?"

"You and I have different ideas about life."

He steered her toward her room. As they crossed the courtyard she noticed men lingering in the shadows.

Troy continued on and she glanced up to be sure he saw them. The grim set of his jaw told her he did.

Four Indians sat before her door.

"What do they want?" she whispered, unable to keep from huddling against his arm and clamping her hands upon the fringed leather of his shirt.

"Let's find out."

Troy paused before the group and secured the release of his arm from her, then began signing to the men.

"They all want you to draw their picture."

He turned back to the men gesturing again. After a long exchange the men departed.

"See the can of worms you opened?"

She pressed a hand to her heart and felt the desperate flutter of a trapped bird.

He drew a long sigh. "I knew you were trouble the first time I set eyes on you, but I misjudged how much."

"Will they come back?"

"Oh yeah, first thing tomorrow. So for good or ill you got your models, more than you'll ever need. I reckon there'll be a whole passel of them waiting on you come morning." He dragged his hat from his head. "I got things to do tomorrow, mules and packs. Damn it. I'll have to hire a man to sit here with you."

She did not argue, suddenly feeling frightened at the prospect of facing so many savages. What if they didn't like her work? Somehow she thought a bad review from these men would be much more disastrous than one in the Post.

He thrust her into her room. Before she had time to object to his rough treatment he spoke.

"Stay inside and don't answer the door or say a word unless you hear it's me, understand? I'll be back after daybreak."

She nodded and he closed the door in her face.

"Good night to you, too, Mr. Price."

His voice came from beyond the heavy door. "Bolt it."

She did.

All night she tossed, imagining one of her models clutching a hatchet and thrusting his fingers into her hair. A man in war paint beat a drum decorated with human scalps. The pounding rhythm went on and on until she thought she'd go mad.

Eleanor sat up in bed. Sunlight flooded the room and the drumbeat changed to an insistent knock at her door.

"Hart! Open this door or I'll bust it down."

She blinked. Where was she? A sweeping glance about the rough-hewn beams on the ceiling and she remembered. Fort Union, the trading post.

"I'm coming."

The pounding ceased. She slid from the bed and grasped her wrap, drawing it closed before she released the bolt on the door.

"What took you so long?" Her scout's scowl dissolved into a dumbfounded stare. His gaze raked her hair, which lay in a loose braid upon her white morning robe. She knew he could see nothing but her toes, but still her cheeks flamed under his scrutiny and her skin tingled from scalp to heel. No one ever looked at her like that. The raw power of his gaze curled her toes.

"You look like a bride," he said, sounding astonished at her everyday attire.

She gripped the closed front of her wrap. "This is an ordinary nightdress and cover, Mr. Price."

"Awful fancy duds just for sleeping. You just rising? Lord, the sun's been up a full hour."

"I didn't sleep well. Nightmares." She was about to say of Indians, when a russet-colored face popped up behind Troy's back. Streaks of sienna lined one cheek and a white dot marked the center of his chin. She screamed.

Troy grabbed her arm and pushed her back into the room.

"What's wrong with you?"

She pointed. "An Indian."

"Course. I told you they'd be waiting. They been there hours already."

"They?"

"Fifteen so far, all dressed for war like you asked. You got Crow, Pawnee, one Oto, two Chippewa and a group of Cree. Draw them together and you can get rid of them faster. Scared the sentries near to death 'til I explained it."

She quaked in his arms from fear and then from the nearness of him. Every time he touched her she trembled. Her reaction was unfathomable. Never in her life had she experienced anything like it.

"They just want you to draw them. Word's out. Your pictures have power."

Her breast swelled with pride as she absorbed his compliment. Others had called her paintings precise and detailed, but no one ever called her work powerful.

In slow degrees his arms collected her and her stomach gave a frantic flutter of excitement. She needed to get away from him before she made an absolute idiot of herself. Instead, she stepped forward and clung to his middle like a child.

He stiffened and her grip tightened.

"I'm afraid of them."

One big hand came down on the center of her back, radiating confidence. "They ain't wild animals. They're men, like all men, no better or worse. Besides, I got a friend to protect you. Name's Black Feather, he's Sioux. Only asks that you paint him first and then he will watch over you." He stepped back and she was forced to release him or be dragged.

"You want to be a painter or not?"

Reluctantly, she let him go. Her breasts and belly tingled in a most surprising way. When she glanced up, she saw his face looked flushed. What was happening here?

"I'll get him."

"Wait." She grasped his arm to stop him from departing. "Are you sure it will be all right?"

"I wouldn't leave you if I thought they'd be trouble."

She gazed up into the certainty of his confident gray eyes and released his sleeve.

"Mr. Price, do you really think my paintings are powerful?"

"You misunderstand me. Wind Dancer told the others how the wind carried your picture to him. He calls you medicine woman and thinks your work has magic."

"Oh, but that's not true. You have to tell them this isn't magic. It could injure them in some way. Please tell them."

"I tried. There's no reasoning with them. Best just to paint as many as you can."

"I need coffee and a moment to dress."

"I'll have the cook send over a tray." He motioned to someone she could not see. "Let me introduce you to Black Feather."

"I'm in my nightdress."

"He won't mind."

Troy stepped outside and reappeared a moment later with a man who looked dangerous and fierce. This is how an Indian should look, dark and savage.

"You can't leave me with him," she whispered from the side of her mouth as she tried to smile at the villain.

"Why not?"

"He looks…" She paused, considering what to say that would not insult Troy, who was Indian as well. "Does he speak English?"

"He understands it."

"Well, why doesn't he speak?"

"Just his way, is all."

"Why should I trust him?"

"I saved his life."

She gave him a doubtful look, wondering what that had to do with the matters at hand. She drew a deep breath and felt no better until she gazed at him. His eyes asked for her trust.

"All right."

"Get dressed. He'll be waiting." Troy led Black Feather from the room.

She bolted the door, leaning heavily against the planking. What had she gotten herself into?

Chapter 4

Troy left Eleanor's door and walked past the line of men all dressed in ceremonial regalia. The scent of bear grease, tanned leather and tobacco filled the air. Halfway across the yard he paused to lift his buckskin shirt to his nose and sniffed. The scent of roses clung to him, as she had clung, invading his senses and intoxicating his mind.

She was frightened. That was all. The woman only needed his protection. The task of keeping her safe filled his belly with chips of ice. He had failed with Rachel. His heart beat fast. *She is not Rachel. You won't fail again.*

He continued on his way, his feet carrying him forward as his mind cast back for images of hope to keep him from his black despair. His mind clasped onto visions of Eleanor dressed in angel white. A nightgown? He'd been to several weddings where the bride had nothing so fine as this woman's sleeping robes. With her hair barely contained in a loose braid and that puffy white fabric floating about her like a cloud, it was all he could do not to scoop her into his arms and toss her onto her unmade bed. But she didn't want him that way. To her, he was not a man, he was an Indian.

Even if she did want him, he knew from experience what her world thought of such a coupling and what could happen as a result. His lips formed a grim line as he continued along, praying that she would not be long in his keeping. His reaction to Eleanor frightened him nearly as much as the possibility of repeating his past mistakes.

His stomach tightened as he considered his dilemma. Even from three paces he had felt her heat. Toes pale and narrow had peeked from beneath her hem. Then she had thrown herself into his arms. Through that thin fabric, he had felt each soft curve and warm hollow. Not like last night when she had huddled against his arm like a timid fawn. Then the stiff cage of bones she wore about her ribs had shielded her lush curves. He'd like to free her from that cage.

This woman hit him with such raw need he could barely think. He swallowed back his desire, now burning hot like the coal in a forge.

She said she wanted to stand on her own two feet and be judged on her own merit. He understood that desire. He'd come west to do much the same, thinking to find a place where men were judged on their deeds. He'd succeeded in that he hadn't died or been maimed by a grizzly and he'd built himself a reputation as a good trapper. But he had failed, too, he thought, jangling his nearly empty purse and thinking of his family. The beaver was gone and he needed to find a new path to survive. His fingers searched the inside of the soft hide pouch until he clutched the gold pieces she'd given him.

Did these shiny new coins come from beneath the feet of his people? The urge to throw the money away raged against practicality. He dropped the coins back into his pouch and continued along. He would take Miss Hart on her little adventure and then return her where she belonged. Where did he belong?

In his wanderings, Rachel's ghost seemed to haunt him. He braced against the waterfall of grief that still washed through him when he remembered the tragedy his love for her had caused.

In his sorrow, he'd run until the land ceased and he had stood on the pacific shores. From a ship's captain there, he'd learned of his people's eviction from their homes. The only home he'd ever had was gone with those he loved.

Troy crossed the yard. As he passed the office, the owner of the post leaped from his doorway like a badger from his burrow.

"Mr. Price. These Indians, I must insist they be dispersed."

Troy shot him a look that sent the man back several paces. "Who's stopping ya?"

"Miss Hart is your responsibility."

"She didn't call 'em." The two faced off a moment before the trader dropped his gaze and Troy continued. "If you're asking my opinion, I'd say it's more dangerous to move them."

He turned the conversation to the matter of storing the woman's gear until his return and changing the gold pieces into silver, glad to be rid of the evil metal. He hated gold. It turned men into savages. He prayed that gold would never again be found under the feet of another tribe. Such a discovery was nothing but a death warrant, signed and sealed.

He headed to the livery to purchase mules and check on his big buckskin gelding named for his home, Dahlonega, Georgia.

Home no longer. His jaw clenched as he pulled his rage deep inside himself. Jackson hated the Cherokee, but he loved their land. Three hundred years his people had lived beside the whites. They understood their ways, but not well enough to save them when gold was found in the ground beneath their corn.

Did the white families who now owned his farm ever think of their neighbors driven out in the dead of winter? He remembered Rachel's family, back before the accident. He pictured Rachel by the stream between their homes running into the forest to meet him, begging him to keep their secret just a little longer until one day she could no longer hide the truth.

He had offered to make her his wife, but she had said there was no place in this world for such a pair. He had pointed to his parents' example and told her they were happy. It was different for Indian women, she'd said. Marrying a white man was not such a shame to her tribe. He had clenched his fists as the deadening sorrow washed through him. His love had shamed her. He had shamed her.

Now he faced the same trap, another white woman who called to his spirit and roused his body. But he was wiser now.

He understood the rules and would not stumble into the same trap. Indians, even half-breeds, could not take white wives.

At the livery, he picked out hearty animals with sound legs and bright eyes, and then restocked his gear including the essentials Eleanor had neglected, like rope, traps, powder, shot and trade goods. He tried not to dwell on the fact that he did not trade for these goods with the efforts from his own hands, but from her vile yellow metal.

He stroked the silky red ribbon he kept to trade with tribes along the way, letting it glide between callused fingers as he recalled the white ribbon of Eleanor's gown fluttering open at her bare neck. Annoyed at her intrusion into his thoughts, he thrust the trade goods in his pack with the remaining coins.

He tried to imagine Eleanor on the trail, draped in her finery as briars tore at her velvet skirts, and shook his head. She was too delicate for such hard riding, just like her mare. The sooner she recognized this, the better for them both. For much as he would deny it, he felt a powerful attraction to this unattainable creature and that made her dangerous beyond measure.

He hoped he could turn her east.

Still, he'd ready for the expedition as if they were headed out for several weeks. A man never knew what he'd run into. Taking precautions went a long way toward coming home again.

His stomach growled, reminding him his breakfast was now a distant memory. He wondered how Eleanor was doing as he headed first for the kitchen and then toward her room carrying a bucket of biscuits and a roast hen. Yesterday's dinner had shocked her. He'd been sure she'd reject his offering, but she surprised him again by cleaning her plate. He'd wager his horse that she'd never eaten such a meal before.

When he arrived in the yard he saw the line down to six men gambling in the dust. Eleanor sat on a chair in the yard studying her subject with complete attention.

Motionless as granite, the man stood. Rows of eagle feathers cascaded down his back, stirring regally in the gentle breeze. Troy glanced at the doorway and found Black Feather sitting in the shadows, watchful as a falcon. Troy nodded a greeting at the old warrior whose chin dipped in return.

Eleanor sat stiffly erect, moving only a paintbrush. Before her lay a perfect copy of Little Buffalo, chief of the wolf band of the Pawnee. He glanced at her work and blinked down in astonishment. How had this prim little miss captured not only the man's features, but also his spirit?

He stared in wonder at the miracle of her creation. With only colored water, she somehow managed this feat. She had talent all right. Had her father never seen her work? For no one who looked at the power of her paintings could deny her skill. In that instant, he understood why these men thought her work such strong medicine.

Troy stood silently studying her, surprised and annoyed that she did not immediately notice him. She seemed transported by her work. A chill rolled up his back. If he didn't know better, he'd be sitting in the dust with the others.

He focused on the straight line of her chin, the slope of her nose and the full mouth in profile. He could not see the mole, but knew it was there, just on the other side of her lovely mouth. His heartbeat grew steadily faster as he stood motionless. The woman was worse than strong medicine; she was poison. Even without so much as a glance, she made him want to tear the brush from her fingers and draw her into his arms.

He stared at Eleanor Hart. Why did he desire what he could not keep? The sooner he took her out on the trail, the sooner he'd be rid of her.

Dissuading her shouldn't take long, with luck, only a few days. Then he'd be out of work again, but at least he'd have his freedom and his sanity.

He thought of the picture he made, gawking, and cleared his throat. She turned her head and smiled. His gut tightened as if she'd kicked him and an answering smile jerked at one corner of his mouth.

"I brought lunch." He lifted the bucket.

"Wonderful. I am quite famished. Just a moment, please." She dipped the brush in a jar and then in green paint. With confidence, she dabbed the brown and then mixed the two. The result looked muddy as Missouri River water until she added it to the page, where it became the ground beneath Little Buffalo's feet. He shook his head in admiration.

She signaled to Black Feather she was done by brushing her hands together and spoke as if he could understand her words. "I am quite finished with this man. Please thank him. I have never had a subject stand so still. Simply marvelous."

Black Feather signed to Little Buffalo, who moved stiffly to see his portrait. He did not smile, exactly, but his eyes reflected his pleasure. He reached in his pouch and drew out a braid of sage grass and laid it before her.

"Oh, thank you very much."

He nodded and departed.

She lifted the sweetgrass rope in one hand and a raven feather, wrapped in red trade cloth and sinew, in the other. "They won't take any money and each one has given me some odd little gift."

Tributes, he thought.

He raised the bucket. "Lunch."

She stood, her eyes sparkling, bright as a summer afternoon as she cast the offerings aside. "Mr. Price, just look at the number of paintings." She motioned to the pages lying about at her feet. "I think one or two have potential."

He glanced about. They all looked good. The aroma of roasted fowl reached him again and he lay his offering upon her chair beside the others.

"I've got our mules and gear ready. We'll leave tomorrow." Her eyebrow rose. "Very good then."

"You got anything suitable for trail riding?" he asked.

She bit at her bottom lip, thinking. His head pounded as blood rushed south in response to this gesture. He wiped the sweat from his brow.

"I have several riding habits."

He had no notion what a habits was, but the riding part sounded promising. "Boots and a coat?"

"A few."

"Lay out what you mean to take—clothes, painting gear, everything. I'll check the load tonight. What we can't take, we'll store."

"Very well."

He hesitated, rubbing the back of his neck. "See you later." Was that disappointment upon her face? He hoped not.

"Won't you join me for lunch?" she asked.

He'd planned on it. But now he found his need to stay clear of her outweighed his hunger.

"Got work. I'll be back in a few hours."

He walked away from the scent of roses as fast as he could manage without making his retreat obvious to all.

He spent the hot afternoon repairing his bridle and making a new cover for his rifle. He had a boy bring the woman dinner. As the afternoon light waned and long shadows fell across the courtyard, he could delay their meeting no longer. But he felt no more prepared after spending the day apart from her.

She opened the door at his first knock and ushered him into her room to inspect her gear. He was struck again with the scent of roses. He moved away from her, facing the bags, bundles and boxes that completely enveloped her bed, spilled onto the floor beneath the window and filled the washtub that occupied more space than the bed. His jaw dropped.

She gave him a helpless look.

"I've weeded through the lot and cut to barest essentials."

He pointed to the bed. "That load alone would kill two mules."

"I'm sure a third mule…" Her voice dropped off under the intensity of his scowl. She lifted her hands in a gesture of surrender. "I have done my best."

He turned to the task and opened an odd-shaped case.

"A fiddle?" His voice rang with building exasperation.

"That is a Stradivarius."

His scowl deepened at her indignant tone.

Memories of his father, stomping one foot as he drew his bow, flashed in Troy's mind, followed by the familiar stabbing grief. The sound of lively music blending in his memory with his mother's lilting laughter. He stared at the fiddle. Could this woman fill a house with music?

"You play?" he asked.

"Certainly."

He couldn't bear to hear the sweet trembling notes, so he pointed to the floor.

She set the fiddle aside.

"What's this?" He pointed.

"A Dutch oven."

He set the box beside the fiddle. "This?"

"Camp chairs, foodstuffs and a portable table."

He placed this beside the oven and pointed at the next crate.

"My painting supplies."

This he laid in a separate pile.

"You are not going to leave these," she cried.

"No. I'm leaving those." He pointed to the oven, furniture and foodstuffs.

"What will we eat?"

He laughed. "Feeding us is my job. I guarantee you won't starve. What's this here?"

"Mr. Thornton's tent."

He let her keep that.

She spoke before he asked about the next. "Bedding."

He kept this and the telescope, but put aside her silver hairbrush and mirror, then turned his attention to her additional belongings.

"Lanterns."

Discarded.

"Easel."

Discarded.

"Oh, no. I must have this."

They faced off again as she hugged the easel, and then placed it in the pile she would keep. It was then he noticed that the hairbrush and fiddle had somehow reappeared in the pile, and glared.

He removed a complete set of ten volumes of poetry, two novels, the glass jar of spices, all the dishes and silverware and several bottles of rosewater.

Eleanor wrung her hands as he attacked her camping gear. He paused at the guns. Each one was masterfully crafted and inlaid with gold. Finely etched hunting scenes decorated the rifle and shotgun. He fingered the outline of a wild boar brought down by hounds.

"Saint's alive," he whispered. Never in his life had he held a weapon of such obvious quality. He aimed the rifle and then reversed the stock to inspect the odd sight. It revolved, changing from a white, to red, to black. The white would be handy against the dark hide of a buffalo, the black good to sight wolf or mountain goat.

"My father had them made for my expedition."

To give a firearm like this to a woman who only shot clay pigeons nearly made him weep. "What a waste."

She stiffened. "Mr. Price, I know you do not approve of my

upbringing. You are right to think I have been pampered. But I assure you, I can shoot and I know how to clean and care for these weapons."

Did she expect a pat on the head?

"That's the barest minimum of the skills you need to survive." He disliked the haughty slant of her chin. "I expect you will know the rest."

"I do. But what happens if I get a fever or step in a hole and break my leg? You gonna bring down enough meat to feed us?"

Her chin remained high, but her hands clutched each other until her knuckles turned white.

"I thought not." He turned back to the gear. "We are leaving tomorrow. I'd say you got one more night to sleep on it."

Eleanor gave him her best aloof stare. If he thought she would turn back now, he was sadly mistaken. He stood waiting. She merely lifted her chin in resolve. He snorted and turned to one of her trunks.

Eleanor shifted, certain he would not delve into her personal belongings. Would he?

"Those are my clothes." She tried to press the lid closed before he had his hands on her unmentionables, but was too late. He held her bodkin in one hand.

"What's this?" He gripped the center insert for her corset in his large hand.

"None of your business, Mr. Price." She extended her hand.

He pointed to the elaborate scrimshaw etched on the whalebone, depicting London sights. "Looks like a picture book."

"That is not its intended use." Her cheeks burned with a mortification of which he was blissfully unaware. One large finger traced London Bridge and she twitched as if he stroked her.

"This near your home?"

Her breath caught and she only managed to shake her head. Her hand remained open and hopeful before her. "No, that is a scene of London and the piece is called a bodkin. May I have it now, please?"

With reluctance, he laid it across her palm. For just an instant the heat of his hand scorched her. He must have felt it as well, that tingling sensation that raced up her arm from point of contact, for his gaze snapped to hers. She stood motionless, his hand blanketed hers and the bodkin pressed between them. Her breathing came in shallow little gasps and his eyes widened as he withdrew, stepping back two paces.

With trembling fingers she tucked away the ivory board, wondering at her strange reaction to this man. When she straightened, she found him poking in a crate of her shoes.

He reached for a box containing her undergarments.

"No, Mr. Price. You will not open that."

He hesitated only an instant, then a devilish smile appeared. She lunged and missed as he flipped open the latch. There on the top was the white lace-and-silk robe she wore this morning when she clung to him like a climbing rose. She thanked God that was on the top and not her corset or bloomers. He paused as if stunned by a simple glance at her sleeping garments, then lifted the robe before him.

His gaze flicked from the robe to her and she felt the heat rise in her from his scorching regard. Her heart accelerated its beating until she could not hear past the staccato rhythm.

She extended her hand, silently demanding the return of her attire. He pressed his face into the white silk and inhaled deeply.

Her breathing stopped. She stood shocked to immobility by the sensuality of the simple gesture. It was as if he held her in his firm embrace instead of her dressing gown. His eyes never left her and she trembled beneath his regard.

"Please," she whispered.

He stepped closer until his breath fell upon her flushed face. "Please what?"

She stood speechless.

He leaned in, inhaling the air about her neck and she closed her eyes at the quickening that urged her to step forward and draw his mouth down to meet her exposed neck.

"What is it you want, Lena?"

Lena? Her mother called her Nora, her father Eleanor, but she liked the way he said it, like an endearment.

"My robe," she whispered.

"You smell like roses." Another intake of breath and the air rushed cool about her and then hot as he exhaled, lifting the small hairs at her neck. Her body tingled with excitement as she realized what she really wanted. A kiss—his kiss.

As if reading her thoughts, one hand closed on the column of her throat and stroked until he held her jaw, lifting to bring her mouth close to his. She came alive under his touch. The simple brush of his thumb sent her insides all atremble.

"Have you ever been kissed?" he asked.

"Certainly." Several men had pulled her away from the dancing to steal a kiss.

His words brushed her lips. "What did you think of it?"

"I rather found dancing more invigorating."

He chuckled. "Did they kiss you like this?"

He dipped to brush his lips gently to hers.

She nodded, thinking he rather had a better hang of it than the others.

"I thought so. That's not how I want to kiss you."

She did not understand the thrill of excitement but rather sensed that something unexpected would happen. Her body trembled like a plucked violin string as she waited for him to come to her. It took every ounce of her upbringing to wait.

"Do you want me to kiss you, Lena?"

A lady would never say yes.

"Yes."

At her word, his lips touched hers then pressed firmly. His hand moved to cradle the back of her head as he leaned over her. Their torsos met and sharp shafts of pleasure radiated from her unexpectedly sensitive breast to the center of her belly.

She gasped in surprise and his tongue entered her mouth. She stiffened at the unexpected intrusion, while his fingers tightened in the hair at her scalp. He had control of her and she discovered that realization as potent as his kiss. His tongue made darting little thrusts that drove her nearly to distraction. All she could do was cling to this man as his kiss filled her with desire, sharp as the stab of tiny needles. All the strength in her arms was not sufficient to draw him close enough to fill the aching need tearing through her quaking body.

She pressed against him as he withdrew, denying her need as he pulled at her clasping arms now encircling his neck.

Bewildered, she released him and stood staring up at this stranger whose touch awakened this terrible monster of need.

"What did you do?" she asked.

"Kissed you the way a woman is meant to be kissed."

She pressed her hands flat over her trembling belly where the worst of her desire now screamed for her to reach out to him again.

"I didn't know."

"Now you do." His voice rumbled in an animal growl that lifted her skin to gooseflesh once more.

With just a kiss he had stripped away all her refinement like layers of varnish from a fine table, leaving only her naked desire. She turned her back and attempted to rein in her emotions. She was Eleanor Hart and he was her guide. She covered her mouth in shock as the scandal of what she had done washed over her like ice water. She stood paralyzed, as her upbringing collided with her new awareness for this man.

Her actions were the equivalent of kissing the stable boy. Her gut twisted at how easily she had abandoned her good breeding. She spoke four languages, knew how to play the piano and violin and did not go panting after servants. It was simply not done.

"Mr. Price," she began, and stopped at the strange tenor of her voice. She balled her fists and tried again, speaking to the wall. "Mr. Price, that was completely inappropriate. You had no right to take advantage of me."

"I didn't until you gave me leave."

Had she? Good gracious, she had!

"I had no idea what you intended."

"Next time you'll know."

How she wanted to strike his arrogant face, but recalled that she had given her consent. She turned to face him, angrier with herself than with him.

"I can assure you that there will be no next time."

"I'll leave that up to you."

"Will you? I have enough concerns without wondering if my guide will attack me."

He made no reply. It was only then she noticed he looked pale and more wary than she'd ever seen him. Had the kiss affected him as it had her?

"I didn't plan that."

She knew at a glance he hadn't and that frightened her even more. If neither of them had the slightest control when in close proximity, it did not take long to see where that might lead.

He stood watchful, his breathing and pallor revealing his distress. If she didn't know better, she'd say he looked rather more disquieted than she.

"I'll ask you to leave my room now." Why had she let him in to begin with? It all happened so fast. Now the rigid rules of propriety snapped into perfect clarity. Never be alone with a man. In only a matter of moments he had her nearly mindless with desire. Who could have predicted such things were possible? Goodness, she didn't even know if she liked him. But heaven knows he did things to her insides—wild, dangerous things.

She shook her head to remove the images from her mind and found he already stood in the open door. What might have happened if he had not pulled back?

"Mr. Price, can you assure me that we will have no reoccurrence of such behavior?"

"I can't. That's just one of the reasons you should turn back."

"Is this some kind of trick to frighten me?"

"No trick."

He handed back her robe.

Tentatively she accepted the garment, careful not to brush his outstretched arm.

"You still fixing to go upriver?"

She studied him, trying to assess his motives. Had he planned this? He stood as far from her as the cramped room allowed, staring cautiously as if suddenly caged with a wild cat.

"Why did you kiss me, Mr. Price?"

His gaze turned serious. She stood bolstered by her corset as she faced him.

"Why did you let me?"

"I don't know."

He nodded. "Same reason."

It had just happened. He had not planned this any more than she had.

"I see." She now realized that the dangers she faced outside the fort walls included this strange attraction between them. But she was a lady after all. She need only follow the rules of social behavior and there would be nothing to fear. She eyed him. Would there?

"Are you the sort that would kiss an unwilling woman?" she asked.

His smile seemed wise and ruthful all at once.

"No."

She drew a reassuring breath. "Then I shall be ready to depart tomorrow."

He nodded his acceptance.

"I'll send a boy 'round to collect your gear so I can load it up in the morning. I'll be waiting at daybreak."

"Very well."

"Lena? Is there something you ain't telling me? Some other reason besides painting that brought you here?"

She stiffened as his question struck too close to the truth. She collected herself and lied.

"I need a portfolio of animals to show Mr. Audubon. That is the sole purpose for this expedition."

Chapter 5

Troy closed Lena's door and made it just twelve steps before his knees gave way. He sank onto the lid of a barrel.

What had just happened?

He'd never experienced this quicksilver reaction to a woman, never felt so out of control. She shook him to the core.

What was that?

Lust maybe, animal attraction.

One moment he'd been holding her sleeping robe and the next he was holding her. Had he lost his mind? After spending the last two days convincing himself to stay clear of her, he pulled a stupid stunt like kissing her.

No good could come from this. It was those eyes. He lost all sense when she gazed up at him.

He pushed back his hat as he recalled her reaction. He had expected her to kiss like a child. Instead she'd burned him up like tinder. He mopped his brow with his sleeve.

She dressed like a lady and talked like a lady, but she sure didn't kiss like one. Underneath all that velvet, there was a woman of passion. She made him lose control faster than straight whiskey. He didn't have the head for either one.

Yesterday, he thought it best to be rid of her as soon as possible. Today he found himself desperate to do so.

For if there was one thing he did not need, it was another woman to break his heart. He couldn't stand to lose one more person in his life and the best way to avoid that was to keep clear of women—particularly Miss Eleanor Hart.

Lena.

His body stirred at the memory of her lips pressed to his. He'd never shared a kiss like that one—scorching, that's what it was.

Troy gathered his resolve and tugged down his hat before making his way to the office, where he made arrangements to have anything left behind in Lena's room stored until their return. Hopefully that would not be very long. Until departure, he thought it best to keep clear of her.

Tomorrow that would not be possible.

It took the boy seven trips to tote all her gear to the stables. He looked at the immense pile, pitying the poor mules. If he handled their departure correctly, none of them would have to bear it long.

This morning he'd been so sure he could convince her to stay put, he bet Black Feather a pouch of tobacco on the matter. Now he was no longer sure of anything.

Troy culled her belongings once more, then headed outside the fort walls to sleep with Black Feather and his family. The man's wife did wonders with mule deer.

He rose before dawn, spending nearly an hour tying her art supplies, clothing and shoes onto two overtaxed mules. Then he waited for her grand appearance, expecting her to be late, which she was, but not by much. The sun just streaked the sky orange when her door cracked open.

Excitement rang in her voice. "Lovely morning for traveling, wouldn't you agree, Mr. Price?"

He scowled, keeping his focus on a final knot. The less he looked at Lena the better.

"Fair enough." He glanced up and his jaw dropped. She wore a silky dress the exact coppery color of her hair. The front of her coat showed more buttons than he'd ever seen on one garment in his life. The vest was so tight it carved into her torso like a hot knife through butter. What kept her eyeballs from bulging, he couldn't say.

"You're gonna faint in that."

Her laughter made his viscera twitch. Why did the sound twist up his insides like this? He never felt so jumpy around a female. It was the kiss. He couldn't keep his gaze from her mouth and that mole sheltered just below.

Her cheeks glowed pink and her breathing came sharp and quick. Was it excitement over their departure or remembrance of their kiss that stirred her?

She seemed inclined not to look at him this morning, focusing instead on the sky and the mules. That was her way of dealing with it, then. Pretend it hadn't happened.

But it had.

He cursed himself again as a fool.

His gaze followed the movement of the tasseled end of the stiff wisp of leather she held, assuming the thing to be a tiny whip. As she requested by way of the boy, he had not saddled her horse. Apparently this was the one way she intended to be useful. He tied off his team and followed her to the livery. There she attached the girth beneath her jittery little mare. He noticed that Lena's cocked hat held a plumed feather and some kind of gauzy fabric bunched about the brim.

He stepped closer and the horse's nostril's twitched as she sidestepped, throwing her head.

"She is unaccustomed to you as yet," Lena said by way of apology.

"How is she with wolves?"

Lena's hands stilled upon the stirrup. "Wolves?"

His unblinking stare met her startled gaze, praying that just this once, she'd show some sense and drag that saddle off her horse's back.

"Lots of dangers outside these walls," he said.

She stared through the stable doors toward the yard.

"Alas, that is where the opportunities are to be found as well." She lowered the stirrups.

His cheek twitched at her stubborn insistence to set out. He didn't know if he should admire her or wring her neck. Instead he tried reason.

"You need a horse that's steady and surefooted, not one that will toss you if it gets a whiff of trouble."

"Scheherazade is extremely fleet of foot."

"Not much help if you are lying in a ditch."

She ignored this and tightened the girth without comment. Then she opened her tack box. His eyes widened as he saw three bridles, each more ridiculous than the next. Green, red and a god-awful pink. Her hand shot to the pink like a streak of lightning and he heard a tinkling sound.

"What's that?" he asked, glancing around until his gaze settled on a series of tassels all along the reins. He poked one. "It jingles."

"Chimes. Isn't it lovely?"

He rubbed his forehead. Then without a word drew his knife and cleanly sliced off the bells hidden within each tassel. Her mouth gaped and she pressed a gloved hand to her heart. He lifted her other hand and dropped the things into her palm. It was a mistake. The action brought him within range of the scent of roses once more. His nostrils flared as he stepped back. He could not remember what he was doing until she dropped her gaze to her palm and he saw the bells.

"Stuff those in a box."

"That bridle is Arabic and quite expensive." Her chiding tone needled him.

"So is your scalp. That horse will draw enough notice without advertising her for miles."

Her shoulders lifted as if protecting herself from imaginary attack. Would she call a halt before even mounting up? He watched her eyes shift from side to side as she considered a moment and then tucked the bells in a saddlebag. He kicked the dirt.

She glanced about the dim livery barn.

"Where is the mounting block?" she asked.

"There ain't one. I guess they figure if you can't mount up solo, you're too damned drunk to leave."

She did not smile at his attempt at humor, but instead leveled him with a reproachful stare. "You are not a drunkard, are you, Mr. Price?"

"Folks call me Troy and I don't drink."

They faced off until he got uncomfortable in his skin again. It was those damn blue eyes, reminded him of a wolf. She might have felt the same, for she fidgeted with the lace at her collar. Was she remembering how it felt to be held in his arms?

"Hadn't we best depart?"

"Reckon so."

He extended his locked palms and she stared blankly for a moment and then nodded.

"Oh, I see. Thank you."

Her foot did not fill his hands. As she lifted her knee, he took the opportunity to gander at her trim ankle. Her fine leather boots, carefully polished and handsomely laced, looked like they'd never seen a day's use.

She rose smoothly onto the horned saddle that smelled of linseed oil and creaked as she settled. He waited for her to drop off, but she managed to gain her seat and adjust her skirts. Her weight left his hands and he slid her foot into the single stirrup, his fingers confirming his suspicion. The sole of the boot was smooth as a buffalo horn. New boots, dress, saddle and bridle—all chosen for her new little adventure. He cautioned himself against involvement with a woman who owned nothing until it wore out. Did she cast off men as quickly as slippers?

He glanced up to see her perched on one side of the saddle as if this were perfectly natural. She smiled, lifting that damned adorable mole. He stared.

"Well?" she asked.

He walked back to his team, dogged by the scent of roses and oiled leather.

As they rode through the gate, he spotted Black Feather standing in the shadow of the fort wall, his expression placid, but Troy saw the victorious glint in his friend's eye and scowled.

Here to collect, he thought and reached in his bag, tossing a full pouch of tobacco to his friend, who caught it with ease, then nodded farewell.

Troy signed that he'd see him by supper. The warrior's eyebrows lifted in doubt.

When he glanced back, he saw Lena clear the fort entrance, riding stiff as a corpse, with her chin erect. He wondered what a trot would do to her, but waited until they were on the soft, sandy bank of the river to find out. Once there, he kicked his mount and the team broke into a rough trot. He listened but did not hear her cry out or fall. A glance back showed her bobbing up and down like a cork in water. Each time the horse bounced it seemed to send her a few inches out of the saddle. He slowed.

"What the hell is that?"

"What?"

"That bobbing thing?"

"It is called posting. It helps absorb the shock of this gait."

He glanced around. "What gate?"

She sighed. "The trot. It is one of the gaits—walk, trot, canter, gallop."

He shook his head in bewilderment. All he knew for certain was that she didn't fall off as expected. He headed for a thick grove of cottonwood. Before he even had the train past the first bush, the insects rose to meet them. His horse's ears began to flick back and forth as the flies landed. The thick tail swished far enough forward to lash his legs. Behind him he heard Lena cry out. He turned to see her waving her hand before her face as deerflies attacked from all sides. Her horse's skin twitched and she threw her head.

"Good heavens, we are under attack," Lena said.

"Oh, don't worry. Them little fellas won't draw much blood."

"Blood!"

Her cry brought a smile to his lips. He faced forward, so as not to reveal the hope blooming inside him.

"We'll only be in the trees a few hours."

"Hours!"

He turned to see her horse rear up. His heart stopped in his chest as he imagined the stupid little mare falling over backward on Lena. Memories of his friend, Reed Palmer, surfaced like wood on water. His horse had crushed his pelvis and there was little anyone could do.

Troy's belly filled with ice.

Somehow she kept her seat, gathering up the reins and leaning stiffly forward as the horse lashed out uselessly with her front legs. Once all four feet hit the ground, Lena used the tassel on the end of her whip to keep the flies off her mare's ears. Then she clutched the netting on her hat and lowered it around herself like a shroud.

"That should help. Lead on, Mr. Price."

Troy rubbed his neck trying not to admit his admiration at her pluck. They took an hour to clear the cottonwood and regain the sandy bank of the river with no complaint from behind him. The woman must have thick skin. Beside the Missouri once more, he saw that she did not. Leather riding gloves the color of her coat protected her hands, the netting, her face and neck, and the skirt her legs.

When he realized he had many more bites than she, his mood darkened. He glanced at the sky seeing the first low clouds sweeping in from the south and smiled.

"Oh, look!"

He turned to see her staring at a jackrabbit crouching low beside a fallen log.

"What about it?" asked Troy.

"Can you shoot it?"

"You got a hankering for roast rabbit?"

"I want to paint it."

"Now?"

She arched her brow. "That is why I am here, Mr. Price."

"Troy," he reminded.

She lifted a palm and motioned at the rabbit.

"I don't think you want me to shoot it."

"But I do."

Obviously the little princess was unaccustomed to having her orders questioned. He shrugged, drew his fifty-caliber rifle and took aim.

"Not in the head," she directed.

The shot tore the rabbit in two pieces. His rifle was always loaded for grizzly and did not transfer well to small game.

"Oh, you've ruined it."

He dismounted. "Taste just as good."

"I need my specimens intact."

"Then next time we better snare it."

"If you thought so then why did you not say?"

He retrieved the rabbit, pausing before her to gaze at her haughty face while trying to ignore the mole that seemed to taunt him. "'Cause you were too damned busy telling me my business."

She had the decency to look remorseful. Her expression caused an uncomfortable squeezing around his heart. He scowled at how easily she influenced him.

"I am sorry, Mr. Price. In the future, I will endeavor to rely on your experience."

"That's what you pay me for."

"Point taken."

Did she always have to have the last word? Likely they wouldn't be together long enough for him to find out. Troy gutted the two halves of the hare, wrapped what was left in buckskin to keep off the flies and tied the bundle on the lead mule.

Then they rode along the river, close enough for the sand fleas to bite. Ignoring the constant whine of mosquitoes, he tied a bit of cloth over his nose and mouth to deter the biting insects. A glance back showed Lena swatting and waving her hand before her face. Obviously the netting did not repel these smaller nuisances. He'd seen mosquitoes drive a bull moose crazy until it ran headfirst into a lodge pole pine and knocked itself cold. Let's see how this woman responded to the same tiny torture.

A herd of antelope tempted him for dinner, but he stubbornly resisted, determined to keep camp as uncomfortable as possible. He'd begin by cooking his small, flea-bitten rabbit halves for supper. The gentle breeze turned cold, driving off the insects for the moment and signaling the approaching storm.

He called a halt long before dark, figuring to allow her plenty of time to hang herself.

He heard her groan as she slid from her fancy saddle. The sound was music to his ears. Judging from her stiff-legged walk, he'd say she wasn't accustomed to a day in the saddle. One night on the ground ought to put a kink in her spine and dampen that dogged determination he found so irritating and intriguing.

"Stiff?" he asked.

"I just need to stretch a bit."

"Life out here is sure uncomfortable. Not like you're used to."

She glared. "I should not presume to know to what I am accustomed."

"Might be more comfortable at the fort."

She sniffed. "But that's miles behind us."

"Actually, I took us in kind of a circle. It's only just over that rise. Three miles, four tops."

Her mouth dropped open as an expression of fire shot from narrowing eyes.

Chapter 6

"You mean to say that we've ridden through swamp and bug-infested forests all day to cover a distance of only three miles?"

He liked her color now. Her lips reddened and her cheeks relayed her emotion by changing to a tempting pink. What he didn't like was her tone.

"Thought you'd quit by now."

She gripped her hands into fists and thrust them to her hips. "How disappointing for you to have misjudged me."

"Just keep in mind, if you want to head back, it ain't far."

She moved closer and he noted the pulsing vessels at her neck. His gut twisted in awareness of her as he resisted the urge to draw her in. Instead he retreated a step.

"I trust that I have convinced you of the seriousness of my intent and that tomorrow we shall continue in a straight line up the Yellowstone."

He was about to argue, but decided he'd best cool her temper, before he did something foolish like kiss her.

"Anything you say, Princess."

He turned his back on her and gathered wood for a fire. When he glanced over his shoulder, he discovered she had moved off a hundred yards. He unloaded the mules, lifting down package after package of her indispensable gear. When he went to skin the rabbit he found her sketching the damn thing. He smiled as he saw how she arranged it behind a branch to disguise the fact that her subject lay in two pieces. He stared at the rabbit portrait. Unlike the original, whose tongue lolled and showed dried blood at the mouth, the rabbit image looked relatively clean, if slightly longer than typical. She could not hide the lifelessness of the dead eyes.

"You still riled?" he asked.

"No. But no repeats of this. I did not come here to survive your idea of some trial by fire, and you are paid to do my bidding."

That raised all sorts of possibilities in his mind, but he only nodded, keeping his expression serious. "Yes, ma'am."

She turned the page in his direction. "What do you think?"

"Looks just like a dead rabbit to me."

Her shoulders slumped. "I know. I can't seem to animate it."

Troy's brow rose. "Nothing on God's green earth will animate that."

He grabbed the two pieces and thrust his skinning knife beneath the hide.

Lena winced and then turned her attention to her work. "Audubon often uses dead animals. He props them up with wire and wood, posing them in natural positions. I can't understand how he makes them appear alive. I am afraid I do not have the imagination to render what I cannot see."

"But you sure can draw what you do see. Don't fuss, we'll catch something tomorrow," he assured and then inwardly groaned. Why did he feel compelled to bolster her? Now, as her spirits flagged, was the time to drive her home. He knew the safest thing for this lady was to head back to her New York parlor before they ran into real trouble.

He spiked the two halves of the rabbit and set them to roast. From the gleam in Lena's eyes as she watched the meat sizzle and drip, he'd say she had worked up an appetite.

Intentionally, he did not stop for lunch, nor offer her any jerky during the hot afternoon. Now they had but one scrawny rabbit, when he knew he could put down that many times over.

After a few silent minutes she rose. "You had best set up my tent now."

He frowned. "You got me confused with one of your servants."

"I beg your pardon?"

"Thought you wanted your independence? That means doing for yourself. Out here a person makes their own bed then lies in it."

Her eyes rounded in shock. He'd rendered her speechless. She stiffened her shoulders and marched toward her gear.

He reserved his smile until her back was turned. For the next hour he watched her wrestle with a tube of canvas, rope and a series of wooden stakes. She gave him an occasional hopeful glance, but he feigned occupancy at sewing a torn moccasin.

With the stakes set, she took up a series of interlocking rods. With all the cottonwood about them, she chose instead to construct this contraption of two poles and a sagging rope, threaded through the canvas sack to form the saddest looking burrow he'd ever seen.

She stood facing her work, hands upon her hips. "There now, that's taking shape." She spun a slow circle. "Where is my mattress?"

"If you mean that ten-pound sack of feathers, it's back at Fort Union."

She frowned and he fought to hold his expression somber.

"Upon what shall I sleep?"

"How about your bed at the fort?" They could in fact be home in less than two hours, well before sunset, due to the meandering route he'd carried them this day.

She crossed her arms before her and cast him the now familiar stubborn expression. "We certainly will not."

"I use a pile of green branches and a buffalo hide."

"I don't believe I have a buffalo robe."

"You can use mine."

She eyed him suspiciously.

He laughed. "I have two."

"I shall use my own blanket, thank you."

For the next several minutes she gathered dead leaves and dry grasses. He wondered how many fleas she'd collected as well. Over the pile she draped a pristine wool blanket and a spotless white bedsheet.

"That should serve."

He glanced skyward and wondered how long until the rain filled the hollow in which she'd staked her tent.

"That'll do." He grinned and held out some of the rabbit.

She accepted the rabbit shank in her bare hand and devoured the flesh to the bones. Afterward she did wipe her mouth on a fine cloth napkin and washed her face in the stream that Troy knew would soon swell to the ground on which they sat.

Lena glanced wistfully at his remaining bit of supper but said nothing as she stood. Her brow furrowed as she glanced about. Firelight now polished her hair like a new copper kettle.

She fingered the mole beneath her lip and he sat forward before he could stop himself, his attention riveted on her face. "Well, I had not anticipated, I mean, I don't have a screen."

"What's that?"

"Where shall I make my ablutions?"

"Your what?"

"Preparations to retire."

"What kind of preparations? Just lay down. That's all."

She straightened, her face twisting in an expression of disapproval. "I need to wash and change and…" She searched the gear before her and then pressed her hands to her cheeks. "Good heavens, you left most of my toiletries behind as well."

"Reckon so." He shredded a branch and polished his teeth.

"Could you make me one of those?"

He did and she sprinkled fine powder upon the frayed end. He extended his branch and she doused his as well. They scrubbed in silence as he enjoyed the taste of peppermint. He could get used to this. His grin allowed white foam to spill from his mouth like a rabid dog and she giggled. The sound stole his humor, replacing it with desire.

He spit. The sooner he was free of her the better. Not just for her sake, but for his.

She focused her pale eyes upon him.

"What was it like where you grew up, Troy?"

She used his first name. He liked the sound of it. What had she asked? Oh, yes, his home. "Farmland. We raised corn and goats mostly."

"Truly?"

He laughed at the evident shock in her voice.

"Did you think I lived in a teepee?"

"Well, yes."

"The Cherokee called themselves the civilized people. We've lived beside the whites since Cortez wandered through. I even went to church on Sundays."

"I had no idea."

He smiled at the confusion that knit her brow.

"Because of your father?"

"Mother made us go."

"Really."

That set her back again. She had ideas about how his life must be and he was bumping up against them.

"What is your father's occupation?"

"Occupation?" He laughed. "He was a dirt farmer and not a good one. Good fiddler, though. Played at weddings. He fell off his horse drunk one night." His smile faded with the memory. "Broke his neck."

He died two years after Troy left for the West. His mother wrote him of the news. He should have gone home then, despite his shame. If he had known he would never have a chance to see them again, nothing could have kept him away. But he hadn't known and had not returned. Guilt poured through him like rising groundwater.

She pressed a hand to her heart. "How perfectly dreadful."

He smiled. "Perfectly."

"Mr. Price, I certainly did not mean to pry. You have the most startling way about you."

"How's that?"

"Well, where I come from people spend a good deal of time covering up such indiscretions. Certainly they would not volunteer that their father drank, even if he were sitting beside them in a stupor."

Troy laughed at the picture her words painted. "Why not?"

"Well it's not done. Propriety dictates that personal matters remain private."

"Secrets, then."

"Just so. Your bluntness is rather startling. If you had asked me a similar question, I would answer quite differently."

"Okay, Princess, what does your pa do?"

"Well, he is in shipping. Owns a fleet of boats. Mother says he could start his own navy. My mother is a descendent of a signer. Her people go back to before the revolution, related to Hamilton. He established the first bank, you know."

"Signer?"

"Of the Constitution."

He smiled. His family went back far before the revolution, though no one cared.

"That's the one that starts, 'We the people' and goes with the Bill of Rights that says 'All men are created equal?'" he asked. But they didn't mean all men. Only white men.

"Very good, Mr. Price. You know your history." She beamed, obviously proud of her ancestry. "And you see? I didn't say a thing that is not common knowledge."

"You also didn't tell me nothing I didn't already know."

"Exactly, let's try another, shall we?" She thought in silence for a moment then asked. "Why did you come west?"

"Trying to find something, I guess. I was looking for a place where a man's character counts more than the color of his skin. Some place where I belonged." He could not keep the hardness from cutting through his voice. "Been to the Pacific and back. There ain't no such place."

"Oh my."

"What's wrong?"

"Why you've done it again. I really shouldn't be privy to such matters."

"You asked."

He studied her pale face and huge round eyes.

"Well, you've just told me something so very personal and I don't know what to say. Wouldn't you feel more comfortable just saying you came west to hunt?"

"If I can't say what's on my mind, I just won't answer."

"How odd." She fiddled with her gloves.

"What, Lena?"

"It's just that I find the urge to say things that I have no right to put to voice."

"You set yourself a lot of rules. Got you laced up tighter than that corset. You're in my territory now. So how about you play by my rules. You ask something I don't want to answer, I'll just tell you straight." He waited but she only tugged her gloves on more tightly. "Go on."

"Did you ever think, well, perhaps what you seek is not a place but a person."

"How's that?"

"A person. Someone to accept you as you are. I believe a person belongs to other people, as I belong to my family. I am a part of them and they are a part of me. Do you feel that way with your family?"

He stilled, absorbing the pain the question raised.

"I have no family."

"Oh, I'm so sorry. Illness?"

"More like greed."

She frowned. "I don't follow."

"You ever heard of Dahlonega, Georgia, in the Appalachian Mountains?"

"I know Georgia, of course.

"Because of the gold."

She dropped her gaze and he knew he was right. That was all whites knew of his families' lands.

"The government took our land. My tribe was forced from their homes and my family sent to Oklahoma in the dead of winter."

Her eyes rounded at this.

"My sisters, Spotted Deer and Little Rabbit, died on the way." That winter he'd spent trapping beaver, while his family marched through snow and ice. Only his mother had lived to see the godforsaken wasteland of Jackson's treaty. Land unfit for white settlers, land without gold. But she had not lived to see the springtime. "My mother died after arrival. I didn't hear until the following spring."

She pressed a hand to her mouth and tears spilled from her eyes.

"I should never have left them."

"Why did you?"

"I left over a woman." He glared at her.

She fingered the broach at her throat as her voice dropped to a whisper. "Is that why you were so angry about my arrival, because I am a woman?"

He met her steady gaze and nodded.

"But I am not that woman," she assured. "Troy, you are my guide. Nothing more."

He gave her a doubtful look.

"What happened last night, well, I choose to overlook it. We both recognize it as a dreadful mistake and agree to not have a reoccurrence."

Her words did not reassure.

"You have to trust me. I will not cross the line society draws between us."

"I hear your words, but I remember your kiss."

She stiffened.

"Will you turn back?"

She breathed deep of the night air and squared her shoulders. "No."

He sighed, then stood to add more wood to the fire. At last he said, "It is time for sleep."

She gathered up a bundle of clothing and headed for the privacy of a two-hundred-year-old cottonwood trunk.

"Best stamp about," he called and watched her halt, showing wide round eyes.

"And why is that?"

"Snakes."

Her head turned slowly toward the unknown menace of the woods and then back to him.

"Rattlesnakes," he added.

With infinite slowness she lowered her bundle to the ground. She would run back to him now and insist they return to the fort. He breathed a sigh of relief, then wondered why he felt so sad.

His brow lifted in confusion as she grasped a stout stick in one hand and her belongings in the other. She swung the limb, beating the bushes and ground as she advanced. He watched with begrudging respect. The girl didn't have an ounce of sense. But she had something more important, something he never expected to find in this fancy little filly—courage.

She returned a very short time later, emerging like a ghost draped in flowing robes. He recognized the same lovely dress she wore at Fort Union and his stomach dropped.

He shook his head. She actually changed for sleeping.

He shoved his hat back on his head. "Can I ask you something?"

"Of course, Mr. Price."

"You gonna sleep in them slippers?"

She shook her head, apprehension blooming on her features.

He did not want to spend the night with her. As evening closed about them he grew more anxious to send her home. Something had to be done.

"And you gonna tie them little tent laces shut?"

"Certainly."

"So how you gonna get clear if a bear wanders in?" He watched his words strike terror in her. First her eyes widened and then her neck stretched like a turtle, as she peered past the firelight into the deep shadows.

Her voice squeaked. "Have you seen evidence of one?"

He stood and stretched, then closed the distance between them until she stepped back.

"There are all kinds of dangers here." And he thought she was the most dangerous of all.

She trembled. The urge to comfort nagged, but he pushed it back. Her tongue darted from her mouth and ran the full curve of her lower lip, pausing for just an instant on the mole.

He twitched, resisting the notion of kissing her.

She lifted a hand, but stopped before laying it on his chest as if remembering she could no longer touch him. He held back his disappointment.

She glanced about. "Why would a bear venture into my tent?"

"That tent is a trap, plus you set up on low ground and rain's coming."

"I couldn't sleep without a roof of some sort above my head."

"I'll take you back to the fort, then. Without the gear, you can be tucked in tight in a few hours. Tomorrow you can paint some more Indians."

She scowled and her voice took on a hard authoritative edge that he hated immediately. "Mr. Price, you have made your opinions on this matter quite clear. You are paid to guide, not harangue. I will thank you to cease in this vein. I shall sleep in Mr. Thornton's tent and that is final."

Far off to the south came a familiar rumble. She did not note it, instead turning toward her tent and throwing back the flap, then hesitating only a moment before crawling inside. He noticed she left both ends of the tent open. She had her escape route, but no shoes in which to run and no weapon with which to defend herself.

But that was his job. He debated telling her to move her tent and then sighed in resignation. As she'd said, he was paid to guide, not harangue, so he turned to her belongings. He lifted her gear, hanging some parcels close to the trunks of the trees where they would stay relatively dry, others he strung from branches, keeping them above the torrent to come. He moved the animals to high ground and secured them against stampede. Finally, he rested by the fire, wrapped snug in a thick buffalo robe upon a nest of green boughs. The breeze arrived first, blowing cold. Far off he heard the rain.

From within her tent Lena said, "How lovely, no bugs."

He gave a snort and curled onto his side.

"Good night, Mr. Price."

"If you say so, Lena."

He gazed up through the canopy of cottonwood. Low clouds blocked the moonlight. The rumble came again, followed by the gentle patter of rain, first on leaves and then on canvas. Gradually, the force of the rain increased. She'd break in the storm. She had to.

Lightning peeled across the sky, turning the clearing green for an instant. Lena's scream came with the thunder. He expected her to flee her drooping teepee, but she stayed even when the water ran through like a river.

For a moment he thought he heard her crying, but the sound was too faint to be certain. He lay rigid, listening.

Any moment she'd quit. She'd climb from her wet bed and beg him to take her home. He would miss her. He admired

proud women and Lena was certainly that. He knew he'd
never see her like again and that was for the best.

"Lena. Come out of there."

He waited, but still she did not emerge, so he threw back
his own dry covers and rose, preparing to haul her out of her
burrow, willing or not.

At last, she emerged, a pale waif crawling from the opening dragging her sodden blanket and a fine linen sheet now
streaked with mud. He stood three paces from her but she did
not see him in the rain. She turned toward the spot where she
had left her belongings. His brow knit in confusion.

She didn't come to him.

The realization stung. He called to her.

"Lena."

She halted, her shoulders rounded in defeat. "I believe I
need a change of clothing."

Something was wrong with her voice. He stepped closer
to where she stood trembling in the rain. The pathetic sight
was just what he expected, but his reaction to it came as a
complete surprise. It was as if an eagle sunk his talons into
his gut and pulled. He crossed the ground that separated them
before he could stop himself, cursing her all the way. Damn
her for not giving up. What did he have to do, tie her up and
haul her back like freight?

She was a white girl whose body called him even as his
mind warned against her soft pale skin. She knew better than
to travel alone with an Indian. He knew better, too. Why did
she lack common sense?

"Come here."

He stretched out his arms and she stepped into them, taking
shelter from the rain beneath his heavy buffalo robe. Her teeth
chattered as the fabric of her garments soaked his buckskin.

"I'm such a bother," she muttered.

He nodded, his chin brushing the wet mass of her tangled hair.

"My tent is a miserable failure."

The twisting talons pulled again.

"Next time pick high ground."

She nestled closer. Remorse changed to desperate desire faster than a swooping falcon. He allowed his arms to draw her in until he felt her softness melting against him like warm honey.

He rested his chin on her head. The wild curling tangle of her hair fascinated him. She was so different than any woman in his past and as unlike him as fur from feather.

"Ready to head home?"

"You want me to quit." She sniffed. "I won't, you know."

"You should."

"Let me tell you something, Mr. Price. I have listened to my father tell me again and again that I am incapable of doing anything beyond breeding and needlepoint. I know you do not want me here, but I shall prove you wrong with the rest and achieve my aim with or without you."

He snorted, pushing her back until she just remained beneath his robe, but did not nestle against him like a lover. "You wouldn't get a mile without me." He gave her a little shake. "Why are you so stubborn?"

Her shoulders drooped, but her voice remained determined. "It is the only way to get what I want."

"And just what do you want?"

"A chance to do one thing on my own. A chance to paint."

"At least tell me why, Lena?"

She straightened and he gazed down at her beautiful wet face. "I don't know what you mean."

"Hell you don't. Your party died, but you kept on. I tried my best to turn you home with no better luck. You come out here alone with a stranger and you faced down a lightning storm that would raise the dead. Still you won't quit. So what's so damned bad back there that you prefer this?"

Her head sank and he thought she'd cry again.

"I just want to paint."

He drew her in. "Lena, you can tell me."

But she wouldn't. Her lips parted only to draw another long ragged breath. She trembled before him. Her lost expression tore at his heart.

He led her to his pallet and stripped off her outer robe, leaving only a thin sheath of fabric as the storm lit the clearing. Her garment clung transparent to her wet skin. If he lived to be as old as Methuselah, he'd never forget the sight of her lush curves. How could a woman be so beautiful?

His gaze took in the hard nipples dark against the sheer veil, smooth, soft skin broken only by the hollow of her navel and a dark thatch of hair. She made a feeble effort to cover herself and he dragged his gaze away. He bundled her in his wolf-skin cloak and then a buffalo robe before laying her on his raised bed of green branches.

Rain pattered on his head. He was a fool for this woman and he did not know how to stop it. The only clear thing was his desire. He was a lone wolf and she a soft hen. He trembled in the rain knowing it was fear that made him shiver. He would not grow attached to this woman. These feelings were just protectiveness and desire. He wished he believed it. Dread seeped in with the rain.

He thought of Rachel. One mistake followed by another until she was dead and he, a thousand miles away when his family needed him. Troy absorbed the clenching pain that rocked him even after all these years.

He would not travel that road a second time.

Troy drew his gaze from Lena and pulled out another robe from his gear, then cut a second bed from willow branches. Finally he lay down a ways off, but not far enough to miss the sound of her teeth chattering. The noise went on a long while. He dreaded going over there to warm her. No man should have such temptation. At last her spasms ceased. He called to her and received no answer. He left his pallet to check and found her asleep, snug as a mole in her burrow while he stood in the pouring rain. Water ran off his hat and streamed down the thick brown fur of the buffalo robe sheathing her. Reluctantly, he returned to his solitary bed.

Chapter 7

Without question, last night had been the most miserable of her life. Eleanor opened her eyes to the gray dawn and saw that the rain still fell in sheets. A shudder shook her shoulders as she sank farther into the soft bedding. The musty odor of wet fur enveloped her but at least she was dry. She sighed, thinking she would stay in bed until the rain stopped.

Last night's strange turn of events fell back into her awareness with the droplets of rain.

She huddled in the downpour and wondered about Troy. Yesterday he'd told her that he had come west because of a white woman. She was fairly bursting with curiosity. But here she had no servants or connections to ply such information. He was so blunt he would likely just tell her if she asked, but some part of her feared his answer.

She felt certain that his determination to turn her homeward stemmed from his experience with this woman. And if it affected her, she felt justified in learning more.

He'd also said he had no family. How sad. She brought her knees up to her chest and considered the injustice he had suffered. He stood alone now in the world. How frightening. What would her life be like without her parents? There would be advantages. The pressure to marry would cease. But disadvantages, too. She loved her mother and someday wished to be just like her. Her father was very stern and austere, but he loved her in his gruff fashion and tried to do what was best for her.

Her mother was determined Eleanor marry English nobility, thus gaining a title for her daughter. It was the only coup left to a woman who was already a queen by every standard but one. Yes, her daughter would be Lady Eleanor if it killed her. But the thought of leaving all she knew frightened Eleanor.

Something pushed at her bottom. She cried out.

"Oh, so you are awake."

She turned to see Troy towering over her, rain falling off his oilskin coat and dribbling down the fringe. Now that she had met him, she found him more intriguing than the character in the novels she had devoured. He fascinated her. This man had unexpected depth and unfathomable sorrow.

She rallied. "Yes. Terrible weather, isn't it?"

"Dawn was a hour ago. You want to stay here all day?"

She did, but could see from his expression that he did not.

Eleanor sighed. She'd come here to paint, but that would be impossible in this abysmal weather.

"What do you suggest?" She tried to sit up, but found he had wrapped her as tight as Cleopatra in her rug.

"I suggest moving before the stream floods us out."

She glanced in the direction he indicated and saw her tent under two feet of muddy water held from the current by one stubborn tent spike. The white canvas rose and fell like a large dirty fish.

"Drat." She struggled to extract herself from the hide, succeeding in clearing her torso before remembering she wore only her thin gown. Cold rain pelted her.

He rolled his eyes and went to his pack, returning with a buckskin cape, which he fastened about her neck with a bone toggle. Then he handed her a brown strip of leather.

"What is this?" she asked.

"Jerky."

She held the leather that now grew sticky in the rain.

"What is its function?"

"Function?" He laughed. "You eat it."

She sniffed, and then nibbled. The flavor reminded her of smoked meat. "Beef?"

"Elk," he corrected. "Eat up and get dressed. I'll pack."

"Where are we bound for today?"

"Just upriver. We'll make what progress we can and see if we can't find you some buffalo. Now get a move on."

She removed her ruined slippers and threw them in the brushes. Then she sat on a sodden stump and drew on her stockings, finding the task difficult over wet legs. The rest of her ministrations went no better. By the time she finished, all her petticoats and her rose-colored velvet riding habit were wet. She drew on a heavy woolen cloak. That, at least, seemed to repel the water.

Price retrieved his cape and then left Eleanor to saddle her mount. Water seeped through the seams of her new boots and mud splattered her skirts as she lifted her foot high up into the stirrup and mounted onto the saddle, which was sticky with moisture. A day of firsts, she thought. First dressing out of doors in the rain and then mounting unassisted. She glowed with the sense of accomplishment until a trickle of rain crept beneath her cloak and slithered down her back.

"Drat."

This was not going at all according to plan.

The dismal rain continued throughout the tedious morning. There were no buildings, no caves, no cover of any sort in which to seek reprieve from the incessant downpour. It was then that Eleanor realized she had never ridden in such a deluge. Occasionally, she sallied forth in a mist or a light shower, but never this unending torrent.

She had little to do but hold the reins and keep her head down as water poured from her ruined hat and trickled through her hair. Mud sucked at her horse's hooves as they slogged along. Eleanor decided the rain had one advantage.

Last night it caused Troy to hold her once again and gave her leave to allow the familiarity. She admitted to herself that she enjoyed that part quite a lot. In the past when a man had pulled her into an embrace she felt only mildly peptic. With Troy the emotions were different. When he'd opened that robe and taken her in his arms, it stirred the strangest sensations, as if she were suddenly home. Wasn't that ridiculous. Her brain must have been numb. But still, nothing had ever felt so right. He comforted and protected her with his body. That was something she had never experienced and found that, despite her assurance to oblige social conventions, she wanted it again.

"Whoa," called Price. He glanced back at her with his piercing dark eyes. "Move up the bank, river's cresting."

The water swelled to a frightening proportion, dragging trees from the bank and carrying them swiftly along. She followed him to higher ground and they continued on.

Eventually her outerwear failed to keep up with the assault and soaked through. She had heard that wool maintained its warming properties even when wet. As her teeth chattered together like angry squirrels, she decided that wool did not suit the American West.

More surprising than the abominable weather was the realization that she preferred it to what awaited her at home. With sickening dread she recalled her promise and determined to avoid payment for as long as possible.

She endured the driving rain well into the gray morning, but faced with the loss of feeling in her fingers and now her toes, she feared for her health. Could one get frostbite without the frost?

In that moment she decided that true happiness can only be pursued if one has dry, warm feet.

"Mr. Price?"

He pulled his gelding to a halt and waited. She expected him to turn, but when he did not she urged her mount along beside his. He sat erect wrapped in a buffalo robe. Water streamed down the furry hide. His broad hat kept his head and hair quite dry. She understood now why he had scoffed at her hats. They were quite the thing in New York, but in a rainstorm they were useless. All her clothing was. Her garments' purpose was to adorn and show her to her best advantage, while proving to all that she kept up with the latest fashion. She studied his attire finding it to be without adornment and existing solely for the enviable and practical purpose of keeping the wearer dry.

"Sorry to disturb you."

He turned his keen eyes on her now, lifting an eyebrow in question. She knew in that instant what he expected. He thought she was ready to quit, to beg him to return her to safety and comfort. He still did not understand how vitally she needed this chance to prove herself. Seeing Audubon's book of watercolors began this yearning in her soul and it would not be doused by a little water.

She straightened, allowing rain to drizzle down her spine and resolved not to speak a word of her discomfort. If he required proof of her determination, she would provide it by not giving him the satisfaction of a complaint. "I wondered if I might have another piece of dried elk to ease my hunger."

His frown deepened. "You want to eat?"

"No need to stop our progress."

His look of amazement did her proud. She accepted the offered elk and returned to the end of the muddy line of mules. As she gnawed away at the leathery meal, the warmth that filled her had nothing to do with the day.

If he could stand it, she could.

The rain tapered off to a drizzle and then quit all together by midday. Troy watched the steam rise off his horse's withers, knowing his little princess was weary and wet. A glance back showed her nearly asleep in the saddle, her skirts hanging about her in flattened masses that reminded him of her ruined tent.

Done in.

But still she had not quit. Doubt crept into his mind and for the first time he considered that she might be a whole lot tougher than she looked.

No, she had to turn back. He just needed to be patient. Why suffer the discomforts of trail living when you had a mansion or two waiting for you at home? He glanced at the fast moving clouds. Too bad the rain had let up so quick.

He picked a spot to camp on the edge of the grove of willows, far back from the dangerous torrent the Yellowstone had become. Eleanor had no tent this evening and her blankets were still wet. He would give her the buffalo robe again.

He watched the herd of forty antelope graze some hundred yards off, lifted his gun and took aim. The shot dropped one animal. The rifle blast sent the others racing over the knoll and out of sight. He headed toward the downed antelope.

"You got one!" she said.

He glanced up to see her clapping her hands. Where were her gloves? It was then he noticed her fingers. They were an unnatural yellowish-white, like wax.

Troy slid off the horse and reached for her hand. It was like holding a block of ice.

"You're frostbit." The accusation was clear in his voice. "Why didn't you tell me you were cold?"

She made no answer, only retrieved her hand and lifted her chin in a haughty posture that he disliked intensely.

"I did not wish to hinder you."

"It's my job to keep you safe. If you're hurt or cold you gotta tell me."

"Very well then, I lost feeling in my feet about midmorning."

He threw his hat on the ground in frustration and dragged her off her mare. Obviously she was too stubborn to know when to say when. Before she could protest, he had her seated on the grass with her heel in his hand. She shouted when he sliced the leather cording, but he persisted until he had her out of the overly tight riding boots. He gawked at her silk stocking.

"What kind of thing is that to wear?" he chided. "Where's your woolens?"

"It is July. I did not know they would be necessary."

He lifted her skirts. What ensued was a quick wrestling match, in which Lena tried to throw down her sodden skirts as he threw them up. Finally he grabbed both her wrists in one hand and used the other to expose her legs. With nimble fingers he drew away the pink ribbon holding the stockings above each knee.

"Mr. Price, this behavior is unacceptable." Her voice squeaked. "I have explained that you cannot cut off any more of my clothing."

"Hush up." He pulled off a silk stocking, then the other before releasing her.

She lunged for the layers of wet fabric and threw them back over her lovely legs. He held her heel in his palm and studied the toes, all white and yellow, but could be worse.

He drew up his long shirt and placed the soles of her feet upon his belly, grimacing at the contact.

"Mr. Price. Please release me." She rolled from side to side, bending her knees in a useless attempt to gain her freedom.

"Now you listen here, frostbite is serious business. This gets much worse and I'll have to cut off a toe or two."

She stilled and her blue, wolf eyes went wide.

He nodded.

"I'm quite certain this is improper," she grumbled.

"I don't give a tinker's damn."

"Really, Mr. Price, if you just allow me to get up. I'm certain…"

"Who's gonna care?" He gestured with his free hand. "Even the antelope are gone. Nobody can see you, so hush up."

She stilled, looking very uncomfortable.

"Feel anything yet?"

"Not in my toes. But your belly is quite warm."

He smiled and rubbed the buckskin over her feet. "Takes a few minutes to bring the blood back."

"They hurt now," she said and began to wiggle again.

"Quit."

She stilled.

"Give me your hands."

She did, extending one as if he offered to dance with her, but retained the other, bracing herself upright on her elbow.

He pointed. "That one, too."

She shook her head, so he made a grab, capturing her wrist. She fell to her back and he brought her hands to his mouth, breathing heavily upon her white knuckles. Her eyebrows lifted, but she said nothing as he loomed over her. The posture they now assumed, intimate as two lovers, brought his mind back to thoughts of their kiss. He'd only meant to steal a kiss and he'd never expected to unleash the torrent of passion this prim little woman concealed. He stared at her lips now, remembering. Why had he not suspected? She showed such passion in her painting, he should have seen that her fire was not contained to her work. Perhaps he had seen and chose to ignore the signs.

He breathed hot air upon her knuckles again.

"I can feel my toes now," she offered.

He slid her feet free and glanced down. The yellow cast had disappeared. He tucked them between his thighs and lowered her hands to his stomach. After a few minutes he told her to put her hands under her armpits and took her feet back onto his stomach. She sat before him with arms folded.

"Can you get your hands on your own belly?" he asked.

"No."

"You still wearing that corset?"

"Of course."

"Damn foolish contraption. You'd be better off throwing it in the river."

"All proper women wear them."

He snorted, then scoffed. "All proper women."

"Of course."

She moved her toes and his stomach twitched.

"You got no notion of what a proper woman is."

She stiffened and tried to pull away. He held her in place with one hand. "I beg your pardon?"

"A proper woman. You think because you dress fancy and speak a certain way that makes you proper? Ever think for just one minute that a woman in a cotton skirt or a buckskin dress might have a whole better grasp on what being a woman really is?"

She lowered her eyes.

"Doesn't take no gewgaws to be proper and it damn sure doesn't take a cage made of whalebone. My mother never even wore shoes half the year. You telling me she weren't proper?"

When she lifted her gaze, her eyes looked huge.

"I never meant to insult your family."

He could see she did not. "All right then."

"Judging from her son, I would say your mother was magnificent."

That stopped him. He wondered if she was pulling his leg, but her expression looked deadly serious.

"All I'm saying is there is more than one way to go about things. Doesn't make one of them wrong."

"Granted."

He let the matter drop. "You need dry clothes and a fire."

"Lovely." She stilled. "I think I am recovered." She tried to draw back.

"Wait."

She did. They sat on the grass, with the animals grazing and the antelope lying still beside them as he examined her little toe, still a blotchy white, and then placed her feet upon his belly once more.

"Is this a common cure for frostbite?" she asked.

"My first thought was to put your hands and feet in the belly of that antelope."

She gasped. "You were not!"

"Works," he said. "I found a Sioux boy after a blizzard once. He killed and gutted his horse and crawled inside. He lived through what killed many."

"How perfectly dreadful. I might rather die."

He studied her. "No, you wouldn't."

"Why do you say so?"

"I've decided you're stronger than you look."

She laughed. "I'm sure you could best me in any contest of strength."

He didn't think so. Not all strength was physical. His mother taught him that. The white woman had a burning desire to stay out here and he admired her for it.

"I'm talking about inner strength—determination."

She gazed at the sky. "My mother calls it stubbornness and considers it one of my most egregious flaws."

She wiggled her toes. His body's reaction was swift and powerful. He stiffened and just had time to yank her feet clear before his erection filled the gap.

She stared at her toes, giving him a moment to recover himself. In all his born days he'd never had such a sudden response to a female.

"My humblest thanks."

"How are your feet, Princess?"

"Why do you call me princess?"

He wondered if he should tell her the truth. "You just look like one to me."

"Well, I'm not. The best I can hope for is duchess."

"What?" he asked.

"Do you know, Troy, this is the first time in my life that no one knows me on sight? I walked into that fort and said I was a painter and everyone just accepted that."

"I think your paintings helped convince them."

"At home, when I enter a room every soul there knows me as Eleanor Hart, heir to the Hart fortune. It's been that way as long as I can remember. It's quite tedious."

"Being rich or being famous?"

"Both. Mother and Father own enough land to practically start their own country for all the good it does them. They can barely stand to be in the same room with one another."

Troy wondered about this. Was that why she left—because her home had no love left in it?

"But they must have loved each other once or they would not have married."

She rolled her eyes in a way one does at an ignorant child.

"Love matches are considered gauche. People of my class marry to combine fortunes or seek some other advantage, such as land, title or acceptance into society."

"Gauche?"

"Beneath us."

"Terrible."

She cocked her head and stared at him as if he'd gone mad. "Oh, not at all. My mother made a very good match. She comes from old money and my father wanted very badly to break into society. She was his avenue. And she in turn became the wealthiest woman in America through her marriage, you see—a smart match. I hope I shall do so well."

He didn't see. This world she inhabited sounded horrible.

Images of his parents rose in his mind. They had loved each other fiercely and after his father's death, he knew his mother mourned. He'd never thought them lucky before, but perhaps the freedom to choose each other was all the luck anyone had a right to in this world.

Since Rachel, Troy never met a woman he wanted enough to give up wandering. Though he had opportunities to put down roots. Even had the attention of a chief's daughter once. Many women, but none of them white; he'd never allowed himself to consider one again. He gazed at Lena, surprised at the regret rolling within him now. She would have her loveless marriage of power and he, his solitude. A pity for them both.

"What happens if you love someone else?"

She pressed a slim hand to her lips and thought a moment. "Well, after I have fulfilled my duty, I could take a lover."

He could barely breathe for the casualness of her tone. Who was this woman before him?

"What duty?"

"Why to produce a heir of course. What kind of question is that?"

"If that is your duty, then why did your parents allow you to come to this place to paint?"

Now he saw the truth in her eyes. She was not cold and indifferent as she appeared. He knew that look, had seen it many times—the look of the hunted.

She lifted her chin and tried for the haughty expression she mastered so perfectly, but instead her shoulders drooped. Lena fidgeted with the nail of her index finger, which was now a healthy pink.

"They agreed to let me go as far as Fort Union and only if accompanied by trusted escorts."

His eyes widened as realization dawned. "You running?"

She nodded. "But only for a little while. I know I must go back."

He realized again how little he knew her.

"How is it with your women?" she asked.

"What's that?"

"In your tribe, the Cherokee, do parents arrange the matches?"

He smiled. "Not often. A man likes to think he picks a woman but usually it is the other way around."

She reached for her stockings and shoes, drawing them on. "Does she choose the best provider or the man with the highest status?"

"Many women are practical. They generally pick a man with their parents' approval and one who can provide for her and her children."

"You mean their children."

"No. The children, home and all possessions belong to the woman. If he does not treat her well, he must leave her clan and his children behind."

"What? That's ridiculous."

"Princess, just because it is different from your way does not make it wrong."

"What about the chief? He has control of the tribe."

"Yes and no. He must listen to his advisors, who listen to their wives. If he does not fulfill his duty to the people then he is no longer chief."

"They assassinate him?"

Troy laughed. "We are civilized, more civilized then the whites, I think. He is replaced by another man elected by the women of the tribe."

"The women? Surely not."

"Surely, sure," he said and laughed. "They select the chief. They choose their husbands, own their land and their children. When a man marries, he leaves his clan and joins hers."

Eleanor's jaw dropped as she considered the stringent rules that governed her life. Up until this day she never questioned them. They were the foundation of all her beliefs. Now they held some noticeable cracks.

Did Cherokee women really choose their husbands?

She stared at him, noting again the straight, narrow nose and the hair that held too much wave and a slightly russet color.

"Your mother chose a white man."

"By your way of thinking. But by the Indian way she chose a man. With them I am not half Cherokee. I am all Cherokee because my mother is Cherokee." He swallowed hard. "Was Cherokee."

"How do you think of it?"

"I use to think I was just a man, but with you I am Cherokee."

"Half Cherokee."

"It is the half that matters to your people."

She said nothing, but her expression told him she knew this was so.

She cleared her throat, but he did not glance her way.

"I wish we lived in a world where appearances were not quite so important."

"I've been looking for that world myself," he said. "People are quick to judge by what they see."

She brightened and latched onto this sentiment. "That's right. I wish to be judged on my own merit. At least that's what I want for my paintings. I know I can get them in a gallery just by signing my name. But that feels like cheating. How am I ever to know if it is my work or my family name that brings success?"

He nodded his understanding. "The fur company don't care what color you are as long as the beaver's plush."

He'd lost some of the morose continence and that cheered her. They seemed to have found some common ground at long last. She dived in, anxious to expand their understanding. "And you have an advantage as an Indian, because you know how to hunt and trap."

His indulgent smile and sad eyes told her at a glance that she'd said something wrong again. She felt the fragile bond between them fray.

"Princess, I spent the first nine years of my life with my head pressed to a goat's side and my hand around a teat. I never even saw a beaver until I came here. But I learned. Now the beaver disappear faster than the Cherokee and this way of being is no more."

What a struggle his life had been. It shaped him as surely as the sea shaped the cliffs. Her life had been calm, allowing her to bob along with the tide. She felt sad and guilty at once.

"Is that why you turned to scouting, because of a shortage of pelts?"

"If I could sell them, I'd find them. But no one's buying. Hear that gentlemen prefer silk to felt now. Good for beaver, but bad for business."

She pondered an entire industry destroyed by a whim of fashion and glanced at the rosy velvet of her skirts, feeling suddenly vain and selfish.

"I'm sorry."

"Don't be. I'll find work. Your people think an Indian— any Indian—makes a good guide. Maybe we do, but only because there's little else for us without our land."

Eleanor shifted uncomfortably knowing she had chosen Troy because she wanted an expert Indian scout. How she had misjudged him. He was so much more than he appeared.

He blew a hard breath and looked about to speak when he stared down at her rumpled, wet attire. Her teeth began to chatter once more.

"Princess, we got to get you out of those wet things."

Chapter 8

"Put this on," Troy said.

Eleanor accepted the buckskin shirt. "Must I?"

He thrust a pair of moccasins at her. "These, too."

She clasped the enormous footwear and shirt, turning to her belongings to select a woolen skirt in indigo blue along with two damp petticoats, before heading toward the privacy of the wild rosebushes. His voice pursued her.

"If you don't take off that damned corset, I'll cut it off and burn it."

"Dreadful man," she whispered as she reached for the buttons of her cloak. Her fingers tingled now, but worked adequately as she disrobed, abandoning the proper for the practical. She pulled off her dress, unlaced her corset and dropped her petticoats, leaving only a chemise. She glanced toward the clearing to be sure Troy remained engaged. He stood with his back to her, unloading the animals. Quickly, she peeled off the last of her saturated wardrobe and dragged the buttery soft leather over her nude body. Other than the feel of his belly beneath the sensitive soles of her feet, nothing ever felt so decadent. She thought back to the sensuality of that moment and wondered if he felt it as well. The experience cut her to the quick. The mere recollection of her feet pressed to the hard definition of his torso lifted the hairs on the back of her neck and made her breathing catch. Then his hot breath fanned her fingers and, just when she thought she'd perish from delight, he placed her hand on the warm velvet of his skin and hard muscle of his belly. It took all her resolve not to stroke him.

She dropped the leather hem of his shirt, surprised to see it reached her knees. The smell of buckskin, and of the man who wore it, rose about her. She tipped her chin downward and inhaled deeply of the heady scent, trying to fix it in her mind. For good or ill, this was a day she would never forget.

Her feet did not fill his moccasins, but she relished the soft rabbit-fur lining and tied her pink garter ribbons about her ankles to hold the footwear in place. She wiggled her toes in the plush interior and sighed in pleasure.

What would her mother say?

That thought straightened her spine as she imagined the disapproving glare she would receive with a whispered chastisement. She shivered and dragged on her wet petticoats. The skirts felt cold against her skin so she tied them over the dry buckskin, using it like a shift. Next came the indigo skirt of wool, smelling as musty as wet sheep. If they encountered much more of this infernal weather, her clothes would surely molder.

Dressed in this bizarre melting of Indian and European style, she stepped from her boudoir behind the rosebush and draped her discarded clothing over the branches in the late afternoon sun, hopeful the breeze would dry them.

Troy glanced in her direction and then froze, skinning knife forgotten in his hand.

"That old shirt never looked so good."

She gave a quick perusal to see that nothing vital was observable other than a strip of skin from her neck and breastbone, no more revealing than her most reserved evening gown. The baggy garment was quite modest, covering her from collar to knee. The soft leather draped over her breasts, but was much more relaxed than her normally snug attire. She found the lack of structure secretly appealing.

"Thank you, Mr. Price."

He glanced at her skirt. "I ought to put you in leggings."

Eleanor stiffened. "You will not."

He shrugged and returned to skinning.

She gazed at the antelope. "I wish I could have sketched that first."

"I'll kill you another tomorrow. Right now, I'm hungry."

He finished the job without wasted effort as she admired the grace of his movements. He'd make a wonderful model, she thought as he turned his attentions to starting a fire.

"I'm sure all the wood is too wet to burn," she observed, feeling sorry at the fact. He gave her yet another of his impatient looks. She scowled back. His censure grew quite tiresome at times. Apparently their truce had ended.

Another meal of dried elk did not appeal. Surely he would not eat the antelope raw. She reconsidered and judged he would.

"Is it true you have eaten dog?" she asked.

"Where'd you hear that?" he asked as he gathered a wooly looking substance in his hand.

"In *Troy Price, Tales of a Trapper.*"

"Lordy, them books again."

"Have you ever read one?"

"No—all stuff and nonsense." His eyes narrowed. "You got one?"

She smiled. "I have three."

"Three." He sounded aggravated again. "I ought to burn them for tinder. Thought I told you to leave the books back at the fort."

She dipped her head. "They're very small."

He sighed and struck the metal ring against a bit of rock, sending sparks into his tuff of wool. Quick as a rabbit, he snatched up the smoking fluff and transferred it to a strip of bark. He kneeled on all fours and blew, causing a wisp of smoke to rise. Then he added strands of dry grass from his pouch. In a moment a flame appeared. She clapped her hands as if she were at the opera.

"I didn't know wool burned so easily," she said.

She detected a note of aggravation in his voice. "It's cattail."

He fed wood shavings from his pouch to the fire and then left the delicate flame to head into the willows. She stared at his fragile creation, knowing it would neither warm nor cook. She sighed and went to retrieve a candle and book before the sun disappeared.

She tipped the wick to the flame. Hot wax extinguished the fragile fire. She held the snuffed candle in her fist as a sinking feeling seized her. At that moment he returned carrying an armload of kindling.

His gaze took in the scene and then pinned her with a look.

"I'm sorry," she said, still clutching the snuffed candle.

"You always this much trouble?"

"Am I? I think I require the usual amount of tending."

He exhaled through his nose with a force that made her certain he disagreed, then he cleared the area before arranging the fodder again. He next relieved her of her candle and only then took steel to flint once more.

"Next time wait until the fire's hot." In a few minutes he had the flames lapping up a pyramid of sticks. "I'm getting more wood. Don't douse it again or I will burn that book."

She kept her distance from the flame until he returned dragging a thick log behind him, which he propped against a tree trunk and kicked. The limb broke neatly in two pieces. She noted that only the bark was damp, the inner core looked perfectly dry.

"Where did you discover dry wood?"

He smiled indulgently. "Don't it say in that book?"

She ignored the jibe. "No indeed."

"Pull dead wood off the living tree. It's off the ground and under the cover of the branches. Mostly it'll go."

"Brilliant."

He laughed. "Never been called that before."

She removed the pins from her hair and combed out the thick mass, attacking the tangles with vigor. Since coming from New Orleans, she had styled her own hair. When she glanced up she found him studying her in a way that made her feel as if she still wore her corset.

"What is it?"

"Your hair is pretty as red fox tail."

Her hand came up to tug at a springy curl wondering if his comment was compliment or criticism. "It has been the bane of my existence."

"That good?"

"No. A curse. So thick and curly. That alone is enough to bear, but also this color. It's dreadfully out of fashion. I look abysmal in the pastels so popular today. I fear it looks distinctly Irish. My father says, 'If not for your expensive attire, Eleanor, you could be mistaken for a scullery maid.'"

She laughed and noted he did not. It was in that instant that she recalled his father was Irish. Eleanor lifted her hands to cover her mouth.

"Oh, Troy, I am so sorry. Could I possibly be more insensitive? It is just so many Irish are servants and…" She stopped before saying her father would not hire them, considering the lot thieves and cutthroats. Up until this moment she had no reason to doubt him. Now she wondered about what else he was wrong.

She stared at her hands, feeling her ears heat as if on fire.

"I'm sure your father was a wonderful man." Her voice sounded choked to her own ears.

"For an Irishman," he added.

The silence stretched. At last he returned to the antelope and she to braiding her hair. Her fingers threaded one section over the next as she watched him cut the flank of the antelope into strips and skewer the meat on spears of fresh willow. As he worked, she mentally listed all the people with whom her parents would not associate. She followed their lead without a moment's hesitation. Now doubt nibbled at her insides. What gave them the right to judge people on sight?

She was desperate to succeed and be judged by her work, rather than by her connections. Yet she judged the world by connections and appearances—the same measures she rejected for herself.

You, Eleanor, are a hypocrite of the first order.

Troy placed the skewers over the coals; she could not take her eyes off the sizzling meat. The aroma was heavenly.

"Have you had antelope?"

"No, but I'm looking forward to it."

He turned the meat twice. Had she ever been more ravenous in her life? If so, she could not remember.

At last he handed her a skewer. She passed it back and forth between her hands until it cooled enough to hold. Gingerly, she bit into the hot meat, leaning forward as the juices ran down her chin. Wonderful—she closed her eyes to savor the taste.

She devoured the offering to the stick. He handed her another portion and she finished this as well. Who could believe her appetite? Her corset did not pinch, giving her the rare luxury to eat until she felt full.

"No fork tonight," he said.

She met his gaze, suddenly mortified. The corners of his eyes wrinkled. In that moment she realized the comment was not a rebuke but a jest. No one had ever teased her before. Her parents were always deadly serious especially on manners and her servants would never presume to address her in this way. She smiled, enjoying the gentle comradeship they now shared.

"A rather serious breach. Are you offended?"

"Relieved." He grinned and she laughed.

The day had been perfectly miserable. Why then was she grinning as if feebleminded? She sighed in the contentment brought by a full belly, dry clothing and a warm fire. In New York, she had all this and more, but never in her life had she appreciated the simple comforts so acutely as when she suffered their lack.

The boredom was gone along with the creeping dread over her future. She felt alive and strong. Her life had purpose. Tomorrow she might see buffalo or bear. He might bring her an otter or beaver to paint.

"What are you grinning at?" he asked.

"I was thinking of the day. I want to thank you."

Confusion contorted his face and her smile broadened.

"For what—nearly freezing you to death?"

"For the antelope and the dry clothes. I can't remember when I felt so happy."

His brow knit.

"What?" she asked.

"Just wondering what kind of a life you been leading when a buckskin shirt and a spear of antelope makes your day."

"Shouldn't it?"

"Always been enough for me. Just figured you'd be looking for something more elegant."

"I left elegance behind with my diamond ear bobs." She folded her arms about her knees and took in the clean air. "I feel completely safe with you."

"That's a mistake. There is danger here. I wanted to tell you last night. You need to sleep dressed. Sometime you'll need to get up in a hurry."

"Why?"

"Bear, Indians, storm. Who knows? Also sleep with a knife and a loaded gun within reach." He stared at her feet and sighed.

She glanced at the object of his newest aggravation peeking out from beneath the hem of her skirts. The overlarge moccasins tied about her ankles with garter ribbon looked enormous upon her feet. "I have boots."

"I've seen. You can't run in them."

"Ladies don't run."

"Then you best be a crack shot."

Uneasiness seeped in, spoiling her pleasant lethargy. She swallowed back her dread as she considered the wide-open prairie in the fading light. Above her, the stars already poked through the velvety blue. All at once she felt very small.

It was then she realized Mr. Thornton's ruined tent lay back in the grove of cottonwood miles behind them.

"Where shall I sleep?"

"I'll make you up a bed of buffalo robes."

She drew the soft leather closed at her throat. "I've never slept out-of-doors."

"You did last night."

"The branches made a roof of sorts."

"You scared?"

"Most certainly, I am."

"Good."

She frowned, suspicious of his motives again.

He stood, folded the hide lengthwise and then placed another nearby. She crawled into the pocket of one, her head closest to the fire. When she glanced up she found him standing with fists pressed to his narrow hips. Did the man do naught but scowl?

"What's amiss?" she asked.

"You sleep with your feet toward the fire to stay warm."

"I want my head warm."

"Do you also want a log to roll out and set your hair on fire?"

She spun in the bed. "Shall I read to you?"

He laid a knife and her pistol beside her wrapped between the fold of a piece of tanned buckskin. "Suit yourself."

She recovered her candle and the first book of his adventures and began to read. The story described him in romantic terms, but quite accurately, she believed, as a leader of men. She skipped over the sentence that described him as a credit to his race, feeling embarrassed but unsure as to why. On his first adventure he faced five grizzlies. By the time his men arrived, he fended off the last two with a knife killing the enormous beasts.

"T'weren't but three," he said softly.

The tale went on to tell of his recovery of goods stolen by hostile Indians and the rescue of a party of missionaries. Finally, her eyes grew heavy.

"You got bears near your home?" he asked.

"I've never seen one, but understand there are a few in Connecticut."

"Deer and rabbits?"

"They frequent the lawn at our summer estate."

"So you could as easily have painted a deer, chipmunk and rabbit there as here. Then have your father send them off to the Audubon feller."

She sat up, suddenly furious. "Can you not understand that I want to succeed without his help? For once in my life I will do something of my own without the benefit of his influence."

"Well, maybe so but you sure as hell didn't go through all this to paint animals found in your own backyard."

She reeled, disquieted now as she considered her future. She drew the fur blanket up to her nose and huddled against the wave of nausea cramping her innards.

Until this moment she never recognized what was so obvious to him. Troy was right. She was running. She turned her gaze to his dark profile. The simple touch of this stranger's hand did more to make her pulse race than all the kisses her suitors had stolen.

Was it because he was forbidden that he raised such desires? She mulled that possibility and found credence in the notion. There was something dangerous in his eyes and she could not deny its appeal. Sometimes, when he looked at her, she knew exactly how it felt to be hunted—the thrill and fear mixing together.

She huddled lower in her buffalo robe and wondered how he knew so much. He didn't really; he only guessed. Intuitive—a necessary skill for a trapper and scout.

Did he share this longing for something he could never have, but wanted in the secret places of his soul?

Why had she come so far from her home?

The answers frightened her. She gazed across the fire to note him watching her. Everything about him was so different from her.

"Good night, Mr. Price."

He nodded and lowered himself to his bed as she did the same. She stared at the stars. They looked different than they did back home. Gazing at the heavens she found no peace, only the cold light of distant stars.

It was her restless insomnia that caused her to note the sound. At first she thought the noise to be Troy snoring. She found the reverberations comforting until the snuffling changed direction and she sat up. A tearing noise came from somewhere beyond the fire.

She was on her feet in an instant and shaking Troy the next.

Troy rolled to his feet, lifting his rifle as he came upright.

Beside him stood the woman, her eyes wide in the dim light of the dying fire.

"What?" he whispered.

She pointed across the clearing and he heard it. An animal—something big—was into their packs.

"Pick up your gun and get to the river."

She did as she was told, without hesitation or questions. He turned his attention to the sound of bottles breaking and inched out of the firelight, approaching downwind.

The black bear disemboweled her pack and rummaged through the remaining toiletries. Troy moved noiselessly in its direction. Even with his silent approach, the creature sensed him and reared for attack.

The bear bellowed and charged.

He fired. The beast never faltered as it leaped forward. Troy struck the creature's jaw with the butt of his rifle as he danced backward and pulled his knife. A woman's scream sent a shiver up his spine. The bear took two more steps before the effect of the bullet registered in its brain. Then it fell forward. He heard a pistol shot and something inside him snapped. He ran blindly toward the river, his long legs eating up the ground between them.

Where was she? His heart hammered in dread as he scanned the black water, fearing the river had taken her. *Not again.*

"Lena! Lena!"

"Here," came her call.

He found her upon her knees beside the carcass of a year-ling cub as big as an autumn hog. She'd shot it through the head with her pistol and by some miracle that small bit of lead had been enough to stop the creature.

He sank to earth beside her and she threw herself into his arms.

"It reared up. I tried to run as you told me, but it chased me to the water. I can't swim." Her head fell to his chest and she cried.

"You're safe now."

But she wasn't.

Her sobs wrenched at his gut. He held her tight and stroked her back. What was she doing out here? The woman had as much business coming into this wilderness as he had holding her in his arms. He pulled her close and the ache in his chest increased. Why did it have to be her? He knew plenty of fine women, beautiful ones and smart ones and ones with kind hearts—but they didn't make him feel like this. Only she did.

After Rachel, he vowed never again to love a white woman. And he didn't. These feelings were not love. He only wanted to protect her and see her safe. But he couldn't do that here.

She lifted her face and clung to him as he pressed his lips to her forehead. He felt her heartbeat and the soft pressure of her full breasts. His body stirred, but he ignored the temptation as she rested her head in the hollow of his throat. Could she feel his pulse pounding there?

Whether she recognized it or not, there was a pull between them, stronger than he'd ever known. Maybe that was why he'd pushed so hard to be rid of her. Damn the stubborn streak that kept her from giving up.

"I'm such a goose."

He cradled her, pulling her up into his lap.

"It ain't safe out here for you. Tomorrow, I'm taking you back."

"No!"

The vigor in her voice startled him.

She drew back. "You're just using this as an excuse to be rid of me. I have until August."

"Lena, that bear attacked you. It could just as easily have been a grizzly. You understand? I can't protect you alone."

"I'll not go back!" She shoved him away, but he hung on. She quaked against him, staring up, her eyes begging him to do something—but what?

Her bottom lip trembled as she spoke. "You were right before. I am running."

Tears streamed down her cheeks and he pulled her in. She came to him, resting against his heart.

"I didn't believe it at first. I thought I just wanted to paint. But then you mentioned all the animals in my own backyard. I started to wonder—why did I come so far? It doesn't make sense."

"It's all right," he whispered.

"It is not all right. I thought I could do as they wished. Now I do not know if I am strong enough."

He lifted her chin so her words would not be lost in the folds of his shirt.

"Strong enough for what?"

"To forego my dreams for theirs."

"Lena, what are you talking about?"

She pulled back, kneeling before him with her head down and her hands folded in a tight little knot upon her lap. He kept one hand upon his rifle and the other on Lena's shoulder, suddenly disturbed over what she would tell him. He'd been trying for days to puzzle her out and now found that he feared the answers.

"I wish I were a man."

"That's crazy talk."

"It's not. A man has choices. A woman does as she is told. If I were a man, I could paint a whole lifetime instead of one short summer."

"Is that what you want?"

She cast him an intense stare and he drew back. "No one ever asked me what I wanted before. Instead they tell me what is best for me and what is expected. Up until now I have always strived to please them." Her gaze shifted about and he saw the simmering rage of a caged animal. "But it is hard to give up one's dreams."

"Of painting?"

Her shoulders sagged. "What does it matter? No one really cares if I can paint, only that I am the daughter of John Hart."

"I care. You're a damn fine painter. Could be great."

She stared at him, her blue eyes dark and huge in the moonlight. Then she set her jaw in a look of stubbornness he recognized. "I'll not have the chance. You were right about me not doing a thing on my own. I haven't, you know. I've never been allowed to try."

He motioned with the barrel of his gun. "You kilt that bear on your own."

Her fragile smile returned accompanied with a look of satisfaction. "Yes. I did."

He'd lost his entire family and thought that the worst sorrow in the world. Now he wondered if it was sadder still to have a family that didn't care a hoot for your happiness. An idea struck and he spoke before he had time to think, trying to keep his tone casual, but thinking his voice carried a certain edge.

"What happens if you don't go back?"

She gasped. "Why, I have to!"

"Do you?"

"They are my family. I can't just abandon them. It would break their hearts. Besides, where would I go? As you've pointed out, I don't belong out here."

But she was considering it now, he could tell.

She heaved a great sigh. "There is nowhere he could not find me."

"Your father."

"Certainly. He is coming in September to gather me up, but if he hears of the epidemic, I should say he'd be here rather sooner."

She glanced into the darkness as if expecting to see him materialize from the shadows.

Lena wasn't afraid of bears. She had much bigger predators on her trail.

Chapter 9

New York City, July 3, 1840

John Edward Hart opened the envelope just arrived by messenger and scanned the scrawling letters of Lord Matthew Thornton. His dear friend had helped convince him to send his daughter on the expedition up the Missouri, giving his personal assurance that he would see to her welfare. John had looked forward to news of their arrival in New Orleans, having had no communication since they left New York's harbor. Instead of reassurances, the letter told of disaster.

Hart straightened, forced upward by a rising tide of wrath and slammed his fist upon the desk with such force the footman standing beside the door left the ground for an instant.

"Get my wife," he shouted.

A few moments later Charlotte breezed into the room, an expression of annoyance clinging to her full lips at being summoned like a servant.

"Yes, John?" Her voice, as always, revealed none of her disquiet.

"Eleanor's ship was quarantined upon arrival. May 12. Cholera."

Charlotte sunk into the chair before his oak desk. Her pale hand pressed over her heart at the spot where white taffeta met the wide lace collar.

"Is she alive?"

He lifted the letter. "As of this writing."

Her hand covered her mouth for just an instant and then she straightened, again the lady of the house. "You must go after her, John."

Troy's shoulders ached from the late-night work of skinning two bears and stowing the best of the meat in the hides high in the treetops. Before beginning the bloody work, he had moved their camp well away from the carcasses that were sure to bring more trouble.

When he returned from stringing up the meat, he found Lena fast asleep in his sleeping robe. He tossed more wood on the fire and crawled beneath the second hide.

He understood her better now, but knowing didn't make things easier. For different reasons, they both needed to prove themselves and both had tried running away. There the similarities ended, for while she might not like it, she, at least, had a home to return to.

He didn't envy her the responsibilities and burdens she carried. He couldn't rescue her from her fate, but he could give her the animals she needed for her work.

Troy glanced down and stared at the face he thought to remember all his life. Lena, peaceful beside his fire. No fears or worries marred her perfect features and in the darkness, she was his alone.

"I'll take you anywhere you want to go, Lena. I'll show you a world you never dreamed of and stand guard while you capture it all in paint," he whispered.

She smiled in her slumber and he wondered if some part of her understood?

The coyotes' call came first and a short time later the high yip of wolves.

He added fuel to the fire and checked the load in his rifle before closing his eyes.

Sunlight danced over his closed lids making everything seem blood red . He startled and took in the clearing, now in filtered morning light, and Lena, again dressed like a lady in a lacy white shirt that tapered to a narrow waist before giving way to wide flaring skirts of crimson. She squatted stiffly before the fire. Damn that unnatural corset. He glimpsed her ankle and smiled to see his moccasins still upon her feet. She wouldn't get far running in those skirts, but footwear was a start.

He sniffed the air, as his nose took in the smell of roasting meat.

"Who's cooking bear?" he growled.

She jumped at his intrusion into her quiet morning then smiled.

"I am."

He threw off the buffalo robe and came closer to inspect her work.

"Right over the coals. Looks about done. Good work."

"I was about to wake you."

She handed him a portion. He devoured the entire piece, filling the emptiness in his belly as Lena observed his progress.

"Is it good?"

"Best I've ever tasted. What did you do?"

"I rubbed the exterior with fresh ground pepper, salt and dried sage, just as Cook does to lamb. Mother insists a lady know how to supervise her servants, especially in the kitchen."

He nodded his approval. "Damned good."

They stared in silence and Lena grew uncomfortable first. She rose.

"Well, I've already had my breakfast. Where are we bound for this day?"

"I figure I can set you a trap for some small critter then scrape these hides."

"So we will remain here today?"

He wondered if she knew how hopeful she sounded and noted the circles beneath her eyes. Likely she was sore from riding and exhausted. From now on he'd make her life as easy as possible.

"If that suits you."

"Why yes. If you don't mind, I'll do some sketches of you preparing the skins."

He hesitated, not wanting to be collected with her assortment of wild Indians and savage beasts, then realizing that was just where he fit.

He nodded his consent then turned to the drudgery of scraping the hides clean. Lena rummaged in her packs and set up her paints on a fallen log, which she used as a seat before her easel.

"Don't suppose you know how to tan a hide?" he asked.

She set her jaw and then gave her head a quick shake. "The sight of blood disturbs me."

He added this to the hundred reasons she was not for him, hoping the weight of them would convince his heart to be rid of foolish notions. A trapper with a woman who shrank from the sight of blood. He shook his head. She was too gentle for this life, too softhearted. It proved as another reminder that she did not belong here with him.

He continued his rhythmic work as she began hers. Gradually the bits of flesh and sinew fell away.

She watched him, her gaze flicking back to the page on occasion. "I admire your endurance."

"Comes with practice."

After a time, he moved beside her and studied her work. There he sat upon her page scraping the hide, another specimen she encountered on her grand adventure. He fought against the ache in his chest.

"What do you think?" she asked.

He gazed at his savage appearance.

"Looks just like me."

She grinned, obviously pleased, and he held in the sorrow.

"Another painting for your collection," he said.

"I like this one the best."

"Why's that?"

"Because it shall always remind me of you."

"Will *you?*" he asked.

"What?" she asked as she gathered her paint tubes.

"Remember me."

She stilled, her fingers temporarily frozen at their task. Lena turned her gaze on him and he felt his pulse quicken.

"Until they put me in my grave," she said.

He cocked his head, wondering if she toyed with him.

"Truly," she whispered. "You are unique."

He felt his ears tingle at her pledge and he grinned. "Ain't we all?"

"No, sir, we are not. The men I know spend all their days drinking brandy and gambling away the fortunes given to them by more industrious ancestors. We inbreed like rabbits and can do nothing for ourselves. Do you realize that this morning was the first time, the very first time mind you, that I cooked a meal?"

"Good start."

She did not appear to hear him for she continued on. "Your life is so exciting. I would give anything to have gone where you have been." She clasped a hand to her breast. "Oh, the memories you must have."

He knew in that moment he'd trade them all for the chance to make memories they could both keep.

She fiddled with the lace on her shirt. He recognized the sign. Something other than breakfast was on her mind.

"Out with it?"

"Whatever do you mean?"

"Princess, I read signs, including yours."

She pressed her lips together. "Your directness takes some adjustment on my part. I have never met anyone who was so blunt."

"You ain't exactly my normal traveling partner, either."

Her laughter filled the clearing.

"I suppose that's true. I just wanted to apologize for last night. I had no right to burden you with my troubles."

"Princess, I'd say you have good reason to run. That's what I would have done."

That's what he had done. Ran from the sorrow of Rachel even as the grief latched on with sharp claws. He never escaped it, only carried it from place to place, inside him like an unborn child. He'd run so far that by the time he heard about the trouble at home he could not reach them in time to save them.

"It isn't as if they have been bad parents, and I do love them. They see to all my needs. I have had the finest of everything. I must be the most ungrateful of children. All my friends say they would die to be in my place. Mother calls me stubborn and unnatural. Father, well, he barely speaks except to find fault. I wish…well it doesn't matter."

"What?"

"It's just that he never shows my mother or I any affection. He's very gruff, you understand. And mother notices only my flaws. I slouch or laugh with my teeth showing."

"Your teeth?"

She giggled, bringing her hand before her mouth and he scowled.

"That's how it's done."

He made a face.

"Well, you got time to deal with all that. For now you can howl at the moon if you've a mind to. Nobody will know any different."

"I'm so lucky to have found you. I've never had conversations like the ones we share. At home no one speaks of what really matters. You are the only person I know to understand my meaning."

The intensity of her regard made him as nervous as a lone deer at a water hole. He thumbed over his shoulder.

"I best see to the horses."

The next day, they followed the Yellowstone southwest until candle-lighting time. As twilight stole the colors from the day, a flock of pintail ducks stretched their long necks as they headed for the center of the water. The birds made an easy target, but he disliked the idea of going for a swim to retrieve the carcasses.

Lena deserved something other than jerky after two tough days. First frostbite, then a bear. This was not the same as looking after an outfit of trappers or guiding the army. Lena had no skills to survive, nothing but her stubborn pride and some internal toughness. Most women would have quit long ago. He grew more convinced that her troubles, not her ambitions, drove her on. Her little excursion made him responsible for her in a way he was just beginning to grasp. How long would she have lasted if that bear had killed him?

The calculating portion of his brain answered immediately—three days, maybe four.

She must know how to find shelter and make fire and learn to shoot game. Most of all he needed her off that damned skiddery pony she so admired.

Even her clothing was dangerous, cutting off her air, keeping out neither rain, wind nor sun. He thought of her saddle and gritted his teeth wondering what imbecile had decided this was the way a woman should ride.

"Troy, it's nearly dark. Hadn't we better stop?"

He nodded. They were well into the prairie. Trees were sparse. For tonight and probably the next several days there would be no wood for the fire, so instead he'd burn the dried

buffalo pies, a trick he'd learned from the Sioux who knew
how to make use of every part of the creature except the snout.
He slid down from Dahlonega. "Here's good."

She gave a sigh of relief that made him smile. He held the
reins as she dismounted, then hobbled the mare's front legs
and left Lena to see to her saddle. When he returned from
gathering circular droppings he headed for the river. The bend
in the river slowed the current here, making the water calm.
The pintails paddled in a great flock, the whites of their necks
glowing bright in the twilight. He slipped off his belt and powder horn, then his shirt and moccasins. Casting a look back,
he found Lena a mere silhouette against the darkening sky.
He drew off his only dry breeches and lifted his shotgun.
Standing naked, he took aim at a cluster of birds before
squeezing the trigger. Buckshot peppered the water. The ducks
not hit rose into the air with a loud beating of wings.

He cast aside the gun and dived into the water. While he
paddled out to retrieve three ducks, he thought of his old
'coon hound, Smoke. This used to be his job.

Once he reached shore, he found Lena waiting on the
bank. He squatted in the waist-deep water clutching three
ducks by their limp necks. She stood waiting as he pondered
his predicament.

Finally he tossed the birds at her feet. "Pluck these."

She did not move, but only stared at the ducks.

He wanted out of the cold water. His privates were shriv-
eling, but she just stood like a stick.

"Well?" His voice did not disguise his irritation.

"I have no notion how to pluck a bird."

"Well, just carry them up to the camp then."

She squatted and used two fingers to lift a duck by a limp
leg as if it had died of something catching. In the last light
that still clung to the day, he saw the look of disgust evident
in her down-turned lips. She made no move to retreat.

"Git."

"What?"

"Go on."

She looked into the darkness behind her. "What if there's a bear?"

"Bears don't roam the prairie."

"Wolves?"

"Wolves follow buffalo. When you find one, the other is not far behind. There's none about. Now shoo."

Still she hesitated, wringing her hands.

"It's cold as a witch's…" He thought better of the comment and his words fell off.

"Then come out," she said, sounding as if it were the most obvious thing in the world.

"I will." He stood and the water lapped his middle. "You ever seen a naked man?"

"Of course not."

He took another step. "Well then, should be a new experience for ya."

She hesitated a moment longer, her brow wrinkled in confusion. Then she dropped the duck, whirled and charged up the bank as if her skirts were on fire.

He chuckled as he stepped onto the grass and shook off, then slid into his breeches that stuck to his wet legs. Once fully garbed, he lifted the three ducks and walked up the bank to find her sitting on the pile of dried dung, her rifle balanced across her knees.

She spoke into the darkness, still unwilling to face him. "I had no idea you were, I mean to say, if I had the slightest inkling that you had disrobed, I never would have lingered."

Pity, he thought. "I reckon not." He wondered if she blushed. "I've been thinking. You need to know a few things, starting with getting a fire lit," he said.

"I have a burning lens."

"Sun's down. Also, it won't work in rain or snow."

"You left my tinderbox in Fort Union."

He slipped his hand into his possibles bag and withdrew a chunk of flint and his iron striker. He hit one to the other and sent a shower of sparks dancing before him.

"Try these."

He helped her position the two and smiled as she successfully made her own sparks. He decided that he and she were like that stone and that iron. Every time they touched there were sparks. He knew that together they'd make a powerful fire.

"I did it!"

"Now you have to get the sparks to hit the fodder."

He dug a fire pit, carefully removing the dry grass and roots from the area. Nothing caught quicker than prairie grass. Satisfied with the fire pit, he cupped a papery bit of cedar bark in his left hand behind the flint and struck with iron. The sparks leap to the fodder. A tiny wisp of smoke rose. He waved his hand in a lazy circle encouraging the fragile ember. Soon more smoke emerged. He lay down the bundle and blew. A flame erupted from the mass. He fed small dry twigs from his pouch to the hungry fire. Finally, the flame was strong enough to add small pieces of dried buffalo dung, which lit immediately.

"Tomorrow you make the fire," he said.

She looked none too eager, but nodded.

"Now, about them ducks."

Soon feathers were flying in all directions.

"This is rather entertaining." She held aloft a handful of down and blew it at him. The tiny feathers stuck in his hair and she laughed.

Only someone who never plucked feathers would find this work amusing and only someone with plenty would waste good down feathers. Another whirl of feathers assaulted him. He held up a fistful.

"You like a wad of these down your back?"

She held up her hands in surrender.

He gutted the first bird. "You do the others."

She shook her head. "I couldn't."

Their eyes met and he saw the look of disgust on her face. She didn't mind eating them, just so long as she didn't get her hands dirty.

"A mite squeamish for an adventurer."

She smiled. "Until today, my only experience with duck was telling Cook what kind of sauce to prepare."

"No sauce tonight."

She smiled. "No matter. I'm quite famished."

After gutting the remaining birds on his own, Troy staked them and set them to roast.

Lena settled beside him on the ground, watching. She poked at the duck.

"How do you know when they are done?"

He stabbed the breast and watched the juices issue forth. "When the liquid is clear, it's ready."

He offered her the stake and there was no more talk for some time. At last she laid the carcass aside and stared at the fire. "I've never seen wood like this."

He laughed, knowing he would enjoy the next few minutes something fierce.

"'Cause it ain't wood."

She leaned forward, unknowingly perched upon her own throne of manure. "What is it?"

"Same thing you're sitting on—dried buffalo shit."

She sprang to her feet as if launched from a cannon, brushing her backside furiously. He laughed so hard his sides ached.

Her chin lifted as she assumed a regal stance. "Oh, I see. You are playing games again."

He clutched his ribs. "No, Princess. It's dung. You've been sitting on it and you've been cooking with it."

She pressed her lips together as her hand clasped her mouth. Her face paled and he thought she might lose her dinner. She gagged and he moved to rest a hand on her back.

"Don't touch me." She slapped at him, whirling toward him with eyes flashing fire. "How could you?"

He grinned. "Just the way it's done here."

"Why did you not tell me?"

"Just did."

Her finger pointed at his chest. He longed to grab her wrist and kiss her until she was breathless.

"This is the most…most, well I am heartily offended…"

Then something remarkable happened. She laughed. Not the small, polite kind of laugh with her mouth covered, but a full-bellied laugh. Side by side they roared. He slapped his knee and she held her face in her hands as her eyes watered.

It was something he had never expected—a woman like her being able to laugh at herself.

At last she could speak once more.

"You are a devil," she said.

He nodded.

"Why not use wood? Was this to humble me?"

"No, Princess. There just ain't no wood here."

She glanced across the plains of grass and smiled. "Gives the duck a distinctive flavor, don't you think?"

His smile lingered. "Reckon so."

She lowered herself to the grass and studied the pile of dung. Her shoulders bobbed again as she clucked.

"I suppose it's just grass, after all."

A warm silence stretched between them. She sat still and erect against the night. He wondered what occupied her thoughts as she seldom went so long without jabbering. A faint snore issued from her.

He smiled. Tuckered out then. That explained it. He removed the remaining duck from the spit and lay out his bed, then hers, placing their feet to the fire. He left a gap between them, but not much. He liked to watch her sleep. Living out here alone, he'd developed night vision to rival a horned owl's. By starlight, he watched Lena's hand slip from her cheek and her head drooped. Another minute and she'd fall in the fire.

His smile faded. She wasn't for him. She'd live in a grand house with hundreds of servants to see to her every whim. She didn't need to know how to pluck feathers or tan leather, because she wasn't staying.

She groaned as he lifted her and slid her between the sleeping skins like a child. Then he knelt beside her and tucked the hide close beneath her chin. Her smile hit him in a deep place in his gut. How did she make him feel protective even in her sleep? She was exasperating, surprising and completely unique. She fascinated him. The urge to slide in beside her tugged at him, but he resisted.

"She ain't for you," he muttered to himself as his eyes drank in the sight of her. Lena was like a rose, gone before first frost.

Chapter 10

After spending half the night tossing as if he slept on an anthill, Troy resolved to keep his distance from Lena. Why torture himself with her scent and the touch of her soft skin? It was like giving a mouthful of water to a man dying of thirst. Maybe if he could locate Black Feather's tribe, he could find a willing woman. He recalled a particular doe-eyed gal who was lithe as a weasel. The thought only further darkened his mood. He didn't want a weasel; he wanted that high-spirited woman who smelled of roses.

Damn her.

Troy rolled from his sleeping skins before sunup and walked the river. Better to be away from camp before she emerged from her bed and stretched. Just the image of her silhouetted against the rising sun made sweat break out on his brow.

When he returned he found her still lying about like the lady of the castle. He sighed. That's what she was, after all. A spoiled, pampered little miss on her first adventure. Despite his best intentions, he stalked over to her bedroll. All that was visible was a shocking wave of orange hair made brilliant in the early morning sunlight. The rest of her huddled beneath the dark fur of his buffalo robe.

What would she do if he slid under there with her?

He clenched his teeth and nudged her with his toe. She groaned and her hair slid across the fur as she curled farther down into her burrow.

"Breakfast in bed, my lady?" he asked, imitating her accent, then waited with his hands upon his hips for her appearance.

Instead, her muffled voice emerged from within. "Just leave it by the bed."

Now he was frowning. Irritation prickled him like nettles as it dawned on him that she was so accustomed to breakfast in bed that she saw nothing out of the ordinary in his offer.

He lifted his foot to give her a hearty shove and then lowered it, stalking away. The robe fell back as she sat bolt upright and stared at him.

He glared from across the cold fire pit.

"Was that you speaking a moment ago?" she asked.

He nodded. "I thought I dreamed it."

The hide lay at her waist and he noted she had released her bodice and loosened her corset in the night. The result was a beautiful view of the lush curve of her breast, bare at the top and contained only by a green ribbon and a thin veil of cotton.

Please God, don't let her stretch.

As if hearing his prayer and ignoring it, she rose to her knees. His gaze devoured her, sweeping upward to fix on the perfect swell of her breast, now in profile. Stiffly she rose to her feet.

Oh, no. He told himself to look away, but his traitorous body wanted the image branded to his memories for all time.

She stretched her arms wide and the sheer fabric clung. Beads of sweat covered his brow as she finally noted her state.

"Oh, dear." She whirled away, giving him her back too late. The damage was done.

He turned to the remains of last night's duck, glancing up to note her lacing her boots before gliding across the yellow grass.

"Were you teasing me?" she giggled.

He glanced at the water, considering diving headfirst into

the current to clear his senses. Removing her from his view did wonders for his equilibrium.

"Yup. I'll have your tea ready as soon as I can find me my new silver teapot."

"You left mine at the fort."

He met her gaze and found an impish expression dancing in her eyes. She wanted to play—God help him.

She perched beside him as he sliced dark meat from the carcass. He didn't have to look at her. He had the duck. Absorbed in the task, the tension in his body began to recede.

"Well, I best be about my morning ablutions," she said.

He hoped that meant moving off, but he did not glance up to see. Finally the temptation grew too fierce. He found her standing behind her horse, which was the only cover for some miles. Her dress dropped to her feet followed by several white petticoats. He counted five, stunned at the number. Then he stared at pale ankles, trim calves and dimpled knees. Damn that horse's barrel chest for blocking the most interesting part. He craned his neck, leaning forward so far that he fell onto the fire pit. Swearing, he rose to see ash now smeared his buckskin shirt.

He glanced back and found her watching him above the horse's withers.

"Turn about, Mr. Price, if you please."

He snorted, but did as instructed, then beat at his shirt, lifting a cloud of ash from his buckskin shirt. When he turned, he noted she was fully dressed in a pink outfit that matched her horse's silly bridle. He sighed in regret. Perhaps he should keep them on the prairie.

There was little here but antelopes and she wanted to paint a variety of game.

After breakfast he headed south, following the Yellowstone as it snaked across the prairie. Over the next six days, he kept his distance, spending much of his time scouting game, for food or her paintings.

He brought her antelope, prairie dogs and a mule deer, but

she was dissatisfied with the results, finally deciding that the method of positioning dead animals with wire did not create what she called "the desired effect" and hereafter got as close as possible to the live animals using her telescope.

They came upon a buffalo herd in the early afternoon of the sixth day. He made camp and left the mules hobbled and then took her toward the herd.

He kept them at a distance from the enormous creatures while she sketched from horseback, holding her paper tucked tight to her belly. Her pencil flew over the page. Buffalo were unpredictable and dumb as dirt. That paired with their size made them a considerable threat. He tried to watch the herd, but found his gaze straying back to Lena again and again, his interest held in particular by a curling lock of hair that danced in the breeze upon the long graceful slope of her neck.

"You're getting sunburnt," he said at last. The cocked hat she wore shaded her face, but not the pale column of her neck.

She lifted her head and gazed at him as if just remembering he was there. Her brief smile hit him in the chest like a barbed arrow.

"You are always looking out for me." The soft velvet of her voice tickled his insides.

"Lord knows someone has to." He gave a mock suffering tone to his words and was rewarded with the tinkling sound of her laughter. "How much longer, you figure?"

She glanced about seemingly surprised to see the sun well on its way toward setting. If they were in the mountains it would be long gone.

"My goodness, where did the day go?"

He noticed that when she was painting or drawing she disappeared into a private place and all concept of time vanished. She needed to be reminded to eat and only quit when the light grew too poor to work. The results astonished him. He knew little about such things, but her paintings seemed to depict more than an animal's likeness. He had to agree with Wind Dancer. These were indeed spirit paintings.

"I'm sorry," she said closing the leather flap protecting her paper and capping her water bottle. "You must be famished."

He nodded and watched her gaze sweep the meadow before them, drawing pleasure from her expression of contentment.

"I read accounts of herds that stretched for miles in all directions. I didn't credit them until now." Her gaze returned to his. "If I live to be a hundred, I shall never forget this sight."

He kept his gaze on Lena and had to agree. If he lived to be a hundred…

Lena put away her gear and he led them from the buffalo.

"You like traveling about, Lena?"

"Mr. Price, you cannot imagine the sense of freedom. After spending my entire life shut up in one place or another. To finally see what so few have witnessed, it is a gift from God above." The look of exhilaration flickered and then her expression changed. The corners of her mouth slipped downward and her brow lowered over her blue eyes.

"What?"

She met his gaze. "I just wondered, after seeing all this, how I shall return home?"

He watched her carefully as he asked the next question. "Well, you can't stay out here forever, can you?"

Her gaze swept the lush valley. She drew a great breath as if to capture the day inside her.

The longing echoing in her voice made his jaw tighten.

"No, of course I cannot."

It seemed she was convincing herself more than him, for she never glanced his way and her words came harsher than necessary.

Of course she could not. What had he expected her to say? Still her reply put him in a sour mood. He said little as they returned toward camp and Lena seemed to be brooding in her own thoughts as well.

"We'll be coming to Pompey's Pillar tomorrow."

"What is that?"

"Big tower of rock. See it for miles. Be in the mountains soon after that. Might see elk or even a grizzly."

She shivered as if afraid, but her smile returned. The woman loved adventure nearly as much as he did.

"The prairie is lovely in a lonely sort of way, but I shall be glad to leave this incessant wind," she said, returning a wisp of hair to its proper place. "How does anyone live out here? My hair is a ruin. I have rarely had such trouble."

He made no comment, thinking the tendrils of hair playing about her neck were as sensual as a kiss.

"How do the Indian women keep their hair in place? Do they wear hats?"

"Hats?" He laughed. "Only on Sundays."

She blinked. "Are you teasing me?"

He nodded and found her smile captivating.

"Some tribes on the plains use oils and grease."

"You have a fascinating knowledge of the people here."

"Comes from living with them, I guess."

Her mood seemed to darken as they returned to the mules. He tried to think of some way to cheer her as he drew out his fire-starting stone and iron. Fingering his assortment of stones he came upon a notion.

"Ever seen one of these?" he asked.

She set aside her sketches and an eyebrow lifted in interest. "What is that?"

Her gaze seemed stuck on one particular stone. He'd found it two years before in the Big Belt Mountains near the headwaters of the Missouri River.

Her eyes twinkled with excitement as she held it to the light.

"Don't know. Found it in a stream."

Her voice came breathless with her enthusiasm. "It looks like glass. I'd say an emerald or peridot."

He achieved his aim. Lena no longer looked downcast. He

rummaged in his pouch until his fingers touched the stone he sought, recognizing it by its sharp point. He drew out the blue one that reminded him of glacial ice.

"Got another."

Her gaze lifted from her treasure.

He handed her the second stone and Lena turned it in her hand then smiled at him. He hadn't realized how much he'd missed her smile until he saw it once more. He thanked the Lord he'd scooped up the bright pebbles that day.

"Have you shown this to anyone else?"

"Just you."

"These could be worth a great deal of money. Are there more?"

Troy scratched his neck. Money again. Her world turned on it. "I never liked digging in the dirt like a hog in autumn. Spotted these in the gravel by a stream after a rain. I thought they might work for starting fires, but they don't throw a spark. Pretty though."

She handed them back. He smiled at her reluctance to release them.

"Keep them. Make a fine souvenir."

"Oh, no, I couldn't. They might be valuable."

"Do you like them?"

"Of course."

"Then they're valuable."

She stared down at the pebbles.

"I'll accept the green, to remember you by."

That thought made him sad, but he accepted the blue, tucking the clear pebble back in his fire-starting bag.

She sighed and glanced skyward. "What a lovely day."

"Nearly done now."

He set his fire and readied the meal. The silence was back. Not the comfortable one he'd grown used to but the sorrowful one that came from Lena, as she stared at the flames.

At last, she leveled her gaze upon him, while her teeth worried her bottom lip. He lifted a brow in silent question.

"What's wrong, Princess?"

She shook her head, denying any worries. That night he lay still listening to her toss. He nearly called out to her. Just 'cause she had something on her mind didn't mean she wanted to talk to him about it.

The next morning she was still chewing her lip as if it was breakfast. He broke camp and headed them downriver across a flat expanse of sand.

He'd decided he'd be damned if he'd ask her again and then went ahead and asked. *Guess I'm already damned, anyways.*

"Want to talk about it?"

"What?"

He lifted his eyebrows.

"Is it so obvious?"

He nodded.

"Might I trust you with a revelation that weighs heavily upon me of late?"

Uncertainty made his skin itch. He didn't know what she was fixing to unload, but from her furrowed brow and the restless motion of her hands, he'd bet nothing he wanted to hear.

"Go ahead." He felt nowhere near as relaxed as he sounded.

She drew in a deep breath as if about to plunge into cold water. He braced himself for what came next.

"My father agreed to this excursion and to present my work only if, upon my return, I conceded to marry a man of his choosing."

His insides went cold and his breath caught. "He picks your husband?"

She nodded.

"Why did you agree to that?"

"A woman must marry."

"Not to just anyone."

"No, of course not. My mother favors an English lord. A

title is the only advantage she could not obtain for herself, so she seeks it for me. I would be Lady Eleanor, a member of nobility. Won't that be grand?" Her voice rang hollow with none of the enthusiasm or excitement of a bride.

"They're just going to pack you off to England with some stranger?"

"Perhaps I shall be permitted to travel the continent and see the great museums."

"That what you want?"

She fisted her reins, sending her knuckles in sharp relief against the kid gloves.

"What does it matter? English, American, they are all birds of a feather." Her eyes sparkled dangerously. "For now I will stretch *my* wings." She tapped her riding crop against her horse's side and the little mare cantered off. She urged more speed and the horse complied, issuing into a full gallop so smooth Troy thought she could tip a jug while riding and not spill a drop.

He imagined her stepping in a 'chuck hole and apprehension tore through him. He followed, kicking Dahlonega to a gallop. She glanced back and her laughter urged him on. He grinned, accepting the challenge.

Her horse was as fast as the wind. Dahlonega was half race-horse and still he did not close the gap. Finally, she stopped, turned the horse, and damned if the animal didn't bow to him. He pulled up on the reins and watched as her mare danced side-ways, crossing one dainty foot before the next. Never in his life had he witnessed a horse do something so unnatural.

Next, her mount reared up. He lunged toward Lena, know-ing he'd never reach her before she fell, but she did not fall. Instead, she leaned forward as the horse rose. Damned if the animal didn't hop on his back legs like a dancing bear as Lena rode along, perched sideways, like a monkey on its back.

He drew off his hat and gaped. She laughed as her horse came down upon all fours and then spun in tight circles upon a fixed front leg, first one way and then the next. Lena gave a slight tug and the horse stilled. She stroked the fine arched neck of the horse and then lifted her gaze to him. He noted the smug little smile and the expectation in her eyes.

Troy kicked his horse forward. "Damn!"

Her smile showed pride. "Isn't she grand?"

He never took his eyes off Lena. "Sure is."

"I told you she was fast."

"Like greased lightning." Finally he glanced at the horse. "What was them moves you was throwing?"

"Dressage—invented for war. That last one is designed to knock attackers away from the rider. I told you, she's a champion."

"I seen Sioux jump off a galloping horse and bounce back on like a rubber ball. I seen Crow fire arrows from a horse while riding backwards. But I never, in my born days, seen a horse hop up and down like she done."

Lena leaned forward and hugged the horse's neck, dropping a kiss to the white mane. "She's a wonder."

"I finally see why you brung her."

She smiled.

"She's kinda like you."

Lena straightened, blue eyes intent. "In what way?"

"First time I seen that little filly, I thought her too pretty to be of any use. I didn't think either one of you were strong enough to last a week out here."

She lowered her chin. "And now?"

"Seems I misjudged you both."

"I've never been expected to be anything but vapid and useless."

"Well, you'll be quite a surprise when you get back, I imagine."

Her sad smile tore him up. With her wild ride finished, her troubles overtook her once more. His attempt at bolstering her spirits failed.

The approach of sunset made him blue. Another day gone and one closer to the day he'd have to turn her loose. Lena felt it, too. Her unnatural quiet drew over her like a cloak.

They reached camp and built a fire against the approaching dark. Soon the yip and yap of coyotes filled the air and they settled before a fire.

He wished she'd never told him. It would be easier to let her go if he thought she was willing. Instead she faced her future like a brave soldier, ready to sacrifice herself.

"You can't save me," she said, as if reading his thoughts.

"I know."

"Where will you take me tomorrow?"

It was all they had, he realized, this journey, her work and their longing.

Troy always preferred the mountains to prairie. They reminded him of his home. The air, though dry, smelled of lodge pole pine here. He breathed deep.

He picked a beautiful spot to camp beside a rock-lined stream. Water cascaded down into deep pools providing places to bathe.

Lena decided the following morning was washing day. Troy sat back and watched her set about the task. After only a few minutes he clutched his mouth in an effort not to bust out laughing.

"And what, may I ask, are you snickering about?" Lena regarded him in the haughty attitude that once irritated him.

"I just never seen a woman rub soap into dry clothes before."

"I suppose you could do better."

"If that's supposed to get me to leap up and wash your dirty clothes, you got me confused with a fool."

Her shoulders slumped. "I've never done this before."

"Now that don't surprise me as much as you might think."

She sat on the rock before her laundry, dresses in one pile and underclothing in another. Her expression of defeat changed to one of hope when she laid her eyes upon him.

"Surely you've seen someone do laundry."

He straightened. "Seen?" Speech failed him. "You mean to tell me you ain't even seen any laundry done?"

"My education did not include it."

"Sounds lacking."

She lifted her chin. "I'll have you know I had the best education money can buy. I can read Latin and speak French. I studied Academies and Socrates."

He lifted his eyebrows as if impressed. "Oh, well, then. Why not just speak some French at them stinky duds. That ought to impress them plenty. Won't make you smell no better though."

She glanced about as if expecting her maid to arrive at any moment.

"Oh, bother," she muttered, then pasted a smile upon her face. The result affected his innards more than he cared to admit.

"Mr. Price, I am not asking for you to wash my clothes, but any relevant observances would be most welcome."

"You asking for help?"

"I am."

"Oh, well, I didn't recognize it past all them two-dollar words. Where I come from, you just ask someone to lend a hand and slap a please on the end."

She considered that. "Would you instruct me, please?"

"If I help you, then you let me wash my hair with that fancy soap."

Her smile seemed knowing. "You help me, Mr. Price, and I shall wash your hair for you."

He couldn't quite keep the glee from his face when he offered his hand to seal the bargain. She hesitated a moment, then reconsidered and clasped his palm. Tingling warmth began at the point of contact and rippled up his arm. He scowled and then glanced at her to see her eyes wide in surprise.

He released her and cleared his throat, wondering why he agreed to let her touch him, when he'd spent the better part of the last two weeks avoiding her touch.

Longing and caution warred within him as he stared at her.

"Shall we begin?" she asked.

He drew a deep breath as if he were about to plunge head-first into the pool before him.

"Now, I ain't never washed anything but woolens and cottons. I don't know how them velvets will hold up."

She nodded. "Understood."

"Since we don't have a kettle we'll have to make do in the stream. Give them all a good soak first."

Lena stood by the falls as Troy moved downstream, already anticipating the next catastrophe. She took her crimson skirt and held it in two fingers, then bent to douse it beneath the falls. The current swept the garment away and down into the pool where Troy waited to fish it out.

"Gad, I might have lost it," she said.

"Try the still water and hold down what you ain't gripping with rocks."

He hadn't meant to help her, but all the talk wore him out more than washing. In a few moments she knelt on the grassy bank as he sat on a rock that rose above the water, his breeches rolled up to his knee. He showed her how to dunk and beat the fabric on a rock. He told her not to twist the woolens as it made them shrink. Troy conserved the soap, using it only on the soiled places.

"Don't daub at it. Rub it." He grasped the nearest garment and showed her, then dunked it to rinse. The bathing soap she used for laundry filled the air with the scent of roses. He demonstrated, lifting the fabric. In that instant he recognized the thing, now as transparent as smoke. He held the source of many hours of lost slumber—her damned sheer sleeping robe. He stared at the thing imagining Lena that first rainy night, naked, wet and exposed to him.

Curse it all; the image seemed branded on his brain. He knew until his dying day, he would never be rid of it.

"Like this?" Lena followed his demonstration.

"I gotta get back to tanning hides." He headed for shore, pausing only to dunk his head. The woman made him hotter than a horned toad in August.

The afternoon passed in the slow torture of watching Lena stoop and scrub her garments, presenting him with a fine view of her backside. Finally, she sighed and swept her forearm across her moist brow.

He helped her twist the last of the garments and then they hung them on the bushes to dry.

"I reckon you'll be glad to get back home, where other folks do the washing."

"I won't miss the washing. But other things I will miss greatly."

"What, for instance?"

He hung the last skirt and rested on the downed log as she considered the leafy cover above them.

"I'll miss my freedom. I'll miss waking up and wondering what the day will bring. At home my life is very predictable, tiresome really. The only joy I find is in my painting."

"You do that real well."

"Thank you, Troy. But soon I shall be back to painting bowls of fruit in the drawing room."

Their gazes met and held.

He was sorry he couldn't do more for her than help her find the animals she needed and keep her safe while she did her work. But he wasn't willing to fall in love with her and lose his heart in the process.

He glanced away. No, she would soon belong to some thin-blooded Englishman who thought her spirit something to be squashed.

He ground his teeth together until they squeaked.

Chapter 11

Lena pressed her fists to her hips and surveyed her drying wardrobe. Then she stretched her back and Troy's mouth went dry. When she turned to him, her eyes shone with an impish delight.

"I am prepared to fulfill my promise, Mr. Price, and play your valet this evening."

"Valet?" He laughed. "I can wash it myself. Just give me the soap."

She shook her head, sending the curls at her temples dancing. How he loved the merry color of her hair.

"Nonsense. We have an agreement."

Well, he'd given her a chance to bow out. If she was dead set, he wouldn't stop her.

Discomfort hit as he stared up at Lena, the lady of the manor, now prepared to wash his hair. He longed for her touch and knew that was why he'd accepted the wager. Imagining her slim fingers delving into his hair, massaging his scalp sent a pulsing of anticipation down his spine. Lena swept toward him then paused.

"Let me just retrieve my soaps." She drew out a satchel and revealed six different cakes: three pink, one purple, one pale green and a strange translucent yellow. She sniffed the first.

"I do not think the rose will suit, nor the lilac. That leaves only gardenia." She lifted the green.

"What about that?" He pointed at the yellow.

She giggled. "That is saddle soap."

He lifted the cake and inhaled. The scent of a new leather rose to him. He extended the bar. "I want this one."

She looked unsure. "If you're certain. I don't know what it will do to hair."

The unease returned as they regarded each other in silence. She cleared her throat.

"Well then." She extended her hand for the bar and he slid it into her small palm. "If you'll just sit on the bank. I'll fill the water skin and bring it to you."

He sat on a rock, waiting for her, listening to his heart pound as loud as a woodpecker on a hollow trunk. She swept up the bank, deposited the skin and then returned to her belongings. After rummaging a moment, she returned with a pristine white linen towel and silver comb and brush he thought she left back at Fort Union. She laid the towel before his feet and then arranged the soap and other items.

She swept a lock of hair from her forehead and stood before him.

"I'm afraid I'll get your shirt rather wet."

"You ever washed anyone's hair?"

Her cheeks pinkened. "I shall be frank, Mr. Price. Before coming here, I never even washed my own."

He laughed.

She rushed to recover. "But I know how to go about it. I'll wet it first, then soap, then rinse."

Troy doubted it would be so simple.

"If you'll just remove your shirt."

He did, standing to pull off the buckskin and set it beside her belongings. When he turned back he found the pink in her cheeks had migrated to her neck and the tips of her ears. Her chest rose and fell in a rhythm far too quick for a woman standing still.

His nostrils flared drawing in her scent. She looked like a woman waiting to be kissed. He realized he never wanted anything more than to draw her close and press his mouth to those full lips.

"If...if you will kindly sit now," she said.

He stared at her lovely, nervous face. He could kiss her. Likely he could do more than kiss her. But he'd never keep her. Not for long.

This magnificent woman would make someone a damn fine wife. Just not him.

He plunked down on the log.

Why did that matter? He'd been with many women and they never cared that he would not stay. He took what they offered and enjoyed their coupling. So what made him care if this little slip of a thing left him at summer's end? Regret he could not fathom pierced him.

"Lean forward," she said.

He did and cool water streamed over his head and down his neck, trickling over his shoulders and back.

Lena grasped the soap and wet her hands raising a lather. Then she placed the soap against his head and scrubbed. Quickly the bubbles foamed. She worked the soap through his hair. He groaned and she stilled. Excitement vibrated from her fingers and radiated up her arms. Did he feel it as well?

She inched a little closer, keeping her fingers in motion as she stood close enough to hear his breathing. Sunlight danced over the smooth bronzed skin of his back. She noted how very pale were her forearms by comparison.

The impulse to touch his neck and rub his shoulders proved hard to resist as she worked down to his nape and then back toward his crown, building a foaming lather.

He sighed.

"How does that feel?" she asked.

"One step from paradise."

She smiled and then frowned as she noted the lather leaning dangerously on his forehead. It slid down his brow and she scooped to stop it, but the suds slithered toward his eye. He reacted an instant later. She knew the moment of contact, for he lifted a hand to rub.

"Water," he ordered.

She retrieved the skin and doused him, sending a torrent of soap streaming down his face.

He sputtered and stood, shaking his hair from his face, both eyes now pinched shut. His hand streaked out.

"Towel."

She handed it over and he threw his head back. His hair flew up, landing in soapy strands on his back.

Bubbles trickled down his forehead, as an untimely mirth struck her. She pressed a hand to her mouth as he swiped the linen across his face. A very unladylike snort escaped her and he opened one eye to peer. Seeing her poorly contained humor, his eyes narrowed.

He fell to his knees upon the stream's bank and dunked his head. Then he stood and shook like a wet dog, causing Lena to squeal as she threw out her hands in vain effort to stop the sudden shower. A devilish grin crossed his lips and he stalked forward to give another shake. She dashed up the bank, but not quickly enough, for he captured her ankle. She fell upon the grass.

She kicked to no effect as he fell upon her in a wink and flipped onto her back, where she thrashed like an upended turtle while he straddled her thigh.

"Mr. Price. Release me this instant." Her best incensed voice did not slow him, but rather only caused a devilish glint in his eye. Her stomach gave a wild flip as she struggled once more trying to push him off.

He clasped her wrists.

"You think it's funny?" he asked.

She shook her head. "No, not at all."

He loomed and water dripped from his hair onto her face.

"You think it's funny. Now it's my turn."

He shook as she screeched and gave one more pathetic effort to escape as he meted out his punishment. Droplets showered her, but still he was not satisfied until he actually rubbed his wet head against her cheek, sliding down her throat.

She stilled as the game changed from playful to sensual. A tingle rippled down her neck, making her chest constrict. The most remarkable, dreadful thing happened next, as her nipples hardened. She would have wrapped her arms about herself, had she had use of them.

He lifted his head, laughter silenced as his gaze met hers. His quicksilver reaction made her pulse race. Suddenly the game turned deadly serious as he held her motionless. His body stilled, except for the heaving of his beautiful bare chest. For just a moment she thought he might kiss her. No, she wanted him to kiss her, hoped—longed for his lips to brush hers, for his chest to cover the dreadful ache his antics brought to her breasts.

He released her abruptly and rolled clear, coming to rest a few feet from her. She sat up and wiped the droplets off her face. He watched her, his chest continuing to work at a rate much faster than necessary for the little exertion restraining her must have cost him.

A satisfied grin lifted his mouth and she thought him the most devilishly handsome man she'd ever seen.

"That was very naughty."

He nodded. "So was running soap through my eyes."

"That was purely accidental."

"It was purely careless."

She regarded him, wondering at the strange tension still tightening her belly. "No one has ever done that before."

"What?"

"My mother called it roughhousing."

"Did you like it?"

She could not begin to tell him how much, so she simply nodded.

"The men of my class are so self-important and, well, the servants would never presume to speak to me as you do."

"Sounds lonely."

She'd never thought of her life that way, but it was true. Once she believed this was just how things were, serious and formal. This man gave her a glimpse of a different life, one full of teasing and laughter. She straightened as she recognized she preferred this.

"Yes, it is rather."

"What about your pa?"

"Oh, no, he is very austere. His position, you understand." She saw from his confusion he did not. "Did your father tease you?"

"He put a garter snake down my pants once."

She gasped. "How dreadful."

"It was funny."

"Funny?" She tried to imagine him as a little boy, dancing about with a snake in his pants, and giggled. "Well, I imagine it wasn't funny for the snake."

"He came out all right."

"That's a mercy." They stared in silence for a moment as they exchanged a smile. This camaraderie…she'd never expected it and had never experienced such ease with anyone, especially not her parents. "I so enjoy your company, Troy."

"Thanks."

"I shall miss you when I leave."

He said nothing for a moment, but his smile faded. "Lena, it's none of my business, but if not for your promise, would you stay?"

How she longed to say yes. It was the truth. If not for her obligation to her family, she would stay with him if he'd have her. But he had not asked that.

She sighed, suddenly melancholy. The foolish game and pleasure of only a moment ago disappeared like a puddle in the sun. She could not stay.

"Why, Troy?"

"I guess I'll miss you, too."

Her smile stood in opposition to the bands of sorrow now squeezing her heart. How unfair of life to show her possibilities that she could not explore, roads she might never tread. She needed some distance from him to think.

"I would like to bathe now."

He nodded and cast his eye to the water.

"If you want a bath, this is the spot. I'm going to set camp up that way." He pointed. "Keep your pistol and rifle nearby. There are bears about."

Her eyes rounded.

"Ain't seen no evidence. But fire a shot if you need me."

He left her, giving her privacy to bathe. She glanced about as she laid her firearms upon the bank as instructed, but saw no wildlife. She remained in her shift kneeling on the shallow sandy bottom, astonished at the warm water that flowed gently by. After a time, she emerged, dried and dressed. Her hair took some struggle to tame and she wished for the assistance of her lady's maid. Finally clean, she donned a pale yellow morning dress she had yet to wear and headed toward the thin wisp of smoke.

Troy glanced up at her appearance and his jaw dropped at the sight of her. His pulse leapt as he fought to keep from reaching out to her.

Lena had let her hair down. The red cascade of thick curls twisted and tumbled about her shoulders in a wild curling mass like water over a falls. His fingers itched to dive in.

What was she wearing? She stood before him in an impractical concoction of silk the color of butter that made her hair look bright as polished copper.

She noticed the object of his attention and fingered a curl. "It's still wet, so I left it down to dry. Do you mind?"

His heart thumped against his ribs like a bullfrog in a bucket. Did he mind?

"It's all right." Damn him, his voice cracked.

He continued to stare. Most of the women he knew had thick hair—straight, dark hair. This unnatural color reminded him of fire and the texture—coarse and full of life. Such wild hair did not suit the proper little daughter of a rich Yankee.

"Is something wrong?" she asked, taking a seat across from him at the fire.

He wanted to touch it and decided this could be his only chance. He would not spend the rest of his life wondering. In a moment he sat beside her on the log. She studied him with apprehension and his hand snaked out to touch her riotous cascade of hair.

"Thick as a pony's tail," he whispered.

She thought of her reaction the last time he touched her and decided she best nip this in the bud.

"Mr. Price, it's not proper for you to stroke me like your pet hound."

He stared into the blue canvas of her eyes. If he didn't do something quick he'd kiss her.

"This is how I pet my hound." He scratched behind her ear.

She slapped at his hand and laughed, giving him the chance to move away.

They shared their dinner and a few stories. He described the time he first faced a bear. "So I shot at it and then ran. Next thing I know it's running past me. Just as it draws even it gives me this look as if to say, 'They're shooting at you, too?'"

Her laughter shook her shoulders and she rocked back and forth with her mirth.

"I don't have anything nearly as amusing to tell. The closest I can come is when I caught my mother with one of her lovers. She was wearing only her nightgown and he a pair of unfastened britches. Still she lifted her chin and said, 'Eleanor, you remember Mr. Woolrich?'"

Troy's jaw dropped. "What'd you do?"

"I curtsied, of course." She giggled.

But Troy did not laugh or even smile. His brow wrinkled

in confusion as he studied her. What did she mean one of her mother's lovers?

"She had more than one?"

"More than one what?" asked Lena, her eyes wide with innocence that he began to suspect was not genuine.

"Lovers?"

"It's rather usual."

"Not here it ain't."

She continued to stare as if there was something wrong with him.

"Did your daddy find out?"

"Of course. But as he has a mistress in Newport and one in New York, he could hardly object."

Troy threw off his hat. "What?"

She clasped her hands about her knees. "I see I have shocked you. Of course this is not the structure of things in the lower classes, but in my world it is common practice. Couples marry to merge fortunes and families, not hearts. One must often look outside marriage to find love."

Troy felt sick to his stomach. "That ain't right."

She cast him an indulgent smile. "If you were forced to marry a woman you did not love, would you not want the opportunity to find love elsewhere?"

"But she'd be my wife."

"Whom you married for wealth or connections. You attend functions with her, expect her to bear your children and look after your home. But you do not expect monogamy. And a wife, well, she certainly doesn't expect it. I know of women who encourage their husband's pursuits, anxious to be rid of them."

Troy slid off the log and landed in the dirt. He shook his head like a hound too close to the fire. Did people really do these things?

"No wonder you left."

He glanced up to see her wise smile. She looked sad and older than her years.

"Some women keep the same liaison their entire lives. It is one of the few areas that they have any measure of control." She looked at him in a way that made him think her words were meant as more than simply informative. She seemed to be asking him something. "This is a man she chooses for love. Though she may not marry him, she may bear his children and spend as much time with him as she can arrange. Occasionally an entire season."

"His children?"

"Certainly, her husband accepts them as his own, but men have little to do with raising their offspring in any case."

The sickness in his stomach traveled to his throat and he swallowed to keep it back as he imagined Lena living such a life.

"Are you scandalized at our wickedness?"

He didn't deny it. "Hell, yes!"

"I'm sorry. But that is what I can expect in life."

A sudden sympathy rose above the abhorrence. "Lena, do you want to go back?"

She straightened. "It's my duty."

"That's not what I asked. If you didn't have a duty, if you were just an ordinary woman, would you stay?"

Lena's gaze lifted from him and swept up to the tops of the swaying Douglas firs. Her expression changed to a look of longing so intense that it made him ache. Then her eyes turned cold and the corners of her mouth tipped down.

"I am not ordinary. To engage in such fantasies only serves to make things more difficult."

He had his answer—if she had a choice, she'd stay.

After they settled for the night, Troy lay still listening to Lena toss. Eventually the exhaustion of her body won out over the disquiet of her mind and she slept.

He gazed up into the stars and wondered what to do? He'd always imagined finding a woman that fired his blood. In his vague fantasies she'd love him as well and then she'd leave her world behind to become part of his.

Now he lay not five feet from just such a woman, but life wasn't going as he planned. She wouldn't or couldn't leave her world behind and damned if he could think of a place for him in hers.

As if reflecting his mood, a hard rain arrived, with cracking thunder and deafening explosions of thunder. The overhang of rock kept out the weather, but not the wind. He glanced over to Lena and found her buried beneath the buffalo hide, curled in a ball. He wanted to comfort her, but knew what would come from crawling under that buffalo hide. She was safer in the storm.

He glanced longingly in her direction, hoping she would summon him. If she came to him, he would not send her away.

Gradually the rain moved along, sweeping away the thunder as it went. He closed his eyes to rest, pushing back his disappointment and cursing her courage.

The next morning he skirted along the river until a tributary blocked their path.

He drew up and considered the fast-moving water. The fording would be more difficult than customary as the knee-deep water now ran fast with the runoff from the storms.

He glanced back at her. Today she wore a dress the color of dried pine pitch and a straw bonnet with the biggest feather he'd ever seen.

In an effort to break the long silence between them, he spoke. "What kind of bird was that?"

"Ostrich," she said. "From Australia."

"I'd like to see one."

"It has pink legs and feathers of black and white, but they dye them to any shade." Her fingers swept over the yellow feather. "The bird stands larger than my horse."

He snorted. "You're pulling my leg."

"Truly. They are enormous."

"Don't have to be too damned big to be taller than *your* horse."

She gave him a halfhearted scowl, then laughed.

The sound tickled his insides.

"Good eating?" he asked.

"My horse? I shouldn't think so."

Now he scowled, though inside he enjoyed her teasing.

"The bird."

Her eyebrows rose. "I'm afraid I wouldn't know. I've only seen them in the pages of a book."

He gave the feather a final glance. "Pity."

Only then she seemed to notice that he pointed toward the stream. Her eyes rounded in worry.

"I'll go first," he said. "Just hold tight, the water is fast."

He gave Dahlonega a nudge and his horse stepped confidently into the coursing water. He held the rope to the mules in his left hand and felt it tighten as the pack animals resisted taking the first step. "Get up there."

They came with tentative strides. Once at midstream the water brushed the creatures' bellies and they grew anxious to be clear, trotting the distance to shore. He turned toward Lena. Her horse danced with mincing steps more anxious than the mules'. He didn't like the way the little mare tossed her head, rolling her eyes over white.

In that instant he remembered Rachel alone on the river, standing in the bow of the little boat on a clear sunny day. She couldn't swim—Rachel couldn't swim. A tidal wave of glacial runoff flooded through him as past mistakes collided with current ones.

He dropped the line holding the pack animals.

"Don't move," he ordered. "I'm coming back for you."

She spoke, but the river garbled her words and then took the reins in a firm hand, using the tasseled stick. His heart dropped as the mare lunged from the bank landing some five feet from shore. White forelegs frothed in the rushing water as the mare scrambled to keep her footing in the fast-moving current.

The horse's rear legs slid and the animal went down hard, rolling toward the rider. Panic ripped through his chest as they fell as one. Faced with the choice of having her mount roll upon her or leaping clear, she released her grip.

Instantly, the water took her, wrapping her heavy skirts about her legs. She clawed for the reins and they slid through her fingers as she went under.

Troy released his holster and threw off his possibles bag, powder horn and shot as he stood on the saddle and dived headfirst into the frothing river. The icy water cramped his muscles as he struggled to swim with the current.

Rachel, I'm coming.

He surfaced and saw her petticoats some feet before him; her head remained submerged. She wasn't breathing. This revelation sparked him to kick with all his might, tearing through the water.

Not again, please God, not again.

Chapter 12

Eleanor tumbled over and over in the frigid water until she no longer knew which way was up. Her lungs burned with desperation for the air she could not reach. She held her breath even after her body demanded she exhale. To take in that cold water would be her death and she did not want to die. She had to finish her work. She clawed at the formless enemy that spun her like a leaf in a whirlwind. The weight of her seven petticoats and the heavy velvet of her dress now wrapped her as tightly as any chains. She reached, but grasped only rushing water. Numb, her arms moved clumsily.

No.

Her skirts snagged and jerked her back. Snagged on what? A tree? Oh, God, if it held her down, please no. She struggled, pulling toward the object gripping her. She broke the surface. Sweet air filled her lungs before water covered her face once more. She kicked, hoping for just one more breath. Her feet dragged against the bottom. She anchored them in the mud and stood, breaching like the dolphins that chased her ship in the Gulf of Mexico.

Troy stood beside her, water streaming through his dark hair as he held her like a drowned kitten by the scruff of her neck. Her ruined coiffure made a convenient handhold. She had not even felt his grip. He shifted her into his arms and dragged her onto the tall grass along the shore. She spit water and coughed as he pounded on her back. Finally, she lay prostrate, heaving, yet unable to regain her equilibrium. He tugged at her bodice as she choked and stared at the dark spots dancing over the stream like dragonflies.

"Rachel, Rachel!"

Why did he call her that?

The sound of renting fabric tore into her stupor.

Her ribs expanded with blissful freedom and she fell back upon the bank.

How long she lay so, she did not know. She shivered in her wet things and her eyes blinked open to find herself once more lying cradled in Troy's strong arms. Relief washed his features. Water dripped from his glorious mass of hair and onto her face. She stared, certain for a moment that tears mingled with the river water.

"You gave me a fright," he whispered and dragged her up against his body in a rough embrace.

His hand lay familiar across her waist and she clasped it naturally, as if they had rested like this all their lives.

She stared up at her savior, still disbelieving her own eyes. By some miracle, he had reached her and pulled her from the jaws of death.

"You saved my life."

"Thank God."

She drew back to stare up at him. Of course he was relieved at her survival, but he looked pale and visibly shaken. His hand trembled as he pushed back his sodden hair. Up until this moment, he seemed invincible. The realization that he was not, coupled with the thought of how narrowly she avoided death, hit her like the icy river water, sending her skin to gooseflesh.

"Troy, are you quite all right?" she asked.

His chest heaved from his exertions and his gaze locked to

hers. She should release him now, but found her fingers entwined behind his neck.

He leaned over her like a lover, his mouth an inch away. She held her breath as he pressed his lips to her temple. The tender kisses fell down her cheek until he found her lips. She savored the contact as his mouth slanted over hers. In his embrace, she forgot the wet velvet pressing cold upon her legs and the terror of only moments ago. In his embrace she woke from her nightmare into heaven on earth.

His hand slid over her ribs to cup her breast. A shard of pleasure sliced through her abdomen at the contact. The urge to draw near overpowered and she pressed herself tightly into his splayed hand. He drew back, forcing her away, and stared down as if he did not know her.

"Troy, what is wrong?"

"Lena?"

"Yes." Had he kissed her thinking she was this other woman? Her lips pressed into a thin line and her eyes narrowed as she considered this possibility and how deeply it disturbed her.

"Who is she?"

Troy stared down at this woman he protected. For a moment, when she had gone under the water, he'd thought she was his Rachel. Only this time he had saved her.

The panic receded, replaced by the grinding loss that tore into him whenever he thought of Rachel.

Lena lay in his arms, dress gaping and the corset strings all undone; his hand lay familiar upon her breast. He could feel her heart beat.

He set her at arm's length, shaking his head to clear it. The action sprayed droplets of water across her face. She wiped them away.

He stared out at the water.

"Rachel," he whispered.

She sat up, hands upon her hips and a scowl darkening her features. When she spoke her tone radiated her irk.

"You kiss me and then call me by another woman's name?"

He frowned. "It was when I kissed you that I recognized you. No one else ever kissed me like that."

She gasped, cast speechless by his words.

"Like what?" she asked.

"Like fire on the prairie."

She lowered her gaze, tugging the edges of her corset back in place and hiding her beautiful breasts from his gaze. When satisfied, she pinned him with a furious glare.

"Who is Rachel?"

Lena had such life in her, such fire. Experience had taught him the damage of this kind of fire. Troy looked away, watching a dead branch spin in the current, thinking back to that awful day. Then he swallowed, but the lump remained.

"She was a woman I loved. She drowned. I couldn't reach her in time."

Lena's temper dissolved and her voice now sounded regretful. "I'm sorry then."

He drew his knees up and rested his chin upon them. His body now drained of power by his grief. He could not muster the energy to rise.

"My accident has stirred bad memories," Lena said. "Did she also fall from her horse?"

"She did not fall. She jumped."

His words seemed to hit Lena like ice water. She gaped.

"Why?" she asked.

He drew a great breath before speaking, searching for the courage to tell this woman of his shame.

"She was yenego, white, like you."

Her eyes widened.

"Yes, a white woman, who promised to be my wife. She begged me not to speak to her father until she had."

Lena shivered and inched away. It was easier to stare at the water. There he did not see the shock in her eyes.

"One night she told me she carried my child."

Eleanor could not contain her gasp. Troy glared as her eyes widened in understanding. Rachel was white. Lena understood now.

There was no worse fate for a white woman than to marry outside her race. But to carry his child—no wonder she could not tell her parents.

Even if this woman loved Troy, she would lose everything. Her family would disown her, her friends turn their backs.

Rachel had drowned herself, literally dying of shame. Lena pressed her hand over her mouth at the horror as she met his gaze.

Troy watched her recoil, reading the abhorrence clearly in her eyes. She understood it all now. He drew his hands through his hair, fingers raking hard along his scalp. "Do you know what she said? She told me that our love would shame her family. Do you know why?"

Eleanor clutched her own throat. She knew. He could see it in her eyes. When she did not answer, he continued.

"Because for a white woman there was no greater shame than to love an Indian."

Eleanor lowered her gaze, but said nothing. Her revulsion burned him like iron from the forge. Given the same situation, would Lena choose death rather than face the world as his wife?

"What did you do?" she asked

"I went to my mother. She said if Rachel did not want this child, then we would raise it without her."

"What did her family do? Did they disown her?"

Is that how it was done in her world? A family abandoned their daughter when she needed them most? He felt sick to his stomach at the thought.

"No. I followed Rachel to her home, but she had stolen her father's boat and rowed far out onto the lake."

Eleanor's hands crept up her neck to rest over her ears as if she did not wish to hear his words.

"She could not swim, either. One large step and the deep water took her."

"How terrible."

"Terrible, yes, that she would rather die than bear my child."

"Did you tell her father?"

He snorted. "No."

He let her secret die with his child. Instead of the truth, her parents were left with only unanswered questions. He thought that was worse.

She met his stare and inched closer. Her hand lifted to stroke his face.

He leaned away, narrowly avoiding her hand brushing his cheek. "No, Lena."

"I only meant to comfort you."

"You cannot bring me comfort, only sorrow."

Her eyes widened as if she reached some understanding.

"But you are my guide. It is a completely different situation."

The insistence in her voice filled his belly with a creeping disquiet.

"Is it?"

"Certainly."

He cast her a look of doubt and she fumbled with the lacing of her corset, drawing the strings closed.

"Is that why you washed my hair?"

Her gaze dropped and her cheeks glowed. She could not meet his eyes.

"You may deny what is happening between us. I cannot."

"Just this once, I wish you would not speak your mind."

He gazed down at Lena as regret filled him like a cistern after a rain. The first time he saw her, he could not look away. Through her paintings he glimpsed her passion. At the fort, he kissed her only to prove to himself that she felt nothing for him, that her passion was only for her work. But it was not true. Each day this connection between them strengthened, putting them both in danger.

"I have given you good reasons to go home. Now I add one more—this force between us grows stronger."

She clutched at her torn blouse and lifted her chin in defiance, but she did not deny his words. His hand still burned from the touch of her skin. He made a fist to drive away the longing, fighting against the need to touch her once more as he waited for her words.

She stiffened her spine and stood as if she was not drenched to the bone. Her hair lay in a sodden mass and water leaked beside her ears to trickle down her long neck and into the ruined collar of her blouse. Still she stood like a princess.

"You raise valid concerns, Mr. Price."

His eyebrow quirked.

"I can assure you that you need have no more worry over advances on my part. I quite understand the importance of decorum."

"Sometimes it is impossible to keep a wildcat in a bag."

She puzzled over this as a chill rolled up her spine. She could not suppress a shiver. Her wet clothing weighed heavily upon her and she longed to step into the warmth and comfort of his arms. She ached inside to realize she could not—ever again.

Up until this moment she allowed herself to believe the excuses disguising her desire. She needed comfort or protection or warmth. How right he was about their attraction. At first she thought him simply intriguing. Now she made up excuses to touch him. But no more. Now she must be strong and do what she knew was right.

Eleanor wrapped her arms about herself as her teeth began to chatter. When she glanced up she saw his pained expression, as if it hurt him not to step forward and hold her. They were both caught in this trap.

Her family would feel exactly the same as Rachel's. How terrible to have to endure the scorn of society and not just upon one's self. Such a selfish act would shame the woman's entire family. How tragic to have to choose between one's family and one's heart. She understood this woman's choice.

It was unfair to them both to prolong their misery. She could finish her painting as quickly as possible and then leave him.

Their gaze locked. What would it be like to be free to choose this wonder of a man?

Her stomach flashed hot and then cold. Sensations danced across her skin like feathers on the wind.

"If wishes were horses then beggars would ride," she said.

"What?"

She glanced out at the dirty water. "I came within a hair's breath of dying. I have a second chance and I shall use it to make great paintings. But right now, I am cold."

She had never been soaked so often in her life. She looked about and found the horses grazing upstream on the far bank.

"Oh, no." She tried to walk, but her sodden skirts dragged upon her and she staggered. Troy caught her elbow before she stumbled. As soon as she regained her balance, he moved away. The heat of his touch remained.

She stared out to the opposite shore. The distance was not far, but now she knew the force of the water and trembled.

"Current's powerful," he said.

"How will we manage?"

"Swim."

She gasped. "Oh, no. I can't."

"I can. I'll swim over and get my horse. Then we'll cross together."

Her knees failed her and she sank to the grass. After nearly dying in that water, she was not anxious to venture out once more.

He grasped her wrist and dragged her to her feet. "Come on, it's near dark."

She glanced at the sky and noted the sun's low angle. Soon the night would catch them on this side of the swollen stream.

Wolves might attack their horses or them. She glanced nervously about. Time bore heavily.

She swallowed but felt no braver. "I cannot cross again."

He gave her a hard look and she felt cowardly and weak.

"Then I'll get the horses and we'll head back to Fort Union."

She grasped his arm to halt him. Beneath her fingers muscles bulged as he paused. Tension crackled between them at the contact.

"No." She stood torn between her desires and her terror. "I'm afraid."

He nodded. "Understandable, but we still gotta go one way or the other."

He was right. She knew it, but when she tried to walk, her knees turned to water. The sodden garments stuck and she shivered. Everything she owned was on the far bank. She took a step and water squished from her boot. He led the way to a place above their destination and stopped to face her, his expression somber.

"So which is it Lena, east or west?"

She pushed the mass of wet hair back from her forehead and gazed at the far shore. Despite her dousing, she discovered that the flame of determination was not yet extinguished.

He waited, still as stone.

She stared at the frothing enemy the stream had become, just one more obstacle between her and her goal. Her gaze lifted to the horizon.

"West."

He said nothing, but nodded as if he expected her to continue, then waded in. Without warning, he dived into the stream.

A cry escaped her at his sudden disappearance into the murky depths. What if he drowned? To her shame, her first thought was of being alone on this shore. She had not even a hatpin for protection. He surfaced at midstream, his arms pulling in strong relaxed strokes that filled her with envy. Still the current dragged him far downstream. She understood, now, why he'd begun so far from his destination and admired how he accurately judged the speed and distance. When he stood on the far bank, relief nearly buckled her knees.

She found herself hopping up and down waving her arms over her head in a most undignified manner. The man reduced her to the most bizarre behavior.

He waved back and then grabbed his horse's reins.

Her breath caught again as he mounted up and forded for the second time. His horse thrashed his front legs at the water, bringing his master safely to shore.

Troy leaned from the saddle, extending his hand. Her legs would not work, but she managed to lift an arm. He grasped her wrist and pulled her up before him, then turned the horse back to the water. She threw her arms about Troy's neck, latching on for dear life. His wet buckskin stuck to her cheek as she closed her eyes. Beneath her, the big horse braced against the surge. At last his mount's withers rose as he lunged up the steep bank.

Troy wheeled them past the mules and herded Scheherazade back to the others.

Then he lowered Eleanor to the ground and dismounted beside her.

"Back on dry ground, Princess."

She sighed. "I think I prefer Lena."

He cast his gaze over her and she cautioned herself to stillness despite the disquiet his consideration caused. Here she stood, dripping wet and still, somehow, her body burned with heat. His warning returned. This time she fought the attraction, refusing to approach him.

"You gotta get out of those duds."

"Yes, I must."

Her teeth chattered as she retrieved clothing from a bundle on the third mule. Glancing about, she found the grass spread out in all directions.

Eleanor crouched behind the animal to peel off her sodden garments until she stood in only her transparent shift, silk stockings and boots. At this moment she glanced over the mule's hindquarters to find Troy standing in a dry pair of buckskin breeches and nothing else. Concern over her state of undress vanished with her modesty as she rose upon her toes to feast upon his lean torso and sculpted muscle. Her breath caught as his gaze locked to hers. The hunger in those smoky eyes overwhelmed. Did her body have the same startling effect upon him?

Was his throat too dry for words?

When, at last, he spoke, his voice seemed deep and husky as if from disuse. "Finish up."

He glanced away, retrieving a pair of ornately beaded moccasins and drawing them on. It was then she remembered she stood next to naked on a prairie with nothing but a horse between herself and the gaze of a man. This is what he cautioned against. This invisible thread that drew her to him and made her forget all her good breeding. He was right to be wary. She must redouble her guard against this dangerous desire.

His warning rose in her mind with a nagging doubt. What if she could not control this longing he raised?

Possibilities flashed in her mind, each one ending in disaster. Had his lost love also felt this unendurable desire until she could no longer resist him? Eleanor feared falling to such ruin. She imagined the horror in her mother's face and her father's censure.

She shivered and then dragged off the last wet layer and rapidly donned a dry shift and petticoats, lacing her corset with extra care. From her pack she chose a chemisette with full sleeves of white cambric and sapphire blue cashmere bodice and matching skirt, mainly for their warmth. When she still shivered she added a black *pardessus* with satin trim.

Again properly attired, her sense of control returned. Her doubt faded. Of course she could control herself. How ridiculous to think otherwise. Thus convinced, she rounded the mule and found him checking the gear.

"Not wet," he said.

She didn't know if she was more grateful that her supplies were undamaged or that he now wore a long fringed shirt. Who would have thought the sight of a naked chest could wreak such havoc?

Then she recalled that she had painted bare-chested Indians at the fort and experienced none of these emotions. She paused as her equilibrium shifted once more.

How strange that the greatest menace here was not the storms or bears or even the raging waters that had nearly consumed her. Her desire for this man proved the greatest peril, threatening not her life, but her way of life. Against that, all other dangers paled by comparison.

Chapter 13

Someone or something watched them. Troy left Lena and the animals in a defensible position hidden behind a bank of rock and scouted the area. He found the tracks of several horses riding parallel to his trail in single file. Not mustangs, judging from the manure spread. Wild horses stop when voiding their intestines, but not mounted horses. He studied the tracks, noting the animals were unshod.

War ponies.

Sioux territory—but he'd had no grievance with these tribes. In fact, they welcomed him. He stiffened as a thought flashed through his mind—Lena. He wheeled about and headed back for her. Before he reached the clearing he heard her scream.

Kicking Dahlonega to a gallop, he charged into the camp, a pistol in one hand and a rifle in the other. A Sioux warrior held Lena before him while another tugged on the lead line of his mules.

The feral cry brought him about too late. He turned to fire at the two men attacking from the rear, squeezing the trigger as one man cleanly slashed both Dahlonega's hamstrings.

His horse screamed and fell, sending Troy's rifle ball wide. Dahlonega rolled over him. Wind whooshed from his lungs.

He lost his grip on the pistol, but managed to spring to his feet, knife at the ready.

The second man dived, catching Troy's wrist and driving him backward. He heard Lena's second scream, but could not disengage his attacker.

"Troy, behind you."

The blow struck him on the back of his head, seeming to split his skull. His legs crumpled. The brave before him lifted his knife. Troy's vision blurred.

"Don't black out," he muttered. But the world went liquid, turning the color of blood.

Lena watched Troy fall in disbelief. She kicked at her attacker with such viciousness he released her and fell forward clutching his groin. She nearly reached Troy when a second man caught her about the waist, whirling her in a sweeping circle as he captured her against him. The instant she struck solid ground she pummeled him with her fists, which he quickly secured.

"Troy!"

He did not move. Blood matted his hair and dripped to the grass beside him.

They had killed him. Tears blurred her vision.

A second Indian took charge of her wrists and quickly lashed them together before her. He spoke, but she could not hear his words above the pitiful screams of Dahlonega.

Five men surrounded his horse.

"Do not touch him," she ordered and for the first time in her life, no one paid her any mind.

The one with red hand prints blazoned upon his chest lifted his knife and slit the horse's neck. Blood poured as if from a pump.

Perspiration covered Lena's face and familiar dots danced before her eyes.

"No. I will not faint."

She breathed faster to make up for the constricting corset.

A man tugged her bound arms to draw her toward his horse. She resisted.

"No. Troy. Let me go! I have to help him!"

She struggled uselessly against the man who lifted her to a rider. He threw her leg over the horse's withers and for the first time she rode astride.

The Indian kicked his horse and they sprang from the clearing into the forest of pines.

Troy rubbed the bump on his head and drew back at the sticky mess of his hair. Struggling like a swimmer against a strong current, he tried to pull his recollections together.

What had happened?

He groaned as he dragged himself to all fours. Something terrible—he knew that. But what?

Then he remembered the screams echo in his ringing ears.

Lena.

They'd taken her.

His eyes flashed open. The crust of dried blood flaked from his lids. He glanced about the empty clearing. And his stomach tightened in dread as he saw the carcass.

Sinking back to his haunches he recognized Dahlonega. His friend's eyes now showed a white glaze and his tongue lolled obscenely in death. Flies buzzed in clouds about his horse.

"Bastards!" Liquid rage surged through him as the nausea rolled the contents of his belly. The pounding in his head increased as he crawled toward the fallen buckskin gelding, finding his flesh still warm.

"Oh, Dahlonega," he whispered, resting his head on the lifeless body of the best horse he'd ever owned. *Why did they have to kill my horse?*

That question fell aside as he wondered why they hadn't killed him? He recognized Charging Buffalo's men. He had no quarrel with them, nor they with him. The fact that he still lived was proof of that. So they wanted Lena or her horse. He rose to his feet and swayed as dizziness assaulted him.

His hand went to his throbbing head, certain the warriors had taken his scalp. His fingers told him he had his hair and a lump the size of a robin's egg. Why didn't they take his scalp after they had struck him down?

He glanced about and discovered that in addition to butchering his horse, they'd taken his mules, weapons and all his supplies. Tears dribbled from his eyes again as he glanced at Dahlonega. How could they slaughter such a fine animal?

They should have killed him because he damned sure was going to kill them.

He walked in a slow circle around the clearing and discovered his possibles bag. They'd left him one more thing, a trail.

The cold sweat on Eleanor's back dried as they rode. Her captors did not speak, as they rode in single file. She counted nine men all painted in red and black. The fearsome appearance froze her blood.

She was their captive. Gall rose in her throat and she forced it down. All the dreadful stories she read rose like ghastly specters to haunt her thoughts.

A short time after they left Troy, her captors had transferred her to her own horse where she rode with hands tied before her. She preferred this arrangement to riding double.

They rode up the Yellowstone River as the sun turned the clouds crimson. Eleanor realized that she might not ever need worry about her future or the inevitable husband. Very likely she would die soon. In that moment of realization she recognized her one regret—Troy. How she wished she had told him of her feelings and permitted herself to share the love she held secret in her heart. She forced back a sob. Tears gained her nothing.

Up until this moment she had not admitted, even to herself, how much he meant to her. Instead she let stupid social order dictate her life.

Regret burned her like acid.

Why had she not told him? Fear. She feared her parents and their scorn. Troy thought her strong, but she was not. She did not have the courage to face the firestorm of scorn that awaited her if she admitted her love for Troy. She would lose everything. Without her parents and her position, who was she?

Her eyes lifted to the horizon as the answer came to her. Whoever she wished to be.

What did it matter now?

Again and again, her mind flashed to the memory of Troy lying in a pool of blood. She could scarcely believe him dead. But how could he have survived such a blow? Until this moment, she'd thought him invincible.

She twisted on her saddle to look back at the man she'd seen strike Troy with a club. She memorized his face, studying the eyes and the curve of his mouth, beneath the black paint. The cold fire of vengeance burned within her. For the first time in her life she felt icy conviction that she would hurt this man if given the opportunity.

The night came and they forged on. She coiled her stiff fingers as they rode by the light of the half moon. The yapping of dogs drew her to alert. Next came the smell of campfires. In the field, strange conical tents silhouetted against the starry night.

They had arrived.

Riders mounted on bareback charged from the darkness. Young men, naked save the merest of leather cloths at their waists, whooped as they circled the party. Their cries lifted the hairs on Eleanor's neck.

Her nostrils flared as she struggled with her breathing and the dratted corset once more. Troy was right. The thing would be the death of her.

Faces appeared from the darkness and escorted them through camp. They stopped at a large central fire.

Her gaze darted around the mass of men and women all staring at her with beetle black eyes. A hush fell, which frightened her more than the piercing cries of the women. Whatever devilish plan they'd formed, she prayed they would not violate her before striking her down.

A man in a leather shirt, stained dark, stepped forward, stopping before her. She gazed down in astonishment. He looked thinner, as if he had been ill, but she recognized him instantly. He was the man she'd painted at Fort Union.

It seemed a lifetime ago.

"Wind Dancer? What are you doing here?"

"I living here, Medicine Woman." He raised his hands. "You come down now."

She slipped her tired leg over the saddle horn and leaned forward. Wind Dancer caught her about the waist. His eyes went wide at the contact. He looked frightened and released his hold the instant her feet touched the earth. He spoke to the others sending a murmur of excitement through the gathering.

Facing her now, he drew his knife. She lifted her hands to defend herself and he sliced cleanly through her bonds.

"You come." He motioned and the forest of Indians parted.

She gaped as the leather fell from her wrists. She rubbed the raw skin before trailing after Wind Dancer.

He led her to a large tent of tanned leather hides. Wind Dancer motioned to the entrance hole that stood a foot off the ground and reached only three feet high. It reminded her of a fox burrow. She hesitated, wondering how to manage such a low opening.

Wind Dancer motioned. "You go in."

Her corset made stooping quite impossible, so she curtsied low. This gave her a view of the solemn men, all peering at her from inside the strange house. Her nerve left her and she lifted her shoulders as if to protect her neck.

Thoughts of Troy came and she wished fervently he were there to tell her what to do. His advice on Indians came back. *They ain't wild animals. They're men, like all men, no better or worse.*

She drew as deep a breath as her corset permitted and the stays cut against her ribs. Then she placed her hands inside the burrow and leaned forward until she fell within. A bare-chested man, his hair shiny with grease, motioned to an empty place across the fire. She rose and walked on trembling legs to the spot he indicated, wondering how she would manage sitting upon the ground in her attire. She decided to kneel, folding her feet beneath her bottom until her heels touched the small bustle. Wind Dancer's entrance was much more graceful. He simply crouched and stepped within, before straightening.

He addressed the group a moment and then the older men who sat at the place facing the entrance.

The old man spoke. Eleanor noted he lacked front teeth. His white hair lay in a braid that reminded her of white rope. A string of crimson glass beads adorned the end of the plait.

The man motioned to someone behind her. For the first time she noticed a woman, young and dark, kneeling in the shadows of the fire. She moved forward with a cup and offered it to Eleanor.

It was not until that moment she realized how thirsty she'd become. But could this be drugged?

She dismissed the thought. After all, they did not need opiates to manage her. She nodded her thanks and drank. The sweet taste of ripe berries filled her mouth. She drained the contents and the woman extended a tray of roasted meat. Eleanor felt strange eating before the curious stares of so many men so she lifted her hand to refuse.

"No, thank you."

Wind Dancer spoke and the woman withdrew from the tent. He waited until the tent flap swung closed and then addressed the gathering, his voice now loud like a herald and she jumped at the volume change. "This is Charging Buffalo, chief of our tribe. He welcomes Medicine Woman to his lodge."

She blinked. "Who is Medicine Woman?"

Confusion pinched his face as he answered. "You are Medicine Woman."

Only then did she recall Troy telling her that the men she painted believed her paintings held some mystic power. "And he welcomes me? I've been kidnapped."

Wind Dancer looked confused. "What is kin-napped?"

"You abducted me, stole me from my guide."

He translated. Charging Buffalo nodded gravely and spoke a long time. Eleanor remembered her upbringing and did not fidget, though the effort rattled her nerves. Her gaze flashed around the group of bronze men. For an insane moment she wished she had her sketchbook and could capture this assemblage. Who would believe she faced a council of Sioux warriors?

At last Charging Buffalo ceased.

Wind Dancer spoke to her. "Rotting Face sickness kills our people. Charging Buffalo say white men not die from this curse, so white medicine protecting them. I come from Fort Union, I have sickness." He lifted his forelock to show the angry red scars left by smallpox. "But I do not die."

Eleanor had the disease as a child, but still she recoiled.

"Your medicine painting protects me. Charging Buffalo bring you to protect his people."

She was about to object and explain that this was stuff and nonsense when a tiny voice within her urged caution. She hesitated and considered her choices as she glanced around at the earnest, serious faces.

If she said she could not protect them, what would they do? An equally terrifying possibility crossed her mind and her breathing stopped for a moment. What if they discovered her paintings held no special powers? Fear gripped her, closing about her throat like punishing fingers. Perspiration dampened her forehead.

What would Troy do?

She lifted her chin and imagined he sat here in her place.

She ceased her attentions to Wind Dancer and turned instead to address Charging Buffalo. "What is it you want?"

She waited for the answer.

"You do paint the chief and his warriors, then his wives and childrens."

Did he say wives? She stared at the man. Had he more than one?

She managed to close her gaping mouth and draw up her courage. "What do you offer for my paintings?"

The men discussed this question at length. At last Wind Dancer made their reply. "We will give you eleven horses of your choosing, eight buffalo robes and two slaves."

Eleanor blinked, wondering if this was a good offer, at the same time knowing she wanted none of this.

"I will tell you what I want. Bring the body of Troy Price to this village for a proper burial. Return all our belongings, including my horse. After my work is finished, you will escort me back to Fort Union."

The men talked. "What about the horses?" asked Wind Dancer.

"I have not yet decided."

More discussion. "Charging Buffalo asks if you want Price killed?"

To even speak of this set a white-hot rage afire within "You've already killed him. Once is certainly enough."

The warriors spoke in agitated voices. Finally she interceded.

"What are they saying?"

"Price alive when we go."

Chapter 14

He fingered the knot and the new scab on the back of his head. He washed the dried blood from his face and neck, then vomited on the bank. The vomiting continued throughout the afternoon as he followed the tracks of the Sioux ponies.

After sundown Troy lost their trail and had to await the moon's rising. Then he continued in a zigzag pattern until he found the way once more.

Lena needed him, so he pressed on until the moon set, finally stopping beside a stream to drink and rest until dawn. He settled against the trunk of a pine as he gnawed on some of the jerked elk he carried in his pouch. His stomach revolted and he lost his meal. Finally he settled for small sips of water from the skin.

He did not flatter himself that he could rescue Lena from Charging Buffalo. The man had over sixty warriors. But he aimed to die trying.

They returned for him in the late morning of the second day. Seven braves. Troy lay flat in the long grass thinking that the sun behind him gave a slight edge. They had not seen him yet, but on that course, they certainly would.

He crept perpendicular hoping to get clear of them, knowing they would spot his tracks. It was obvious that they had come back for him.

Regret hollowed his innards. He wished he could have seen Lena once more. He waited until they were nearly upon him and then leapt from the grass and clutched the nearest man by the leg, dragging him off his pony. The others shouted as he swung up in the fallen man's place. He turned to face the warriors' attack. Instead of charging forward, the men pulled up on their reins and waved their hands.

He charged forward and they retreated.

Troy knew the Sioux. They did not retreat, especially not when the odds were seven to one. He lowered his reins and stared at the man now standing before him in the grass.

"Hello, Wind Dancer."

"You strike like a snake," he said swiping the bits of grass from his damp body, then turning his attention back to Troy. "We are searching for you."

"Come back to finish the job?"

"Medicine Woman wants you."

Troy rubbed the knot on his head beneath his hat. "Turns out I was headed that way, but seeing as how you killed my horse it was taking longer than customary."

"I am sorry. Charging Buffalo say you pick from his ponies."

Damn wild, skinny-hipped unbroken mustang. Dahlonega was half thoroughbred.

"Now, you ride this horse." Wind Dancer motioned and Troy saw that there were only six braves and seven ponies. He swung off the brave's horse and handed the rein to Wind Dancer.

"Medicine Woman is well?" he asked.

"Yes, but she will not make a spirit painting until she see you not dead."

Troy lifted his eyebrows. "That so?"

"Yes. She is very stubborn woman."

Now he understood why he was getting the royal treatment. Somehow his little princess had stared down the Sioux. He was impressed.

"Best get on then."

"We bring our Medicine Man, Red Eagle, for your wounds," said Wind Dancer.

The old man dismounted and poked at the knot on Troy's head. Troy gazed at the man's sour expression. He looked like he just swallowed a bug.

"What's eating him?"

"He say the spirit paintings are evil medicine. But Charging Buffalo sees the truth."

Troy winced as the man pressed harder. Lena's arrival was stepping on this man's toes. Troy studied the healer.

Being supplanted by a woman surely hit hard. Troy wondered what the man was willing to do to regain his authority.

He knew an enemy when he saw one. Lena needed someone to watch her back and get her the hell out of there as soon as possible.

The old man gave him water laced with a bitter root Troy recognized as treatment for pain. Then they mounted up and headed north.

The River Otter band of Sioux summered on the Yellowstone, on a wide plain, inside a bend in the river. He was shocked to see so few teepees staked along the grassy banks.

"Where are the rest of your people?"

Wind Dancer's jaw tightened before he spoke. "Gone to our ancestors, taken by the Rotting Face disease."

"So many?"

"Nearly all. Here a few remain. We need white magic. The council decides that Medicine Woman will protect us from this sickness."

Troy knew it would not. This disease once attacked his people in the time of his great grandmother. He knew its power and that if it had destroyed Charging Buffalo's numbers already, the survivors would not likely sicken again. That meant he and Lena might just live long enough to see the Missouri.

They rode past the sentries and into the center of the village. Women left their work to gather and stare at the man summoned by the Medicine Woman.

Troy didn't know if he should be please or shamed. It sure the hell beat riding in uninvited.

Then he saw her. She wore that new dress. The pale yellow silk shone like the sun. Her hair hung in sausage curls about her ears, and upon her head was a gauzy little cap with matching silk flowers above each ear. Her skirts were far fuller than he was accustomed to seeing and stuck out about her like a water barrel.

She beamed at him, as she seemed to float over the grass in his direction. The women moved aside as she came. He slid off the pony and somehow managed not to run the distance separating them.

She halted before him as if unable to take the final step. He held out his hands and she leapt into his arms. Her wrists locked about his neck and she raised her head and tugged.

His mouth dipped and he kissed her on the lips. When he drew away he found her crying. Confused, he set her aside and tried to step away but she clung like that first morning at the fort.

"When I saw you lying there, I gave up hope. I thought they'd killed you."

"He thumped me good. But I got a head harder than a mountain goat's."

She released him only enough to clasp his chin and study his face.

"You look so pale."

She drew a handkerchief from a sleeve. He stared at the scrap of lace, as out of place here on the prairie as she was. Her hand moved to dab at her eyes.

"But all the blood. They hit you so hard. And your horse. I'm so sorry. This is all my fault."

He didn't deny it, but she could hardly have predicted how the Sioux would take her paintings. Wild as wolves, the Sioux. His people understood whites. Had lived peacefully with them for nearly three hundred years, but all that fell away with the gold. Damn that filthy metal.

Lena stroked him. "I've never been so happy to see anyone in my life."

"I imagine so," he said, thinking of the terror she must have experienced.

"Not for that reason. I was afraid, certainly, but the grief when I thought you dead. I don't know how I survived it."

She didn't look worse for wear, but he didn't say that. Lena always knew how to turn herself out and he was certain looking so different only helped increase the Sioux's awe of her. She hesitated, biting her lip as though she were itching to say something more.

"Well?" he asked.

"Did I place you in jeopardy? If I hadn't sent them, would you have reached safety by now?"

"I was coming after you."

Her eyes widened and she began to cry again.

"Best stop that. You need to appear strong."

She lifted a gloved hand to her eyes. The tears disappeared into the cotton cloth. Troy glanced about and saw Red Eagle's eyes narrow as he watched Lena like his namesake.

"They want me to paint, but I said I could not until I saw you safe."

"Explains why they captured me alive," he said, scratching under his hat.

"I also told them that you would negotiate the terms of my work."

"What terms?"

"They offered me eleven ponies and…" She pressed a finger to her chin. "What else?"

"Eleven!" He could not keep the shock from his voice.

Her finger dropped. "Is that a great deal?"

"I never heard them offer more than five and that was for a captured daughter of a chief."

"Well then, I should be flattered." She leaned forward and whispered. "Troy, they also offered me slaves."

He snorted. "You got enough of them in New York."

She stiffened. "I beg your pardon. Those men are free."

His eyes narrowed. "Lena, you ever work a day in that kitchen of yours? There's little difference. Your world stands on the backs of others."

She shifted uncomfortably.

Troy drew his arm across his forehead. This was neither the time nor the place for that. "What about your paintings?"

"They think they will protect them from smallpox."

Troy frowned. "I heard. Anybody you paint gets sick while we're here and it's all over but the shouting."

She worked her hands together as if washing them. "What do I do?"

"Don't see no other way but to paint who they say as fast as possible. We can't hornswoggle them for long. Maybe we'll get clear before they figure the truth."

Wind Dancer stepped forward. "You will paint now."

Lena's smile showed a courage that made Troy's insides swell with pride.

"I will."

Troy took a position beside Lena as she set up her easel and paints. Red Eagle worked grinding roots into a paste as a woman cleaned the blood from Troy's head. Soon he had his hat back on. The sticky mash made the cut itch, but he refrained from scratching.

Lena painted Charging Buffalo first and alone. He stood in his full regalia and Troy admitted he cut a fine figure, every inch the chief.

He glanced from the light lines and gentle washes of Lena's paper. As the afternoon wore on she added the bold reds and greens of his costume. She even captured the proud angle of his jaw and the intensity of his eyes.

As the sun grew hot, Lena retrieved a collapsible parasol,

but could not hold this and paint. One of the men lashed the handle to a spear and staked it so as to provide her with shade.

"Thank you," she said and gave a curtsey. Then she returned to her painting.

She painted as if alone in her drawing room, ignoring the entire village as they gawked at her. She stood still and composed beneath the lace parasol canopy as a queen among her subjects.

How did she do it? Was it her upbringing? He thought of all the women in his life. Most would have dissolved into useless wailing faced with capture by Sioux. Courage, of course, but this was something else. Confidence and a single-minded focus he sorely admired.

Lena lowered her brush and said, "It's finished."

She stepped aside, full of assurance as the chief approached. It was only then that Troy noticed Lena's hands choked her skirts and her breathing came in sharp little tugs. Lena *was* frightened. She just knew better than to show it. His regard for her increased again.

He scowled at her narrow waist, knowing that corset squeezed the life out of her, but he couldn't get her to give it up. Stubborn, willful and confident as an eagle, Lena was all that.

"Easy now. Deep breaths. He'll like that fine," Troy murmured, just loud enough for her to hear. She glanced at him and seemed to draw reassurance from his eyes.

The chief shouted and Lena stepped back, her eyes flying to Troy.

He smiled.

"Shouting shows he thinks you're important. A sign he respects."

She removed the painting and placed a new page on her easel.

"I loathe shouting. Reminds me of my father."

Her voice was so low he almost didn't hear her. Did the man bully her? Certainly he would force her into marriage. Troy disliked the man without ever laying eyes upon him.

Charging Buffalo gathered his council together and they waited for Lena to begin again. The next painting took her until the light began to fade.

She spoke to Wind Dancer. "They understand that water will destroy these paintings? They must stay dry and away from fire."

"We understand," said Wind Dancer.

Lena rolled her shoulders and then lowered the brush. "I'm finished."

The men crowded about. They nodded gravely. The Medicine Man pushed forward, shouting at the men and then at Lena. She backed away as he advanced. Troy stepped between them to intercede, knowing that if he put the Medicine Man down, it would mean his death.

Chapter 15

Eleanor's heart pounded in her ears. The old Medicine Man advanced, lifting his staff as if he meant to strike her. Troy stepped between them.

What could she do to stop this?

Charging Buffalo interceded, facing Red Eagle. The great blood vessels in the Medicine Man's neck pulsed as he faced his chief. Her gaze went around to the council members, who now shifted nervously as if uncertain what to do. Wind Dancer grabbed Lena's arm and drew her away, back to the tent where she had spent last night in miserable worry. Troy followed without invitation.

In a moment they ducked inside.

"What's going on?" Troy directed his question to Wind Dancer, who did not enter, but crouched outside. Behind them Charging Buffalo's stern voice reached them followed by the higher tones of the Medicine Man's reply.

"Red Eagle say Medicine Woman not protect our spirits but steal them." He straightened a moment, giving her a view of his lean, muscular legs, and then he stooped again. "Charging Buffalo say medicine protect. The council are not sure. I go."

He rose and darted away.

"What do we do?" she asked.

He glanced outside. "Wait."

"We could run."

Troy stuck his head out of the teepee then ducked back in, closing the flap behind him. His alert gaze darted about the enclosure. "No place to run where they can't catch us."

The shouts went on and on, finally fading as the group moved away.

"Sounds like they're going talk it out." Troy threw his hat aside and itched his head then he sat upon the yellow grass within the circle of leather.

At the sight of the dry yellow mud on his scalp, Lena suddenly remembered his injuries. She crouched beside him, stroking his head.

"How are you?"

He lowered his chin for her to take a look. "I ain't ate nor slept since they cracked me on the noggin yesterday morning. The headache is better though."

"I can't see anything but this paste they've rubbed into your scalp."

He held her gaze a moment and a tingling awareness fluttered in her belly.

"They'll talk a while to decide." He replaced his hat.

The voices receded, but she knew they continued out of her hearing, deciding her fate and his.

"Will they torture us?"

He sighed and lifted an arm She snuggled in the nook he offered. Her skirts billowed up, covering his legs as well as hers as they sat side by side.

"You was real brave out there. Now, you have to be brave a while longer."

"Red Eagle hates me."

She felt his chin brush her hair as he nodded. "You're a threat."

Eleanor straightened. "I did not ask to come here."

"You're here just the same. Red Eagle was head man. Now

the tribe is looking to you for their medicine. Don't sit right with him."

"What can we do?"

"I'm working on it. They already got two braves outside the teepee. I'd have to kill them to run. Odds are I'd only get one before they raised the alarm. That's a sure way to get killed. You stood your ground out there. That can't hurt."

"If Charging Buffalo is chief then his word is law."

"No. The council will decide. Red Eagle is a powerful man. They will listen to him and to their chief. They won't come to a decision tonight."

"How do you know?"

"The Sioux are many things, but never hasty."

"I don't understand Indians."

He sighed. "We ain't all the same, you know."

She realized he took offense to her comment and why not? He considered himself Cherokee and she continued to disparage his race.

"I didn't mean to insult you. I am shocked and embarrassed at my ignorance."

He drew away to face her, his gaze serious. "Tribes, languages, cultures, religions. Lots of Cherokee are Christians, some been farming side by side with the whites for three hundred years, did you know that?"

She shook her head. "I did not."

"Throwing us all in one basket—that ain't right. They're no more the same than Germans and Irish."

She laughed. "They're from different countries."

"This is much the same."

"I see."

"I don't think of you as Cherokee any longer."

"What then?"

"I think of you as a **man**." She wanted to say her man but did not dare.

"I'm not ashamed of being what I am, man along with the rest."

His eyes glowed with an intensity that made her tremble. She regarded him. This could be her last night on earth and God had seen fit to allow her to spend it with the man she adored.

A call came from outside the tent. Two women arrived carrying a trencher laden with cooked meat. One stirred the coals and revived the fire until it danced once more. Wind Dancer entered a moment later, stooping to enter.

"The council is decide what is right. You waiting here. After this meal you go out, then stay in all night. No come out or killed."

"What's going on?" asked Troy.

Wind Dancer's expression gave little hope. "You stay in."

Alone with their meal, Troy tried the meat. Lena's stomach heaved with worry.

"Eat," he insisted.

"I can't."

"It's buffalo."

She shook her head.

"Lena, you need to eat and sleep. How you gonna face them all starving and tired?"

He lifted a morsel and she opened her lips to allow the bite to pass. They did not speak, but focused on consuming what was given.

Afterward Troy stood.

Lena's heart pounded as fear threatened to consume her.

"Where are you going?"

"Privy, actually probably a grove of cottonwoods. Sit tight. When I come back they'll take you."

"I can't…" She blushed. "I wouldn't be able to, to—well, not with a man watching."

He gave her a measuring look and ducked out of the raised opening. She sat still in the tent listening to the sounds of strangers coming and going. Dogs barked and a baby howled.

She added logs to the fire and watched the flames lick the bark. What would tomorrow bring?

Voices came from just before the tent. She clutched her throat and waited.

Troy ducked inside. "I got four women to go with you. Best I could do."

She peered out, but could not manage to stand.

He gripped her wrist. "You're the daughter of John Hart. You best act like it."

Eleanor nodded and stood, shaking out her silk skirt before bowing out of the entrance. Her unwelcome companions flanked her, one taking the lead. Maids, she told herself until she noted the sheathed hunting knife tied to the belt of each woman.

They did not speak, only motioned to the grove, giving her the privacy of a large bush. Squatting in the dark, she considered running. She glanced down at her skirts and her pale yellow dress glowed in the moonlight. She would never elude them and if she did, her clothing would snag on the brambles all about. Troy's words came back to her. *Dress for running.* She sighed, remembering her scornful response that ladies don't run.

She glanced skyward at the waxing moon, reminding her of the night she made her promise to return and marry.

How far away that seemed now. She would be lucky to survive the next day, let alone return to fulfill her pledge.

She understood now all her father's reluctance to her journey. If possible, the West was more dangerous than he had imagined. Had she turned back at New Orleans, she would now be safe at home. But then she would never have met Troy.

They might have only one last night together. She straightened. This time society and family had no dominion here. Tonight, she would allow her heart to lead.

What would he say if she told him she wanted to know him as a man? Her face heated and her ears tingled as she considered broaching such a delicate topic. She was no fool and knew that to sleep with a man now could bring her ruin.

Faced with the risks presented by the Sioux, she thought the possibility of a bastard child suddenly seemed less momentous. She might not live long enough to bear a child. That thought lifted the hairs on her arms. She considered another possibility—she conceived and returned home with child. This same situation brought Troy's love to end her own life. Lena would never take that way out.

Such a scandal would rock her family's foundation. If she became with child, they would send her to the continent. She had heard the whispers to that effect about Amy Grace's daughter, Nancy. Rumors only, but she was gone the correct number of months. At the time, Lena had speculated with the rest upon the woman's return. Now she considered something that had never occurred to her. What had happened to the child?

The thought of leaving behind her own flesh and blood turned her cold. But she did not know if she could deny herself what might be her only chance to know this wonderful man on the most personal of levels.

One of the women called.

Eleanor returned to the group, who now swept along like shadows seeing a path invisible to her. Firelight glowed from within the buffalo skin houses. The woman before her halted and Lena blinked in surprise. Was this her tent already?

Her jailor called and the hide flap lifted. She peeked inside and recognized Troy's familiar fringed leggings.

"Thank you and good night," she said.

One woman lifted her hand and they departed. She stood in the dark before the portal, wondering if she were alone. She could not see them but rather felt their presence in the dark. Eleanor walked away from the tent and made only four steps before a man appeared to bar her way, motioning the way she had come. She halted. Troy was right about the guards.

She returned to Troy.

Eleanor stooped and entered the circular room. Now she

must decide if she was to remain chaste or offer herself to him. She felt the need to be held by him, to feel the protection of his embrace and forget the nightmare outside the circle of their fire. Didn't she deserve one night of happiness?

Yes.

She straightened and gazed at Troy. His eyes were shut and the soft sounds of sleep issued from his parted lips. Her mouth gaped and she sunk to her knees before him.

"Troy?" she whispered.

He did not move.

Disappointment rounded her shoulders. After all the anticipation, she felt like weeping. How could he do this to her?

Then she recalled the fight, his fall, the gash to his head and that he had walked all night to find her.

Her fingers swept back the hair from his forehead. "You came for me."

She knelt before him and pressed a kiss to his forehead. He did not stir. It took a few moments to release the laces from the buttons on her shoes. Next she struggled with hooks and eyes hidden at her side. Finally she pulled off her corset and, sighing in relief, scratched her ribs and belly, then dragged the cotton chemise free from her skin for the first time all day.

She hung the bodice and skirt on a peg on the tent pole and placed her shoes neatly beneath, as if this was her new armoire.

Then she released the veil and pins from her hair, brushing out the ringlets beside her ears with her fingers. Her hand paused as she considered how foolish it was to dress her hair here. The Sioux knew no different and she was certain Troy did not keep up with the latest styles. So did she do this for herself or others? She determined to release herself from the rigors of styling her hair.

In stocking feet, Eleanor walked across the yellowed grass to the skin where Troy slept. She lay beside him, cautiously sliding an arm over his broad chest as her head found the pillow of his shoulder.

Troy's arm snaked out and, without waking, he dragged her to him, holding her tenderly as if he had loved her all his life. She sighed and breathed his scent, feeling instantly comforted.

Last night she had tossed and paced, finally giving up all together. The meager comfort of her sketchpad did not console her and finally she wept.

But tonight the fire seemed warm and Troy's arms cradled her in safety. She gave a stifled yawn and blinked up at him, noticing the dark shadow of whiskers spread across his jaw. Two days' growth.

She rubbed the line of his jaw with her knuckles savoring the rough texture, so different from her own.

Was this what it would be like to marry for love? Would she sleep each night wrapped in the loving comfort of his embrace instead of alone in her lonely ornate chamber? Would he hold her even in sleep and never be parted, save by death?

Her hand fell to the flat expanse of his chest. The steady beat of his heart sounded in her ear and vibrated beneath her palm.

Danger lay all around her. But somehow they could not reach her here in his embrace. Tomorrow would be soon enough to face the decision of the council. Tonight she would sleep beside this man as his wife.

"I love you, Troy," she whispered.

Troy opened his eyes at the gentle call from outside the tee-pec. The woman's voice announced herself again. He glanced at the closed flap entrance. He blinked his eyes and saw it was full light.

He called out for her to enter in what little of her language he knew.

The flap lifted and a woman appeared. She smiled at him and then her eyes went wide. She did not enter, but only lowered the tray of food to the ground and retreated.

What was that about?

Something wiggled beside him. He glanced down to see

Lena cuddled up against him like a kitten on a cold day. Her leg draped his thighs. A slender pink calf poked out from beneath the buffalo robe. Her arm looped familiarly across his belly and an ocean of wild red waves cascaded over his arm and onto the buffalo robe. Troy swallowed hard.

Lena's hair was down. His breath caught at the sight. Pale pink dusted her cheeks and her beautiful lips turned in a secret smile as she dreamed on.

He should wake her—shouldn't he?

Then he noticed she wore only a slip and petticoat. His body pulsed to life. The squeezing ache quickly settled in his groin. Why had she done this?

Didn't she know every man had limits to his control? She'd crossed that line when she removed her armor and let down her glorious hair. He stroked her back and she made a purring sound. His fingers tangled into the curls. Thick as carded wool. Rich—just like the rest of her.

Her fingers flexed, gripping the hide that covered his belly and he twitched.

"Great God almighty," he breathed.

His eyes flashed to the peg where her garments hung. He either had to get her into that dress or out of this shift in a hurry.

One way or the other, right now, he decided.

He wrapped his arms about her and her eyes blinked open. Her hand descended as if reaching for him. No—she couldn't.

He nudged her and her eyes blinked lazily open. Her smile dazzled.

Trying to look cross, he said, "Lena, what are you doing?"

The smile never wavered. "Sleeping in your arms."

"You can't go crawling into a man's sleeping robes without knowing what will happen."

Her smile changed from languid to sensual, sending a raw sexual energy flooding into his bloodstream.

"I know."

Did she? For she was about to find out. He rolled her to her back. She offered no resistance as her hands looped about his neck. The soft fragrance of flowers wafted up from her pale body as he lowered himself to her. He nudged a knee between her thighs. To his utter astonishment, she parted her legs, allowing him to nestle there. Pressing against the core of her brought a moment's sweet pleasure followed by a rising, unsatisfied ache.

Propped upon his elbows, he stared down into her expressive eyes. She showed no fear or hesitation. His body trembled with want, but he would not force this. He was no savage to take an unwilling woman.

"Is this what you truly want?" he asked.

He watched her mouth, pink and full as she spoke. "I've dreamed of you all my life. I just never expected to find you here."

He didn't understand her words, but her acceptance was clear. He stared down at the tiny mole beneath her lip. That little dark spot had giving him many hours fascination. Now, at last, he dipped, running his tongue over the slightly elevated flesh. His tongue brushed the full swell of her bottom lip and then explored the hard surface of her straight teeth, parting now to admit him to her sweet mouth.

You'll never keep her. His mind flashed a warning. He knew that she would only break his heart, but still he could not resist her.

A voice came from somewhere far away.

He deepened the kiss, feeling her arms tight about his neck, urging him closer.

The voice again, and this time he heard the words.

"Price? I come in now."

He rolled away from Lena, leaving her exposed and breathless. She panted, her eyes wide with confusion, her legs still splayed. Her petticoats gathered at her knees, spilling into the gap where he lay just a moment before. Crouching, Troy faced Wind Dancer, who scowled at him.

Lena lay between them, her gaze going from one to the

other. Coming to her senses, she scrambled to her seat, tucking her slender legs beneath the ocean of white linen.

Wind Dancer spoke to Lena. "Council decision is reached. You come."

"What did they decide?" asked Troy.

Wind Dancer's solemn face gave little hope as he stared at Lena. "You come."

She pressed her arms protectively about her. "Yes. As soon as I am dressed."

Wind Dancer nodded, sending the feathers in his hair a flutter. Then he stepped back and dropped the flap.

Their gazes met.

Lena reached out and grasped his hand with fingers suddenly icy cold. "I wish we had just a little more time."

He helped her dress. Then, Troy stepped first from the opening and Lena followed. The instant his head cleared the entrance, two men seized his arms and dragged him aside. Unable to run, Lena stood alone before the assembled warriors.

Chapter 16

Troy twisted, preparing to kick out the legs of the braves that held him. He'd die before he'd see them harm Lena.

Wind Dancer spoke, "Be still or I open your head again."

Troy ceased his struggles.

Lena stood regal as a princess before the gathering. Her eyes widened as she noted Troy's capture, but she did not weep or beg, instead turning to Wind Dancer as if she were a condemned queen. He motioned her to follow. Troy stood rigid, preparing to escape if they harmed her. He knew he could not save her, but he could go down fighting.

Wind Dancer led Lena forward and then to a halt. He left her there, facing the village. Troy saw Red Eagle standing tall and triumphant. The cold fingers of dread crept up Troy's spine. Had the man won?

Then Red Eagle spoke to the assemblage. No translation was offered by speech or sign. The words were not for him.

Beside the old man, Charging Buffalo looked grim. The two moved aside, leaving Lena looking bewildered and alone. Her gaze strayed to him.

Helpless, he stood before her. His eye caught movement and turned to spot the archer draw back his bowstring.

"No!" he shouted.

The man released his fingers from the cord and the arrow shot into the air. Troy jerked his head to see Lena have time only to gape before the point struck her in the center of her chest.

Troy wrenched himself free. The braves beside him did not resist his efforts but stood dumbstruck beside him. Troy took one step, then another, running the ten paces to her side.

Lena did not fall. The arrow quivered and stilled, sticking outward from her body like a tree limb. She turned to Charging Buffalo, whose eyes rounded in astonishment. Red Eagle sunk to his knees.

Panic shook the assemblage. Screams and shouts mingled as the people fled in all directions. The Medicine Man dragged himself to his feet and ran after the rest.

Only Charging Buffalo and a few of his braves stood their ground.

Lena turned to the chief. "What have I done?"

Why didn't she fall?

She grasped the arrow and pulled, but it remained embedded in her body.

"Lena—how?" he asked.

Her color drained away until her face shone pale as the surface of the moon.

"My corset. It's stuck in the bodkin."

"What?"

"The picture book piece of London Bridge," she whispered.

Understanding flooded his mind as possibilities sparked.

"Are you injured?" he asked.

She gave a shake of her head. "I don't know."

"Hold on."

The village now cleared except for the five brave men before him, Charging Buffalo and Wind Dancer among them. Unease and astonishment blanketed their features.

Charging Buffalo signed one word, "How?"

He signed his answer, his hands moving in even strokes.

Medicine Woman saves the most powerful medicine for herself. Bring our horses and mules. We go.

The chief spoke and Wind Dancer translated. "One of our women has sickened with the spotting disease. Red Eagle says Medicine Woman brings this white man's curse with her. Charging Bear says the woman was not protected by Medicine Woman's spirit painting."

Lena leaned heavily on Troy and he grabbed her elbow to support her. They had to get out of here, right away.

"You shot at Medicine Woman. She will not work her medicine here again."

Charging Buffalo spoke for a long time. Wind Dancer explained that he was sorry for the mistakes of his council. There had been so much bad from the whites: diseases, liquor and guns that could kill a man before he even saw his enemy. They agreed this was some evil trick. Now they saw Medicine Woman's power and were honored that she had shared it with the River Otter People.

"Not anymore, she won't," said Troy.

"This we regret. You pick of my horses," Wind Dancer translated for Charging Buffalo.

Troy wanted to leave immediately. "I accept your choice."

The chief spoke to his braves, who departed a moment later. Troy glanced at Lena and noted her labored breathing. He had to get that arrow out before she could ride. He hesitated, wondering if the arrowhead acted like a cork. He clenched his teeth together, knowing that, either way, it must come out.

He grasped the arrow thrusting from Lena's chest and pulled. A tremor ran through her as he expelled the point, but he noted no blood. She shivered as if freezing cold.

The chief stepped back as Troy hoisted the arrow. "We will keep this as a reminder of your hospitality."

The warriors returned with the mules packed.

He squeezed Lena's elbow. "You gotta stand up tall. I'm letting go."

She bit her lower lip and nodded. Troy released her and waited a moment, then hurried to saddle her filly and check the mules. He scowled at his new mount, an Appaloosa stallion. Upon the creature's speckled back was not the small, austere saddle of the Sioux, but Troy's old saddle. They couldn't ride double on her little Arabian and he did not yet trust this new horse. With no choice but to move forward, Troy mounted the Appaloosa who bore his weight calmly.

"Lena," he said, extending his hand, and she reached up.

He hauled her up before him and she fell heavily against his chest.

"Lena, are you hurt?"

"Yes."

"Hold on."

With his right hand he held her and the single rein of the Sioux bridle. His left pulled the line of animals strung behind him. It seemed to take forever to clear the village. At last, all sign of the Sioux vanished behind him and he pulled to a stop.

Lena's eyes blinked open as he eased her away from the safety of his chest.

"Hold the horn," he said and swung down. In a moment he had her sitting on a buffalo robe, as he worked the impossibly small hooks and eyes disguised beneath a flap on the side of her dress. She did not protest when he drew the silken fabric down about her waist, and that worried him. He moved before her and studied the corset. A tear in the fabric was the only evidence of the assault. His breath returned. She reached to a gap between her full breasts and withdrew the bodkin from its sleeve, revealing the finely carved scene he had first admired the day they met. The reason for her embarrassment that day was now clear to him. Her fingers trembled and the ivory fell in two. She let out a strangled cry as the ivory slid through her trembling fingers.

He noted the etched bridge in the center split cleanly by the arrow. Small wonder she was as pale as milk. His gaze shifted from her trembling hands to the spot of crimson blossoming on the clean white linen of her corset. It was the size of a half dollar and spreading outward.

His stomach clenched as if mule-kicked.

"Great God almighty." He reached for his knife only to find it missing. He never got it back from the Sioux.

He scrambled behind her, tearing at the cording. She cried out and he forced himself to take care as he unlaced the contraption.

Now he moved before her, dragging the shift down below the orbs of her breasts to find blood welling from a slice at the center of her chest. The corset hadn't stopped the arrow, only slowed it.

Had the point split her breastplate as neatly as it had the whalebone?

He drew back the skin flanking the wound and saw the glistening sheath covering the muscle beneath, bloody, but intact.

His heart beat so loudly he could not hear his own words.

"Flesh wound."

He pressed her breastbone, above and below the slit, and she winced. Bruised likely, but that was all.

"It ain't broke."

Her sigh of relief was audible.

"But the skin's cut."

"Is it bad?" she asked glancing down at the wound.

"It'll mend."

Her head sunk forward to look. "That's a mercy."

"Best bandage you up."

"I have a medicinal salve."

Troy retrieved the ointment and then tore one of her numerous petticoats for a clean pad of linen. She placed a dollop of the cream upon the cloth and then he pressed the fabric over the wound. She drew her chemise back in place. Troy tried to wind strips around her ribs to hold the bandage, but her full breasts prevented the binding from touching the pad.

"Them things are starting to irritate me," he muttered.

Her coy smile removed the scowl from his face.

"My mother calls them one of a woman's few advantages."

"I can't get the pad to stay put."

"Use the corset," she said.

He did and found that it held the dressing perfectly. "So it finally comes in handy," he said.

She lifted the split bodkin. "Twice in one day."

Their gaze met and held as he realized how nearly he had come to losing her.

"Lena, if anything had happened to you. I don't know what I would have done."

She smiled, seemingly pleased to be the cause of his torment and he realized that he would lose her soon enough.

How had he let himself become attached to her after warning himself against making such a mistake again? Lena was no different than Rachel. A month from now, if he passed her on the street, she would likely walk by without acknowledging him.

But he would never forget her.

"Troy?" she asked.

He snapped back from his musings and checked beneath the pad.

"No bleeding," he said. "Lena, we gotta move downriver 'fore them Sioux change their mind about letting us go."

Her eyes widened, seeming huge in her pale face.

"I'll tie your horse to the others and you'll ride with me." He arranged the horses, unsure about his new mount, but equally unsure if her little horse could carry them both, not to mention what would happen if he slapped his saddle on the creature. He eased her up on the Appaloosa again and then mounted behind, cradling Lena against him as he led the group downriver.

"Rest now." He stroked her head. "That's my girl."

"Am I?"

"What?"

"Your girl."

He glanced down at the top of her head. "Do you want to be?"

"More than anything." She held his arm, now snug across her waist. "I thought I would die today."

"You were brave. Never showed them no fear. They respect that."

"I've never been more frightened."

"That's what courage is, going on, even if your knees are cracking together. But don't you worry, Lena. I'll bring you home safe."

She began to cry.

"Lena. What's wrong, does your wound pain you?"

She shook her head. "This morning, I could have had you. Now I've lost you again."

"I'm right here."

She sniffed and he felt his throat tighten.

"Only for a few more days."

He couldn't stand to see her like this. There must be something he could do to ease their parting for both of them.

"Been known to rub on a person's nerves. You'll be lucky to be rid of me." He knew he'd never grow tired of her. *Never.*

"I will not."

His heart squeezed tight at what she said. Then the reality of their situation returned.

"You don't know what it means to keep hold of something until it wears out. You'd grow weary of me over time."

"Never."

"That coming from a woman with more shoes than there are days of the week. You ain't never done without. My whole life has been making do. Believe me. You don't want a life with me."

She extended her hand, placing it over his. "But I do."

He scowled. "I should dress you in buckskin and beads and see how you like it."

"If only it were so simple."

"Nothing ever is."

She cast him a look of longing and he pressed his lips into a grim line, refusing to let her take his heart and toss it away.

"Lena, I ain't the one leaving. I ain't the one that's got promises to keep. You got choices to make and one is which way we ride. So do you want to stay with me or not?"

Chapter 17

Lena wasn't staying. She wept that night as he tossed beneath the weight of the buffalo hide. The next morning he found her eyes red-rimmed.

Troy helped Lena onto Scheherazade's back and then mounted his new Appaloosa stallion. The horse was big and strong, and Troy hated him.

He'd ridden Dahlonega all over the West. His mount was only seven and had good years left before Charging Buffalo's men killed him.

He glanced back at Lena, finding her head hung low. He never meant to hurt her. Seemed he caused women trouble no matter what his intentions. But she was leaving him, damn it. So why did he feel guilty?

He only knew he wanted her with an acuteness that pierced his heart like a thorn. He was taking her back before they did something they'd regret.

Still, as they rode into the late afternoon, he pondered how to get her to stay with him. To do so she would need to forsake her promise to her father and abandon her family. It was a hard choice. What would he do in her place? If his mother and sisters lived, what would he give up to keep from shaming them?

He sighed.

His family was dead. He had no further obligation to them, while Lena had nothing but obligations to hers.

He drew up in a grove by the river, choosing to make camp early. He needed to check Lena's wound. How he dreaded facing her again.

He slid off the Sioux horse and hobbled the stallion's front legs, then turned to Lena, but found she had already dismounted unassisted.

The silence stretched as he unloaded their gear. He saw her lift her arms to remove her saddle and wince.

"I'll do that." He brushed her aside and slipped the weight off her little mare.

By the time he had a fire going the day was nearly spent. He extended a portion of dried jerky, but she waved away his offer.

"Lena, I hate to see you so blue."

She made no attempt to smile.

"When you get back east, you can show your painting to that fellow, Audubon."

She sighed. "Yes."

"Think he'll like 'em?"

She thought a moment. "I believe so."

"That's why you came out here, isn't it?"

Her eyes spoke of her sorrow and his gut tightened at the sight. "It was."

"If he includes you in his next venture, you'll be heading back here."

"Oh, no. Once I marry, I shan't be allowed such liberties. If I am fortunate, I will paint the background for his work from New York."

This news struck him like a second blow from the war club of an attacking Sioux warrior. Anger simmered. Lena deserved her dream. She risked so much, came so far and should never be a background anything. Why didn't anyone back home care about her talent or her wishes?

His mood sunk as well.

"You'll be caged up like a canary."

She nodded. "Just so."

"Is that what you want, Lena?"

Tears brimmed in her eyes and spilled over the dam of her lids, coursing down her cheeks. She spoke in a strangled voice. "What I want has nothing whatsoever to do with it, you see. I can't break my parents' hearts."

She reached out and grasped his hand. Cold fingers gripped his with surprising strength. "If I did not have to go, would you marry me, Troy?"

He lifted her hand to his cheek, pressing a kiss to her palm. A lightning bolt of pain streaked through his heart as he ached over losing her. Another woman shamed by his love.

Life was cruel.

She stroked his face, her fingers dancing over his ear and down his neck to rest upon his shoulder. He lifted his gaze to meet hers.

"Lena, I'm not going to covet what I can't have. You're going back. I'm staying."

"Yes—how practical of you to guard your heart. Mine is already broken." Her hand slipped away.

"I'm sorry, Lena. I never meant for this to happen."

She nodded. "I think I would like to lie down now."

"Does your wound pain you?"

Her fingers rubbed over the spot. "The ache is somewhat deeper. I feel as if I have been shot twice today."

"I best have a look."

She turned away. "No. I will see to it. Just lay out my bed, please. I shall call if I need assistance."

He did as she requested and gave her privacy, busying himself with checking on the animals before returning to the fire. "How does it look?"

"The bleeding has ceased."

She slipped between the buffalo robes until all that remained in view was the curling waves of coppery hair glowing to rival the fire.

He climbed into his own bed. Last night she lay in his arms. This morning she had offered herself to him. He was glad he hadn't taken her. She wasn't his and never would be.

Then why did regret stab at his belly like a dull blade?

She gazed up at the night sky. "I wonder what it would be like to pick a man for love alone."

"Some folks here marry for the same reason as you. Wealth, land—it's common enough."

"Would you come sit beside me?"

Her eyes told the rest. She wanted him. He set his jaw as he considered her sorrow. "Lena, if we was to make love, one of us will have to choose."

"Choose?"

"I'd have to leave my world or you'd have to leave yours."

Her gaze dropped and she nodded. "Yes. That's so." Her long sigh echoed in his soul. "My family has high hopes for me."

"Your pa is forcing you to marry." He felt compelled to point that out.

"It is every father's responsibility to see his daughters well-settled. I will not fault him for it. I feel sorry for him. He so wanted a son. I know I have been a disappointment to him."

Troy wondered how anyone could be disappointed with a woman as magnificent as Lena.

"He does not understand this need I have to paint. I think he hoped that by indulging me, I would outgrow it somehow, like a girl outgrows her dolls. But nothing changed in that regard." She turned her gaze on him, increasing his disquiet. "Do you remember when I mentioned my mother's lovers?"

He shifted uncomfortably and then nodded.

"I will likely do the same someday, after I produce an heir for my husband."

He waited, wondering if she was heading up the trail he suspected. His stomach knotted as he considered life in the shadows of her world.

"I know you love the West. I understand it. But perhaps you would come east?"

"Are you asking what I think you're asking?"

She swallowed. "I would like you to come back with me. I could see all your needs met, a townhouse with servants, monthly income."

"You got that much money?"

"More than I could spend in many lifetimes. My mother saw to it that I have my own funds so I am not at the mercy of my husband—in addition, I am my father's heir."

She waited, her hands clasped tight before her on the buffalo robe.

"Lena, I don't want a house and servants. I want a means to make my own living and my freedom." But he also wanted her. He wanted her badly enough to consider what she offered. Then he remembered something else she said. "What if we have children?"

"I would raise them."

His gaze narrowed. "But I won't."

"Troy, please understand. I would have to maintain a facade of respectability."

"Even if it's a lie?"

"This is how it is done."

"You're asking me to give up my world and my children to live as some kind of male whore."

Her eyes rounded. "That is certainly not at all what I am suggesting. I only seek a means that we might not be parted. I have feelings for you. I am not experienced with such things but I know that what we share is unique. This way we can be together."

"Call it what you like." He glowered at the fire. "What if I asked you to stay?" He waited, watching the indecision play across her features. Longing, yes, he recognized that and then what?

She lowered her head. "I cannot."

Anger cooked his insides. "You're shamed by me."

Her head snapped up. "No."

"You want me in the darkness. Come daylight, you want respectability."

"That's not true."

"Shamed by me. An Indian lover—a savage. You're strong enough to take a Sioux arrow, but not strong enough to admit you love me."

"You are wrong, Troy. I love you. I love my family as well. If my love for you steals all their hopes and dreams, how can I live with myself?"

Troy drew a deep breath. It was as he'd known from the beginning. He could not keep her without losing himself.

"You're willing to ask me to give up everything for your love."

"Yes."

"Stay," he whispered.

She dropped her chin peeking at him through tear-soaked lashes. "I cannot."

He nodded. "Then you appreciate what you're asking. I guess I ain't man enough to live like you're suggesting. I always made my own way. It don't sit right to be your fancy man."

"I understand." Her eyes glowed bright with the tears that remained unshed.

They faced each other. She spoke first. "So this is all we have then—this night, a few more days?"

"Reckon so."

She drew a ragged breath. "You said that I did not understand doing without. Perhaps you are right, but I fear I will spend my life doing without the man I love."

He didn't know if he should send her back or try to keep

her. Up until this moment, he knew with certainty what was best for them both. But now, things had gone too far.

"We only known each other a short while. The ties between us ain't too tight to break, over time." The sorrow in her eyes bored into him like a weevil on a corncob. He tried another lie but his heart wasn't in it. "If we did stay together, we might grow to dislike each other." He didn't believe it, but thought it might comfort her.

"Familiarity breeds contempt?" She shook her head. "Please don't diminish our feelings as some summer's fancy. I know what it is. A day will not pass that I do not think of you and wonder if you think of me."

"I don't see no way out but for you to leave your life or me, mine."

She nodded and lay back on her solitary bed. Her eyes closed and tears streamed from beneath her lids.

Troy watched her by firelight, but she said no more. After the fire burned to orange embers and he could no longer make out her features, he fell into a fitful sleep where he dreamed he was a raven trapped in a tiny cage.

He woke to the scream of her horse and rolled to his feet, rifle aimed. What he saw brought him back a step.

Lena recognized the call of her horse and staggered from her sleeping robes. She would have sworn she had not slept a wink all night, but here it was morning as she rose from the ground, pistol in hand. Beside her, Troy lowered his rifle.

She turned to see his new Appaloosa stallion bite Scheherazade's neck to still her as she danced on the end of her line. Somehow the brute had broken his hobbles and now reared up to throw himself upon the tiny mare's back. The stallion bit her horse again and leaped forward on hind legs, thrusting into her mare.

Lena screamed. "Get him off."

Troy ran forward.

The stallion bucked now, in frantic rhythm as the mare staggered beneath his weight, twisting and screaming in a vain effort to dislodge her attacker.

In an instant it was done. The stallion withdrew from the mare's quaking body and dropped back to all fours. Scheherazade kicked him in the chest and danced away, circling around the tree and tangling her line. The stallion came at her again, but this time Troy captured his harness and dragged him away.

Lena rallied to go to her horse.

Her mare trembled as Lena stroked her neck, whispering assurances. "There now. You poor dear."

She glanced at Troy and found him tying off the stallion some distance away, before returning to her.

"She all right?"

"She is terrified." Lena realized that she shivered as well, overcome by the violence and raw power of the creatures' coupling.

"Now that she's in heat, they'll be no keeping him clear."

"Oh, but you must. She is a purebred. That monster will ruin her. I cannot allow her to breed to that." She pointed to the spotted brute now happily munching the grass about him as if he had not just raped her horse. When she turned her attention to Troy, she discovered a look upon his face as if she had just kicked him in the stomach.

His flat tone did not seem at all right. "We don't want to mix their blood lines."

"Exactly. What if she gets with foal? Oh, what will Father say?"

For a moment she did not comprehend the cold censure glaring in his eyes. Understanding dawned and she shivered. He was the stallion and she, the mare.

She gasped. "Troy, I am sorry. I did not mean to imply."

"But you ain't ashamed of me. Same thing, isn't it? Common everyday horse and a princess. Never mind that she's in heat and calling to him. He ain't good enough for her. Never will be."

He spun away.

"Troy, wait. Please."

From then on, he kept the mules between his stallion and her mare. At night he staked the Appaloosa a good distance from Scheherazade on a double line and he slept across the fire from Lena. He never touched her again, nor did he smile or joke. Everything they shared was ruined and she had no idea how to make things right.

How could loving a man bring them such terrible heartache?

Chapter 18

For the next eight days and nights, Troy kept his hands off Lena and he kept his stallion off her mare. The incident only increased his hatred for the Appaloosa as it reminded him with each glance that he was a wild mustang and she a purebred. As the fort grew nearer his mood darkened. He couldn't have Lena unless he gave up everything he was. He glanced back. Damned if he wasn't tempted.

Letting her go would take more strength than he had.

What if he went?

He'd live in comfort like her favorite hound. Perhaps she'd give him a stall next to her horse. He could bear it for Lena. Because despite her humiliating offer, he still wanted her. On the outside they were opposites, inside she matched him in courage and something else—a lust for independence. She wanted him, too, but not for a husband. That tore his heart wide open. For despite his efforts to avoid it, he'd again fallen in love with a woman who could not or would not acknowledge him.

She'd marry, but not to him. She'd have children and they wouldn't be his. That was the one fence he could not jump.

Lena finished a painting of a flock of turkey vultures on a bluff. He sat close enough to watch her work, but far enough back that he could not smell her floral fragrance. The scent of roses was now forever linked with images of Lena.

"Do you have enough paintings now, you think?"

She paused in midstroke as if frozen by his question. Slowly she lowered her brush and turned to face him. Apprehension flashed in her eyes as she gnawed her bottom lip between white teeth. That adorable mouth sank with her frown.

His stomach clenched at the quickfire jolt of lust that hit him each time he studied her mouth. Would he ever taste her lips again? Yes, he decided. He would not let her go without a kiss.

But then he would let her go, she to her world, he to his.

"Why do you ask?"

"Summer's dying, Lena. Time to head back."

Her chin dropped to her chest. "You've been bringing us back for days and days now."

So, she did know and had said nothing.

"You got your wolf and buffalo. Hell, you even got a bear and a lynx."

"I only painted the bear from memory."

"Good likeness."

She favored him with a sad smile. "Will you be glad to be rid of me?"

He'd be glad to be rid of the pain that came every time he looked at her. But he doubted it would leave him when she did. Likely it would only get worse.

"I don't think I'll ever be rid of you."

Her brush dangled from distracted fingers. "I wish there was some way."

"There is."

She did not move except to speak. "How?"

"You'd have to run off with me. Leave your family. I'll take you to the Rockies or the Pacific. It's a big territory. Easy to get lost."

She sank to her knees, nearly disappearing in the tall yellow grass. "Yes, I'd thought of that."

"Could you live knowing that you deceived them, that you broke your word and ran off with a man beneath you?" He hated himself for suggesting it. She deserved better than lies. But his desperation made him reckless.

She stared off into space. "Not beneath me."

"There wouldn't be no maids or servants. Not ever. You'd have to learn to do for yourself."

"Troy, are you offering to marry me?"

He yanked a blade of grass and chewed the sweet end. "I am. But I want what's best for you and I don't think I'm it."

"My father deserves an heir."

"Why?"

She gaped at him. "It's my duty."

"If you say so."

"You disapprove."

"Do they think you no better than a breeding stock? It sends a chill down my spine. You deserve some happiness."

"A daughter should be obedient and marry as her parents wish."

"Well you ain't obedient or you wouldn't be sitting out here in the prairie grass talking to me."

"All the more reason to return."

"That's fine. When your mare has her foal you can think of me and be glad you didn't taint your bloodline."

Her chin dropped and he heard her crying. Why was he so cruel? This mess wasn't her fault. Oh, but it was. She came here and invaded *his* world. She'd stalked him like a panther and he'd fallen in love with her. Damn her for dangling a prize before him only to snatch it back.

"You shouldn't have come to this wild place." He stared at her, relaying his intentions.

"Why are you looking at me like that?"

He took a step forward and she rose to her feet, senses alert like an antelope the instant before flight. All the days and nights without her crashed in upon him and now he stalked *her*.

"Troy, stop."

She turned to flee and made it only three steps before he captured her, molding her backside to his loins. He swept away the proper little curls of her ridiculous hairstyle and grazed his teeth along her neck, holding her tight to his chest.

He registered her gasp as his hand scaled the armor of her corset to cup the soft flesh of her breast.

"What are you doing?"

"Exactly what you want me to do. When you're lying in your clean sheets with another man, you can think back on this."

He scored her neck with his teeth. She shuddered and arched back, giving him access to the long column of her throat. He captured the soft lobe of her ear and sucked.

She stilled, trembling now, resting her head against his shoulder.

He skimmed a hand up her throat to her cheek. It was then he felt her tears.

He stumbled back as if struck.

What had he done?

"Lena?" He reached for her, grasping her delicate arm. "Lena, forgive me."

She turned to him, weeping, and he dragged her into his arms.

"I never meant to hurt you." He froze then, knowing it for a lie. She made it known she was too good for him, wounded him to the heart. He wanted to hurt her, too. He thought he might vomit from self-loathing. She was right. He was no better than an animal.

She spoke to him. He tried to make out her words past the choking sobs. "I—I want you, t-too. Oh, God help me, but I would not have stopped you. What have I become?"

He held her close as his heart bled with regret and shame. "It's my fault, Lena. I don't deserve you." He cradled her in his arms and they rocked together.

"I love you, Troy, with all my heart. But I love my parents, too. I can't break their hearts to save mine."

"I'm taking you back. You have to go home."

They held each other, tears mingled and dried in the warm prairie winds.

He lifted his head and inhaled, then straightened. Smoke—why had he not noticed sooner? Listening now, he heard no bird song.

Lena stirred beside him. "What is it?"

He stared. She blushed and he shook his head.

"Something's wrong."

It took only a moment to spot the menace.

"What?" she asked, turning in the direction he stared.

"Wildfire. We got to cross the river and pray the water stops her."

"Fire?" She drew her hands to her mouth. "Look at the smoke."

Black as soot and stretching a half mile, the wall of smoke rose hundreds of feet into the sky. By the time he had the animals packed and saddled, ash fell about them like snowflakes.

"Have you seen this before?" she asked.

"No. But I've heard tell. Saddle up."

He led them to the river and glanced back, recalling her last experience fording water.

"Want to ride with me?" he asked.

She shook her head, revealing the mess he'd made of her hair. "I shall hold tight."

Lena turned back to watch the smoke, already feeling it thick in the air, burning the back of her throat.

He kicked his stallion and the beast waded into the river. Her mare followed with no fuss, seeming to sense their peril. Lena clutched the saddle as Scheherazade's hooves left the river bottom and she began her lunging stroke. Lena's skirts dragged in the water, tugging as the river tried to take her. At last they scaled the bank and she could breath again, coughing now.

They rode northeast along the far shore, dogged by the wall

of smoke. All along the far bank, creatures she never expected could swim now leapt into the river. A bobcat and coyote, mule deer and elk all paddled with noses raised, their movements urgent. Wild turkeys beat past them with clumsy strokes of their giant wings. The birds rose higher and turned off to the north.

"Should we follow them?" she asked.

Troy sat with his head cocked. "Listen."

She did. At first there was nothing, but then came a distant rumble like far-off thunder.

He stood on his horse.

"What are you doing?"

He raised a hand to shade his eyes.

She watched him and the smoke in turns. Where the black smoke met the grassland she thought she saw some movement.

"What is that?"

His jaw fell and he pressed a hand to his forehead. Stillness changed to frantic motion as he dropped onto his stallion.

"Ride!" He wheeled his horse about and tugged on the lines to the mules.

"What is it?"

"Buffalo—thousands of them and they're heading right for us."

"Buffalo?"

"A stampede. Now get that horse going like I know she can." He kicked his heels on the Appaloosa's sides. Scheherazade leapt to follow without the slightest urging from her.

Behind them, the wall of charging flesh rushed closer.

Chapter 19

He found no cover, no ready trees in which to escape the buffalo. He could see them now, numbering in the thousands and running together before a wall of fire. Impossible to turn them and their width, they stretched beyond his vision in both directions.

The herd would cross the river and crush them beneath their hooves. He reined in, refusing to waste his energy in a vain attempt to flank them. The line was too wide. He must think of another way.

"Hurry, Troy, they're gaining."

"Horses can't outrun buffalo. They don't have the stamina. I've seen herds run for days."

"What will we do?"

"I'm working on it."

"Even if we could outrun them, how will we escape the inferno behind them?" Lena studied the horizon. "We will never escape both."

The fire, an idea flickered in the recesses of his mind then leaped to life like a spark on fodder. "That's it!"

She drew alongside him and stared at the approaching threat. "I think I would rather be trampled than burn."

He grabbed her by the neck and dragged her over for a swift kiss. "We'll use the fire to turn the herd. Come on."

He led the horses and mules back across the river and she followed, rivulets of water running down her skirt as she mounted the bank once more.

He was off the horse and on his knees clutching his fire-starting gear. In a few minutes he had a thin line of gray smoke and then a flame. Instead of carefully placing it in an earthen pit, he laid his fragile fire on the yellow grass. Smoke billowed as he blew on the flames. Soon the blade ignited.

"What are you doing? You will kill us both."

She tried to wring her skirts on the flame, but he dragged her to the river, then retrieved the horses and brought them into knee-deep water as well. His fire burned in a widening circle of flames. It reached the river and raced along the bank. The wind drove the smoke at them, but the water held back the flames. She held her skirt to her mouth and breathed through the wet fabric. The ground beneath her trembled. She stared through the wall of smoke and fire before her to see the buffalo thundering closer, their outlines hazy through the smoke.

"Lena, you're on fire!" Troy dunked her.

She came up sputtering and inhaled smoke. It burned her lungs and singed the hairs in her nose.

The horses screamed and reared up. One of the mules broke free and bolted across the river.

Troy held the other three and his wild-eyed Appaloosa. She grabbed Scheherazade's muzzle and reins. The herd disappeared in the wall of flames before them.

Troy soaked a buffalo hide in the river and threw it over her horse's back and then threw a second over the Appaloosa.

"Crawl under there," he ordered.

She clasped the reins with one hand and squatted in safety with the hide draping her head and stared into the billowing wall of black smoke.

"What if they run through?"

"They won't."

Something crashed into the water. Far down the bank the first buffalo exploded into the river, followed by more and more. They forged first on the right and then the left, churning the water with a thousand thrashing legs until the river frothed, like beaten egg whites.

Scheherazade shrieked and danced. Lena stood to quiet her mare and Troy covered the horses' heads with a wet hide. Blinded, her Arabian stilled, quivering in silent terror.

The buffalo charged up the far bank and onto the prairie, merging again as they thundered along. They seemed to cross for hours, beating the ground with thousands of hooves. She stood motionless as the herd rushed by in a moving wall of bellowing brown fur and lolling pink tongues.

The last of the lot appeared from the smoke, their coats ablaze. The flames doused in the river, showing patches of angry pink skin.

All about her lay scorched earth. Beyond the flames the approaching fire met and merged with the wall some five hundred feet beyond them. With the buffalo gone, she noticed the roar of hot wind, blasting her like a furnace. She thought of the burning buffalo and sunk in the water to her chin and doused her hair once more. Ash and burning embers drifted down upon them in a scorching shower that sent the mules into a frantic dance.

She helped Troy soak the buffalo robes and drape them over the mules. The creatures no longer tried to run. They stood trembling, their heads swaddled and their nostrils flaring pink.

Before her the fire went out. She blinked to be sure her eyes did not deceive her. The smoke and flame separated like a drawing orange curtain. Beyond, the earth was scorched black to the horizon.

"You set one fire against the other. Brilliant," she said.

He smiled and then sunk beneath the river again for a moment.

"Getting easier to breathe now," he said.

The fire raced along the outer circle of remaining grass, meeting the second fire and burning out. Far down the river-bank the flames reached the water.

"Oh, no." As she watched, burning embers sailed across the river, pushed by the winds of the fire, and ignited in the dry grass on the far bank.

She watched in horror as the fire kindled anew and began its awful path of destruction once more.

Lena stood facing the fire and watched the smoke and flames move on, still astonished at her escape. All around her the black stubble of grass stretched.

"We should have died here," she said.

He wrapped an arm about her. "But we didn't."

"Because of you." She turned to face him. "You saved my life."

"Getting to be a regular habit."

She nestled close to his wet shirt. "Each day forward is a gift."

He let her cling a while, but did not release his hold on the animals. At last she shivered and he led them to dry land. To-gether they climbed the bank where they began. He relieved the horses of their blinders and surveyed the destruction.

"Lost that mule."

"Will we go after it?"

"She's crushed or burned. Nothing on that side could survive."

A shot of fear ripped through her. "Where are my paintings?"

He grinned. "Don't worry, Princess. That mule only had my ammunition, trade goods and all our food."

Her shoulders sagged in relief. "I don't know what I would do if I lost my work."

Troy chuckled.

She realized what she had done and her expression grew apologetic. "Oh, I am truly sorry. I didn't mean your belong-ings were less important. We can replace them."

"Everything's replaceable, right?"

She dropped her gaze and he did not pursue his somber musings.

"Nothing important, I guess. But I will miss that mule."

"That could have been us. It would have been, if I had not trusted you. I never would have faced that herd."

He sighed. "You did face them, Lena."

Her wet skirts clung heavily to her legs and she did not think she could mount up. He scrutinized her a moment and shook his head in dismay.

"No fuel for a fire. We'll have to dry out with the sun. Maybe we can ride out of this mess by sunset if we head due east."

She rummaged through the packs and found her paintings dry within the oilskin case he made for them. She fingered the soft tips of her sable brushes and smiled, her precious paints were intact.

Her wardrobe did not fare so well. She elected to change her clothing. Then they rode due east for five miles before she saw the first green blade of grass. He followed a stream until they could no longer see the blackened earth.

Here they halted and unloaded all the remaining gear. Everything smelled of smoke. She lifted a lock of her hair and sniffed.

"Oh, I must wash," she said.

Troy glanced up from his work of collecting wood. "I'd like to check that wound."

A spark ignited in her at the look he sent and she nodded. In all the turbulence of the past several days, she'd quite forgotten about her injury. She rubbed it now and felt a twinge.

"Call me when you're ready." He headed up the bank as she retrieved her rose-scented soap. Her gaze followed him until he disappeared into the cottonwood grove. She hesitated only a moment and then peeled out of her garments. Dressed in only her shift, she lowered the neckline to study the bandage and found it stuck to her wound. She tugged. The sensation made her stomach roll. She stiffened. If she did not do this, he would. After soaking the cloth, she tried again. The bandage peeled free revealing the healing wound, now pink and clean.

The distasteful task done at last, she waded into waist-deep water and washed the scab, then turned her attention to her hair. After several scrubbings, she still detected a hint of smoke. Well, it would have to do.

Scheherazade nickered and she turned to note the call was not directed to her, but to Troy's stallion. The brute tugged vainly upon his lead and her mare walked to the end of hers. Lena frowned. Troy said she was in heat. Had the stallion attacked her mare?

Doubt nagged.

The quiver in her belly returned as her mind danced back to the image of the large Appaloosa mounting her small Arabian. She shivered with a shameful thrill at the memory. How had her little horse accommodated the stallion?

She glanced toward the woods. By all rights she should be dead now. Instead she was alive and free and quivering with anticipation at Troy's touch.

In heat.

Yes, that's how she felt, burning hot while standing in the cold water.

Of course she'd noticed Troy's efforts to avoid any contact between them. It had weighed heavily upon her. The fort might be only days away now. For the first time she noted the yellow leaves already turning toward autumn and recognized this might be her last chance. Soon her father would arrive.

She loved Troy. Of that she had no doubt. But to act on a doomed love, was that selfish? She knew he did not wish the life she offered and she could hardly blame him. If she made love to him, she might live to regret it. Would she regret not loving him even more?

She sighed. At last she decided it was selfish to take this step and that she would take it. He had asked her if she did

not deserve some happiness. This one small thing she would
have for herself if he'd allow it. She would love him and capture that memory like a burning ember on a cold December
morning. At that moment, he stepped from the wood as if
summoned, his hair wet and clinging to his neck and his arms
loaded with several logs. As he sighted her, the load fell to
his feet with a clatter.

From instinct her arms rose up to cover her naked breasts
as the stream lapped about her hips. Their gaze met and held.
She lowered her arms, offering herself.

He stalked forward pausing at the water's edge.

His voice came in a tortured whisper. "What are you
doing?"

"Waiting for you."

Like a water sprite, she rose from in the river. His gaze
scanned over the perfect torso, hesitating at the clean pink
scab bisecting the skin of her sternum.

She lifted a hand to him and he was lost. He followed her
into the water, still wearing his buckskin clothing and moccasins. She smiled.

His mind flashed messages, tugging to restrain his body
like a bit in a horse's mouth. *Go slow. Treat her tenderly. She's
a lady and used to gentle treatment.*

He stood before her now, waiting. His body fully aroused
and ready, his mind hesitant. What if he hurt her?

No, he'd never forgive himself if he did.

She lifted her hand and stroked his cheek, letting her cool
fingers trail over the burning flesh of his neck and chest. She
paused just below his belt.

He swept her into his arms, carrying her to the shore and
up the bank to set the camp. There he laid her upon his wolf-
skin cloak. She sank into the lush fur as he fell to his knees
before her.

She stretched like a cat in the sun and his mouth went dry.
He tore at his gear, tossing away powder horn, pouches, bags,

holster and knife. Next he dragged his shirt off and threw it on the rest, his hands settling on the lacings of his breeches and he paused, glancing at Lena.

No, that would frighten her. She smiled up at him as she nestled into the plush furs. He kicked out of his moccasins and stretched out beside her.

Lena rolled, draping a long, slim leg over his and lifting until her thigh brushed his erect flesh. She licked the shell of his ear and he shuddered with desire. How could such a little thing make his pulse pound like the hooves of stampeding mustangs?

"My God, but I want you."

Her lips drew into a perfect smile, lush and inviting. "Kiss me."

He did, gently at first, taking in her scent of smoke and roses. She writhed, delving her fingers into his hair as she demanded more. He pressed her to the earth, deepening their kiss.

Slowly, he cautioned. Don't frighten her.

He moved to kiss her cheek and then stroked the shell of her ear with the tip of his tongue. She trembled and a satisfaction grew within him. His hand cast over the plane of her stomach and up to the jutting angle of her ribs to settle at last on the outer swell of her breast. A groan of pleasure issued from deep in her throat as he caressed her.

Both hands now stroked her tender flesh, beginning at her neck and then running up and over the lush territory of her breasts, down the flats of her stomach pausing to scout the narrow canyon of her navel before exploring her hips with feathery strokes.

She moaned and rocked towards him. He recognized desire blazing in her eyes. She reached for him, but he captured her wrist, laying it gently upon the fur, before kissing her forehead.

"Slowly, Lena. You must be ready."

She squirmed and whined in frustration, and still he resisted the call of her body, returning to gently kiss the soft flesh of her breasts. His tongue flicked out to stroke her nipple and her arms wrapped about him, pulling him close.

"Please love me. I cannot wait."

He slipped his hand down between her legs and found her thighs wet with her readiness. She did not squirm or avoid his exploration, but instead boldly rocked her hips to meet his delving fingers.

A long sigh escaped her lips and he kissed her again, stroking her tender flesh with one hand as he captured her neck with the other. She lifted herself as he stroked, her breathing becoming frantic. Her fingers gripped the muscles of his back as a cry escaped her. She arched and then collapsed to the furs, exhaling a long shuddering breath into the cool evening air.

He'd brought her to her pleasure. Satisfaction coiled within him even as his own body throbbed with need, but he would not take her. She was not his, would never be his, not completely. He knew he didn't have the courage to do what she asked. His pride could not stand it. How could he take her and then let her go?

Her eyes blinked open and a look of astonishment crossed her features.

"What was that?" she asked.

"The pleasure a man can give his woman."

She smiled. "Did you feel it?"

He shook his head.

Confusion knit her brow and then sorrow appeared in rapid succession. "Because you did not join with me. I want you to find your pleasure as well."

"I'm not your husband," he reminded.

"I do not care. I want you."

His little princess. All her life she'd gotten everything she wanted. Why should this be any different?

He shook his head. "That is a gift for your husband."

"My husband may well be twice my age, he may be hairy

or hairless or any number of vile possibilities. I wish my first time to be with a man I love. I would marry you if I could. Instead, I give you this bridal gift."

Still he hesitated. She brought his fingers to her lips and sucked them. His breathing stopped as his eyes widened.

"Please," she begged.

He rested his forehead upon hers. "Lena, how can I let you go?"

"We are together now. Do not lose this chance."

He rolled away and released the laces of his breeches. She knelt beside him, capturing the buckskin and dragging it down as he lifted his hips. He waited for her reaction at seeing him naked. Her gaze fastened on his groin and he felt his face heat. Her eyes widened a moment and then she tugged his breeches free and tossed them aside.

She slid along his body like a snake, brushing the soft orbs of her breasts over his thighs as she came, until at last she lay upon him.

He captured her shoulders and rolled her to her back, slipping his knee between her thighs and pausing when he felt her tense.

Their gazes met. "Lena, we don't have to. It's not too late to turn back."

He saw the flash of courage she'd shown on that first day and every day thereafter. He saw the woman he'd grown to love and respect. The woman he would soon lose forever.

"I am not turning back."

He closed his eyes to savor the sweet sensation as he slipped forward into her. At her barrier, he hesitated. He found calm assurance shining in her eyes.

"Go on," she whispered.

And, God help him, he did, swallowing back his doubt and plunging forward until his hips met hers. There he hesitated, trembling with the energy it took to remain still, fighting against his body as every fiber of his being screamed to move.

She did not cry out or struggle to escape. He lifted his gaze to find a frown upon her brow.

He hurt her.

He clasped her jaw in his big rough hands, feeling clumsy in an area he customarily felt at ease.

"Not like this," she said.

She didn't want him. He understood. The first time was hard for any woman. His princess should not be expected to couple in the woods like an animal. She should have a bedroom, clean sheets scented with flowers and a man as refined and perfect as she. Still he did not want to give her up.

"This is how it's done. The lady on her back and the man above."

"No, I won't lie still on my back while you move over me."

"I'll get off, Lena."

She held him, grasping his buttock with a firm grip that startled him with its boldness. Then she rolled. He allowed himself to fall to his side still connected to her in the most intimate way possible.

She stared into his eyes, begging him to understand, afraid and shocked by her need.

"I will have years of lying on my back like a corpse, staring up at brocade bed curtains. A lady is not supposed to enjoy this, did you know? A proper woman reclines still and silent beneath her mate." She stroked his cheek. "But I am that no longer."

His lopsided grin gave her courage. "All right, I'm game. What's on your mind?"

Her voice failed her and she tried again. Would he think her crude, repugnant? Uncertainty warred with desire and she swallowed back her fears. She trusted Troy. If anyone would understand her need for wildness, it was he.

Still, she only managed a whisper. He leaned forward to hear her words.

"Like the horses. I want you to take me like your stallion took my mare."

His jaw dropped and she covered her mouth as heat flooded her cheeks. Her gaze dropped and she pushed at his shoulders, needing to escape that shocked expression on his face. Why had she told him? Now he'd think her wicked and low.

She struggled and he captured her wrists, stilling her frantic efforts at escape. His gaze locked with hers. Now his expression reflected seriousness. His nostrils flared and his eyes flashed wild desire.

He understood.

And he would take her.

Her breathing stopped as he withdrew and rolled her, drawing her up on all fours. She trembled with excitement as his fingers stroked her quivering flesh, running over the curve of her buttock. His chest pressed to her back. Taut muscles tensed over her and she understood his raw power. Rather than terrify, the comprehension thrilled. He would use his strength to give what she asked.

She cried out as his teeth sunk into her neck, sending her back arching as shivering delight danced along her spine. He drove forward with force enough to send her to the ground, but his strong grip upon her shoulders held her for his advance.

Another scream issued from her and in that instant she understood. Her mare did not cry from pain but from an ecstasy too grand to contain. She pushed against him as his teeth scored her neck. He bucked, sending sweet shafts of pleasure through her once more. The need came again, building as before, only this time with the speed and intensity of wildfire.

Together they rode, each stroke building upon the last until the pleasure burst within her, stealing her breath in a long shuttering cry. Her arms went weak and again she would have fallen, but he held her for his pleasure, thrusting deep, and somehow she accommodated him, half-delirious as the waves of pleasure continued to issue through her. His cry was sweet music. He rose up, clasping her hips and drawing her close.

She gasped at the sensation of his body pulsing within

hers. He rocked forward, suddenly unable to keep them aloft and they sank to the earth, he upon her back, crushing her into the soft carpet of furs.

He stayed so for several ragged breaths and then dragged her against him, to rest in the pocket of his chest and legs. She sighed. Nothing on earth could ever compare to their fierce coupling. She knew in the marrow of her bones that only he could stir the wildness she locked within her soul.

Chapter 20

Troy fell hard, his entire body drained of power. He only just managed to land on his forearms, shielding Lena from the entirety of his crushing weight. Too depleted to move, he lay panting like the wild animal she'd summoned.

After a few more rasping breaths, he rolled, dragging her with him.

My God, what had he done?

All his life he'd considered himself a civilized man, a man in control. How did this woman—no, this lady—strip him to the marrow of his being and reveal the savage within?

Images and sensations ripped through him and he groaned, pulling her close. His jaw rested in the curve of her soft neck. He drew back and saw the angry red marks of his teeth on her pure white flesh. He closed his eyes against the evidence of his brutality.

Humiliation burned him like hot ash. He could not even do right by asking her to be his wife. She made it very clear that she would not have him, and after this who could blame her?

She overwhelmed him. He'd meant to go slowly, use a gentle hand, not fall upon her soft, sweet flesh like a wolf to a spring lamb.

When she'd asked him to take her like the stallion, he swore his heart had stopped. That she should ask such a thing shocked him nearly as much as the realization that he wanted her like that, too—wild and fierce. He wanted his woman to have the same furious desires and greedy appetites. To have her ask this of him, it was too sweet to be believed.

And he shouldn't have believed.

And that would be best for them both. If she didn't want him, their parting would be easier. Because, damn him for a fool, he still longed for her.

Her hand slid over his forearm as he tried to move away, but she captured him, lacing her fingers into his and guided his hand to the soft, warm skin of her stomach.

"Lena, will you speak to me? Did I hurt you too much?"

She gave a sound like a sigh, but with a rumble at the back of her throat. Her fingers continued to guide his until she pressed his palm to the contracting button of her nipple.

He bit his lip to keep from groaning at the pleasure of it. His body stirred again, lifting to press against the curve of her buttock. She rubbed her backside against him and he gasped.

Was she mad?

"Lena, stop now. I don't want to hurt you again."

He heard the sound, but did not credit it. But he could have sworn she laughed.

Troy pulled his hand free and rolled her to her back. She stared up at him with luminous eyes that called him once more.

"Are you all right?" he asked.

She stroked his chest. "I want that again."

His eyebrows lifted as he stared in shock. "But I marked your neck and—and—Lena, I was too rough."

"No, I can match you in this. I am stronger than I look. You said so. I have never felt such passion and I will never find it again. Please, once more."

And then the little vixen reached out and wrapped her slender fingers about his shaft. His pulse jumped like a cornered jackrabbit.

"Guess I have to, when you put it that way. But gently this time."

Her face contorted in a pout. "No. Like before."

He hesitated. She kissed him, pressing her warm curves to him, and he was lost. He could as soon take her at his leisure as he could stop a summer storm. Lena was the lightning and he the thunder.

He rolled her away, until her back nestled against his belly, and slipped his shaft between the heat of her thighs. They lay on their sides as he nuzzled her neck. Her breathing grew frantic and she arched to give him access. He clasped his arm about her and slipped himself into her passage from behind, impaling her, relishing her cry of pleasure.

When she tried to move, he held her still, running his hands over her soft breasts and the sensitive curve of her belly. At last he separated the folds of skin at the juncture of her thighs and caressed the tender bud.

She groaned and writhed as he stroked her, holding himself back until her cries told him she neared her summit. Then he thrust as he touched her, trapping her exquisite body between his stroking hands and his delving shaft.

She arched, crying out his name as her body convulsed, squeezing him. The force of her release destroyed his controlled pace. He held her hips, gathering her to accept his thrusting, mindless once more in his frenzy to take what she offered. She cried out a second time. His last conscious thought was the hope that she had found her pleasure again, even as he feared his wildness was too great.

Lena woke to find the twilight creeping over the wooded grove. Beneath her, soft wolf skin caressed her naked body. Behind her, Troy's slumbering breath fanned her neck. She nestled in the warmth of his embrace and remembered their lovemaking. Certain now that Troy was her match.

In any other time and place, he would be her choice. The easy lethargy left her as she recalled that he could never be her husband. Again, she chafed at the necessity of returning to her obligations. But her family was more than that. She loved them. Until she met Troy, they were her only world. Why must she choose?

She gazed up at the branches of the cottonwoods, seeing them rock gently in the evening breeze. Here society's rules fell away. Allowing herself to listen at last to her wild heart, she had abandoned responsibilities, tasted his love and now bitterly regretted her decision to make love with him.

Not because she was ruined. No, she did not give a whit for that. Such things were easily staged. The trouble lay in her. She was not naive enough to believe that such emotions came with just any man. Oh, no. To fly up to the heavens and then fall shattered to the earth only to be born up again from the ashes—this was a rare gift. Such things occurred only once in a lifetime. No, not even that, not so often. She rested her cheek in his palm, ignoring the coursing tears that issued from her. He was all she had ever dreamed of in a man and she was throwing him away.

How could life play her such a nasty trick? How could she find him and then give him up?

Oh, why had she promised to return?

Her heart ached. Why did she feel such duty? She no longer cared for her old world. She only wanted to paint. Now, she would give up even that. But that loss paled next to the pain of having to abandon the man she loved.

The strangled cry escaped her before she could recall it. Troy stiffened.

"Lena? Are you crying?"

She nodded.

He sat, peering down at her with concern lining his sweet

face. "I knew it. It's my fault. I never should have taken advantage of you. Lena, forgive me."

He thought she regretted their joining. She saw it clearly. Guilt, no worse—shame burned his cheeks. She rose to sit beside him and pressed her hand to his chest, taking comfort from the steady beat of his heart.

"I am not sorry, not for an instant. I'm weeping for the future, not the past."

He cocked his head, as confusion wrinkled his brow.

"I want to stay with you. Even in this wilderness I feel their tethers. I cannot seem to break free."

His voice held cold certainty. "You're going back."

"Forgive me." She pressed her hands over her eyes and wept.

He grasped her wrists, tugging them away, then lifted her chin until she met his gaze. His nostrils flared as his look intensified. A chill of dread straightened her spine.

"What if there's a child?"

Her eyes widened. If any man could sire a child, it was Troy. She'd never met a man so virile.

"There may not be."

"But there may."

She did not deny the possibility.

"You can't raise a bastard. They'll take it from you."

Fear gripped her and her breathing quickened.

"What will I do?"

"Give it to me."

"You can't raise a child alone," she said.

"Then I'll find help."

Did he mean to take a wife? She gaped at him. Of course, he would marry. Had she expected him to pine for her his whole life long?

Yes.

She did. If the situations were reversed she would never choose another. But they weren't reversed. Did he try to break her heart? She stared, slack-jawed, and saw the cold glint in his eyes. Yes, he did mean to hurt her as she hurt him. That was right.

"Do you mean to marry?" she asked.

"If need be."

Her lip trembled. She could not prevent it. Her heart twisted at the pain.

His gaze turned cold. "A child deserves his mother. You tell me you can raise our baby and I'll leave off. But if you mean to pass my child to another, hide it like something secret shame, it's mine. I'll not lose a child again—not again."

"Troy, we have several weeks left. By the time we reach Fort Union, I will know."

"You don't leave with my child."

"But I have to."

"Then I'll follow."

She thought of the scandal. "No. You mustn't."

His expression darkened. This was dangerous ground. She cautioned herself to tread cautiously.

"Why's that?"

"It could cause…difficulties."

He nodded, his gaze hard as flint. "I'm good enough to take out for stud, but not good enough to show at auction—that it?"

"That is certainly not it. Oh, you do not understand my position."

"I told you if we did this thing, one of us would have to choose."

"If you follow me to New York and tell the world of my indiscretion, I'll be ruined."

"So you might like a tickle out here in the great wide open, but you sure as hell don't want me popping up in your life back East. Half-breed trapper—you'd sooner die than let them society fellers know we had a dance or two."

"I am not ashamed of you. I am trying to protect my family. Why should they suffer for my indiscretions?"

"Is that what I am?"

"Come with me then. I will take care of you. A house, horses, everything."

"Everything but my children."

She clasped his hand. He must understand. "Troy, I explained to you. I have a duty."

"That's right. You have a duty to any child that might now be settled in for the long haul."

She rested a hand upon her belly. Her father would be furious and her mother so disappointed. But they would take care of this, she would travel the continent until the child came and then—she sighed. Then, they'd expect her to forget her baby and return to wed. Her head dropped.

How could something so glorious change in an instant to a dirty little secret? How she hated her life.

"Yes, you are right. I will give it to you, gratefully. I wish I could stay forever with you." When she tried to stroke his chest, he pulled away.

He grasped his breeches and thrust his legs angrily into the openings.

"Troy?"

He slid into his breeches and moccasins with his back turned and then donned his shirt, before collecting his gear and stalking off into the night.

The air grew cold. She hesitated at the edge of the furs. Would he come back? Her clothing lay down by the river.

She wrapped the wolf skin blanket about her shoulders and dressed in a damp shift she recovered from her packs. Her stomach growled. She gave up her pride and called for him, waiting in the stillness, but receiving no answer.

Her body ached as if from a long day's riding. In truth she had been ridden. She shifted her weight and felt the dull ache between her thighs. Finally she rose and washed away the evidence of their coupling.

She tended the fire and set out the buffalo robes as she had seen him do many times. Setting her rifle by her side, she slid beneath the hide where sleep captured her at last.

When next she stirred, purple clouds streaked the wide sky, the fire lay consumed in a pile of ash and the hide beside her remained vacant. Fear brought her upright. In an instant, her gaze settled upon his horse. He had not abandoned her.

She roused the embers to a delicate flame, feeding it until the fire warmed, then found the jerky in his pack. She gnawed at the tough meal and then stilled, feeling a trickle between her legs.

Closer inspection found blood upon her thighs, but not the bright spotting of virgin's blood she'd seen last night. A moment later the dull ache in her lower back confirmed her suspicions. She stilled, thinking back.

Yes, that was right, about three weeks had passed since her last flow. She slumped on the bank as relief and sorrow warred.

Would he be thankful to break this last tie between them?

Chapter 21

John Edward Hart sat in a crude little chair in the trading post of Fort Union. Before him stood a savage. Hart stared down his nose at the heathen.

"You speakie English?" he asked and then waited a full five seconds for the reply. The man simply stared. "Apparently not."

Hart turned to the guide he had contracted in New Orleans, a dirty little trapper named Jeb Macey.

"How can he be of use? I mean really, it may take an Indian to find an Indian, but I hardly think a mute tracker will do."

Jeb Macey slid two fingers beneath his hat and scratched. Hart retreated a step as he wondered if the man was as lice-ridden as he appeared.

"Well he understands sign and he can speak to any Lakota we meet up with."

"Lakota? What the devil is Lakota?"

"Sioux, a tribe of Indians on the plains, Sir."

"Tell him I am searching for my daughter." Macey nodded. Hart had told his scout this in New Orleans. "She is with a half-breed scout named Price."

Macey's eyebrows lifted, disappearing in the shaggy mane of hair. "Price? Troy Price?"

"You've heard of the scoundrel?"

The man gave a shrug. "Everybody's heard of him. He headed one of the most successful outfits in the Rockies, saved a party of men in the Sierra Nevadas and killed more grizzly than any man I ever knowed."

"You can add kidnapping to his litany of accomplishments. He's taken my daughter. I mean to find and kill him. What do you make in a year, Mr. Macey?"

"Reckon in a good season I could bring down five hundred dollars worth of pelts."

"I'll pay you seven and give the savage here whatever trinkets and weapons you think appropriate."

"Reckon Black Feather might prefer cash."

"Fine, offer him a hundred. I dare say that's more than he'll see in a lifetime."

The little trapper and the Indian began a rapid exchange of gestures so comical he had trouble not snickering. Instead he sipped his brandy, letting the warm liquid scorch the back of his throat.

The fire in his belly burned with the desire to find his errant daughter and drag her back home by her hair. He had known this excursion was a mistake and wondered again how she had ever gained his consent. Women were masters at manipulating men and Eleanor had learned from the best, her mother. The woman cost more to maintain than his house in Newport.

It seemed his daughter had graduated from childhood and already mastered the art of feminine wiles. Now his hunting trip was ruined, for instead of buffalo, he was forced to hunt Eleanor. She'd been damned lucky to survive the outbreak of cholera. He could not conceive why she continued upriver. He never thought he raised a fool. Until this trip, she'd always shown remarkable good judgment, for a woman. Damn that Italian tutor and his box of paints.

What was the matter with the girl? Now a savage had her. If anyone in New York got wind that she had traveled unescorted, he'd never find her a suitable husband.

It was imperative that he bring her back. Then no one need know about this unfortunate episode. Plans could move forward. She would marry and he would have his heir.

Troy returned to camp at dawn to find Lena sitting beside the fire clutching her pistol. What had they done?

He gazed at her, every fiber of his being screamed to run to her side and press himself once more to her sweet body.

But he would not. He should have thought with more than his body the first time. Coupling brought consequences. He moved to her mare and stroked her ribs, considering her belly. Did she carry the Appaloosa's foal?

Did Lena carry his child?

He told her he'd have it, and he would, but with or without a child, he did not want to lose her. He spent the night trying to think of some way for them to stay together. His only answer was to follow her East or to take her captive.

He did not think his pride could stand living as the male version of a mistress. It would kill everything that made him a man. But if he took her, wouldn't that kill everything she was?

Would she grow to love him or hate him?

Clutching the grouse he brought for their meal, he stared across the plains. Should he go east or west?

That was when he saw the dust. He focused on the spot and recognized movement far off. Retrieving her spyglass, he saw a party of more than thirty men riding hard in his direction.

He turned to see Lena on her feet, staring at him.

"Company's coming."

She blinked at him. "What?"

"A large party heading our way."

"Who are they?"

"Don't know. Not trappers, not Indians."

"Should we hide?" She stared at him with red-rimmed eyes, her expression etched with worry.

He smiled. "Hide? Where? Besides, we ain't done nothing wrong."

As soon as he said it he wished he could call the words back. He'd done something very wrong. He had taken a woman, knowing he could never keep her. One look at Lena's tearstained face forced him to confront the truth. He had hurt her deeply.

"But we don't know their business. What if they're after us?"

He lifted the glass again. "Doubtful, but if so, they found us. Running won't help. They outnumber us fifteen to one and I see no pack animals. They're traveling light."

She moved close, wrapping her arms about his waist. "I'm frightened."

He patted her back. "Get your pistol ready and stay close."

They stood together watching the riders bear down.

"Troy, I have to tell you something. There is no child."

He took his gaze from the approaching party and stared down at her as a deep sorrow swelled within him. He would have nothing of her when she left him.

"Truly. I am certain and I am sorry," she said.

A flame of hope, that he had not even known he harbored, snuffed out.

"Likewise."

He could hear them now and turned. Their position was a poor place for a fight, him with his back to the stream and the grove being too small to allow them to elude pursuit. Also, their timing made him suspicious, arriving at his camp at daybreak. That was a trick the army used—attack at dawn, before their opponents were awake or armed.

He pushed Lena behind him as the riders thundered into camp. One horse in particular grabbed his notice. It was a small black stallion with the same narrow face and arching neck as Lena's Arabian. He lifted his gaze to the rider and saw a rotund man dressed in a tailored black suit and silk top hat. He'd never seen a stranger costume. Yes—he had, on Lena. Behind him, she clutched the buckskin at his shoulder.

Her voice rang with urgency. "My father."

"He looks like an undertaker."

Lena's tone was hushed and her words hurried. "He's found me unescorted."

"I'm escorting you."

She bounced up and down, clutching his arm. "Do you not understand? He will kill you."

At this moment the man in question drew a sword and shouted to his men. "There is the blackguard. Seize him!"

Troy didn't go quietly. He aimed his rifle at the center of her father's chest.

"Don't come no closer," he advised.

Several of her father's personal army now trained their guns on Troy, but he kept his hand steady, focusing on the man in charge.

"Release my daughter."

"I ain't got a hold of her now."

Hart's face burned scarlet. "Eleanor, come here."

She cowered behind Troy, but did not go to her father.

"If you do not come this instant, I shall shoot him where he stands."

Troy wondered how he'd manage that, as Hart held only a sword, while he had a bead drawn on the man's heart. Then fear gripped him as he wondered if the fellow was stupid enough to order his men to shoot with Lena standing right behind him?

Lena clearly believed her father's threat, for she moved forward. "Promise you will not harm him."

Spittle flew from his mouth as he shouted. "You dare make conditions to me?"

Lena tried to step before Troy. He blocked her with his body, as both his hands held his rifle.

She stood beside him now and lifted her pistol toward her father. He paled and Eleanor's hand shook.

"Promise me."

Hart dismounted and stalked forward, his eyes glittering dangerously.

"You would shoot your own father?"

She hesitated, then dropped her arm, her head hung in defeat. When she lifted her chin, the determination shone like hell's fire. Her hand, now steady as any scout, pressed the barrel of the pistol to the soft flesh below her chin. Troy's stomach dropped several inches.

"Promise me," she shouted.

Hart blanched and halted.

Lena cocked the trigger. The click echoed in Troy's soul, sending terror vibrating through him.

Troy lost his aim as he shifted his gaze to Lena in astonishment. The woman he knew would never take her own life.

Taking in the wild look in her eye and her finger constricting the trigger, he registered her grim determination. He thought of her stubbornness and a jolt of panic ripped through him. This was no wild threat.

She glanced at him and spoke through gritted teeth. "You do not know him. He will kill you and take me."

Troy didn't care. The only certainty was that Lena must not die. He released his finger from the trigger. He would not watch another woman he loved take her own life.

Her eyes turned to her father. "He goes free or I will shoot."

"All right," shouted her father. "I will not kill him."

Troy's hand shot out and knocked the barrel of her pistol, sending it flying from her hand.

Her jaw dropped as her astonishment registered and then her gaze flashed forward. He caught the movement from the corner of his vision, lifting his rifle to block the thrust of her father's saber. The steel of Hart's blade screeched across the barrel of his Hawkins and the blow missed his heart, cutting instead across his chest and then slicing Troy's belly.

Lena screamed. An instant later the pain came in a rush like the cold wind before a storm. He thought the man had spilled his innards, but a glance down showed only blood spilling from his middle. The air held no scent of punctured intestine.

He swung his rifle with all his might, sending Hart to the ground, and then Troy dropped to his knees.

Lena reached him. With one hand, he clenched the rifle like a crutch. So much blood. His ears buzzed as if he stood surrounded by a swarm of angry hornets. His fingers tingled, suddenly burning hot as his grip failed. The gun slid from his hand and he fell to his chest in the grass.

Troy now viewed Hart's boots, as shiny as if they just came from a shop. He probably had as many shoes as Lena. One boot drew back and kicked him in the ribs.

Lena's hysterical cry lifted the hairs on the back of Troy's neck.

She gripped his arm. Troy turned his head, shocked at the effort of so simple an act, and saw Lena reaching for him as her father dragged her away.

"Hold her," he said, thrusting his sobbing daughter to one of his men. "And burn those damn paintings."

Get up. You have to get up now. Troy closed his eyes.

Hart spoke again. "Cooper, shoot him."

"You promised not to kill him," cried Lena as she struggled against the men who gripped her arms.

He had to help her. Troy succeeded only in moving his arms beneath him.

The arrogance of Hart's tone penetrated the red haze, even as he lay prostrate and bleeding before his enemy.

"No, I promised *I* would not kill him," said Hart. "And I will not."

A second pair of boots stopped before the first. Though still cleaned and polished, this pair showed some use.

"Well?" Hart sounded impatient.

"I'll not shoot an unarmed man."

Hart again. "This scoundrel is a kidnapper and a villain.

Shoot him." Silence for a moment and then Hart stamped a boot heel like a child. "Andrews, you do it."

Troy closed his eyes. The next voice seemed familiar, without the harsh eastern accent.

"I'll do it."

He blinked at the moccasins beside the pair of squeaky new boots.

"Help me get him up, Black Feather."

Black Feather? He knew that name. He gasped at the pain ripping across his middle as two sets of hands dragged him to his feet. He blinked in astonishment at his friends, Jeb Macey and Black Feather.

"Thought you was selling shoes in Philly," said Troy, frightened by the weakness evident in his voice.

"Hush up now," said Macey. He grasped Troy's shirt and twisted, then sliced a hole the size of a silver dollar in the buckskin.

"For God sakes don't fall down until you hear me shoot."

Troy nodded. Falling down should be no trouble, but standing proved a challenge that took all his concentration.

Macey stepped away and Troy tipped. Black Feather's hand steadied. In slow degrees the fingers slipped off and Troy swayed like a blade of grass in the wind.

Ten feet before him, Jeb Macey lifted his rifle and aimed at Troy's heart.

The black powder exploded and smoke belched from the barrel. Troy clutched his belly and lurched forward.

The last thing he heard was Lena's high-pitched cry.

Lena screamed as Troy dropped lifelessly to the ground. Her legs failed her and she crumbled to the grass. Her captor released his grip and she crawled on hands and knees to her lover.

"Troy—Troy, please answer me." She shook his shoulder; his arm flopped like every lifeless carcass she had ever seen. The cry tore from somewhere deep in her soul. "No!"

Her father nudged Troy with his boot. "Is he dead?"

Lena grabbed her sire's heel and twisted. Her father up-ended and she tore at him like a wild animal, trying to reach his face, his eyes.

"Pull her off. Eleanor, are you mad?" He lashed out, striking her across the cheek with the pommel of his sword. The blow sent her reeling.

Hands gripped her. Someone shook her shoulders as she swung again at her captors.

"Take her to the horses."

Her feet never touched the ground as they dragged her from Troy. She kicked and struggled as hands bit cruelly into her upper arms. Her voice failed and still she screamed as the feral cry turned inward, piercing her insides with needle-sharp talons. Her fault, all her fault.

"Laudanum!" cried her father.

He held her nose and forced the thick bitter liquid down her throat. The sky blackened as night fell in a curtain all about her. Alone now, in the dark. Alone and screaming as the horror tore her to pieces.

Chapter 22

The smell of lemon polish and the sound of her mother's voice finally roused Lena from her stupor.

"My God, John, how long has she been like this?"

"I told you she went mad. I drugged her for her own protection."

"How long?"

"Nearly three weeks."

Her mother gasped.

"What happened to her face?"

Her father cleared his throat. "I suppose that half-breed beat her."

Her mother stroked Lena's cheek. "My poor angel."

Eleanor closed her eyes and a tear issued from her eye.

"Has she wept?"

His face appeared before her and she blinked.

"I stopped the laudanum yesterday. Eleanor, can you hear me?"

What was he saying? What savage had beaten her? She lifted a hand to her face, touching the raised scar on her cheek. It curled beneath her left eye like a sickle. The wound left by the pommel of her father's sword. Why did it not pain her?

Then it came. The steamer, locked in her room as her father poured that vile fluid down her throat to stop her pounding upon the door.

Troy.

The dam burst and images flooded her. She convulsed, as if the bullet that ripped him from her had struck a second time. Her father ordered Troy shot like a rabid dog. She sunk to the plush carpet of the drawing room that she only now recognized.

Her mother tried to collect her. "Eleanor, my dear. Sit here now. There's my poppet. Mamma's here."

Eleanor stared at her father, wanting to condemn him, to strike him down. Betrayer. She saw the scars upon his cheeks. Claw marks at his temple, still shining an angry red. Pride rolled through her.

She had done that.

Her fingers curled into claws as she gathered to open his face again. For him she had been willing to leave her love. For this lying, self-serving tyrant, she had been willing to give herself to any stranger in marriage.

No longer.

Sensing attack, he backed away. "I told you. Snapped like a dry twig. I expected better from my daughter."

Her mother pressed Eleanor's head to her breast. "She suffered a terrible ordeal. You obviously upset her. Move away, John, out of her vision if you please."

"I upset her! I am her own father, her rescuer."

Eleanor tracked him as her mind flashed the image of Troy falling, shot by one of her father's minions. He broke his pledge not to harm Troy with a trick of words and then burned her paintings. He had no honor, only wealth and power that he used to do as he pleased.

Her father's voice disturbed her musings. "How can she make a match looking like this? I mean, a dowry will only go so far. At minimum a man of quality expects a woman fit to bear his children. Look at that scar, for God's sake."

"John, dear, it will fade in time. She has lost so much weight. But Cook will fix that. Won't she dear?"

Eleanor did not answer.

"Lost weight? She looks as appealing as a street urchin."

"Now, why not take yourself off, John, and leave us to reacquainting ourselves?"

Eleanor glanced up to see her father scowling down at her. She sneered at him, curling her lip like a wild dog. The obligation to him burned with her dreams on the prairie beside Troy. Now there was only ash.

"She looks as if she hates me, when I saved her life," he said.

"Don't be silly. Of course she doesn't hate you, do you Eleanor?" Her mother gazed hopefully at her.

Eleanor turned her head away from them both.

"Come now, dear." Her mother pulled and Eleanor rose, shocked at her body's weakness. How she could walk when her heart was broken?

Charlotte drew her along past the huge gilded mirror in the entry.

Eleanor gasped. Her mother held a small, frail female with her.

Her mother's gaze met hers in the mirror. "Don't fret, Nora. You have been ill. But you are better now."

Her father's image appeared. "Better. Ha. I've seen better looking women on the docks."

"John, have you no compassion?"

"Compassion?" His voice boomed like cannon fire and his wife flinched. "What I have is an empty nursery, thanks to you and your daughter. Well, I'll not have it. Enough nonsense. She is to marry at once."

Her mother cowered beside Eleanor. "Yes, of course, John."

Her father took a menacing step in their direction. Her mother abandoned her grip on Eleanor's arm and moved quickly to stand behind her, leaving her daughter to fend for herself. Eleanor straightened her tired body.

He halted and stared at her as if confused by her refusal to cower. At his hesitation, her mother resumed control of Eleanor's elbow.

"Would you like a bath, Nora?"

She waited, but Eleanor remained mute.

"Well," said her mother, forced cheerfulness turning her voice musical. "We will talk later, after your bath."

But they did not. In fact, Eleanor refused to speak to anyone except Scheherazade.

The rest of them be damned.

Chapter 23

As soon as his wound knit enough for Troy to ride, he turned east, arriving at Battery Park in New York City by steamer on the eighteenth of November. By midday he stood before an enormous townhouse on Fourteenth Street owned by one John Hart. A snippy maid at the side entrance took one look at him and told them they were not hiring before closing the door in his face.

He learned from a delivery boy that the family had extended their stay in Newport and were not expected back until the end of the month.

He walked to the river and found a trim sloop that carried him north up the Hudson River a few miles to the farm of James Audubon.

Troy arrived at the door of the three-story clapboard house without an appointment, carrying a hollowed out tube he made from the trunk of a young oak. Inside were the paintings Lena had made while at Fort Union.

The man who answered his knock turned out to be John Audubon's son, also named John.

"I'd like you pa to see these paintings."

The man sighed. "Just leave them with me."

Troy lifted the tube out of his grasp and shook his head. "Don't think so. How's about I show you one?"

Carefully he withdrew the painting of Wind Dancer. The man stilled. This time his reach seemed eager. Troy let him take the page.

He turned, not looking at Troy, his attention focused on the painting before him.

"Follow me."

Troy walked behind him to an artist's workroom, the walls covered with paintings of birds. A black crow stared out at him with a glinting black eye and curious expression. As Troy gazed from one familiar bird to the next, he smiled. Understanding dawned. These were exact duplicates, in every detail of the creatures he knew and loved. He paused at a strange pink bird with a twisted neck that seemed impossibly long.

"Ostrich?" asked Troy.

"Flamingo," said John. "From Florida."

"That's a sight."

John lifted the portrait. "So is this. What is your name, sir?"

"Troy Price."

"Wait here, Mr. Price."

Troy felt at home in the company of this colorful flock. He walked about as the scent of watercolors reached him and paused. His breathing changed as he forced back the urge to weep.

Lena.

Was she safe? Had he hurt her?

Behind him came the shuffle of boot heels on carpet. He turned to face an old man with shining white hair and bright blue eyes.

"Mr. Price? I'm James Audubon." He extended his hand and Troy shook. "Your painting is wonderful."

"Thank you. But it ain't mine. I'm just the guide."

"Where is the painter?"

"I'm just scouting for 'em."

"I see. May I ask where this was painted?"

"Fort Union on the Missouri River."

Audubon exchanged a meaningful glance with his son. "Are you familiar with this area?"

Troy dropped a dime novel on the table. One of the many possessions left behind after Lena was stolen from him.

"I'm the best scout west of the Missouri. Been trapping all the way to Oregon and back."

Audubon lifted the story. "I've heard of you."

Troy pointed to Lena's painting. "Think you might have a spot for that artist on your next venture?"

Audubon smiled. "I have a spot for this artist and am in need of a guide."

"Well that sounds mighty good to me."

"Won't you sit down, Mr. Price? I'd like to hear more about this artist."

"Why did you not invite him to a dinner party?" asked Hart. "Then at least she would not be the center of his attention."

Eleanor gritted her teeth. They no longer spoke in hushed tones or moved to his office to have such discussions. Instead they talked openly as if she was deaf as well as mute.

"Primarily because she no longer compares favorably at such affairs," said her mother. "I am frankly astonished he accepted my offer at all. He has just arrived in Newport, but he must have heard the rumors."

"The man's only a baron. He should be grateful I am even considering his suit."

Her mother lifted her brow, but said nothing further as her husband paced across the carpet as if drilling for a parade.

Lena looked out the window at the carriage halting before their door. Mud flecked the coach and the driver, whose face looked as worn as his clothing.

"He's recently widowed, two young sons and a proclivity toward gaming." Her mother's voice floated across the room.

"I don't approve of gambling. Shows a weak character." Hart paused behind her. "Can you not get her into some color other than gray? She looks drab as dishwater."

Her mother's suffering sigh did not escape her.

Beyond the window, the driver held open the door and out stepped Baron Edward Mayberry. His white cravat pinched his fleshy neck, making his head look overly large. Through the distortion of the ancient glass, she took in his gray whiskers and waddling walk.

Hart's voice came from just behind her and dripped with censure. "This is the best you can do?"

Her mother clasped her hands and squeezed until her knuckles turned white. "If you have another prospect, John, please do present them for I have run out of options."

The two exchanged a long stare.

"He is the last," she said.

Eleanor returned her attention to the street. The man seemed to be favoring his left foot.

"Why is he limping?" asked Hart.

"I believe he suffers from gout."

Hart spun to face his wife. "Great chattering monkeys, how do you expect him to get the girl with child?"

Eleanor's stomach tightened in disgust.

"He has two young sons."

The man in question mounted the steps with painful slowness.

Hart clasped his hands behind his back and rocked from toe to heel.

The knocker announced the Baron's arrival.

"How did this happen?" said Hart to his wife. "Your sister has eight children—eight! And you give me this."

Hart spun about and left the room.

Her mother perched beside Eleanor on the window seat and grasped her daughter's chin.

"Nora, I know you understand me. I am sorry I could not bring you a better match. This one said he would marry you.

I think he plans to take you to London. I know you can no longer abide your father's company, so this is best. Please do try to make a good impression for our sakes."

Eleanor scowled. She would sooner wed a monkey than please her father. A good impression was out of the question.

Hart escorted the baron into the parlor and made introductions. Eleanor stared into space as her father tried to convince the baron of the advantages of the match.

"Naturally," said Mayberry, "I am ready to find a new baroness. Not so anxious, however, that I would concede to marry one who is addled. Your lovely wife insists the child is only mute. But she is the girl's mother, and mothers tend to overlook certain deficiencies."

Eleanor glanced at her father to see him redden. How badly did he wish to show this man the door?

She smiled at his dilemma. The last chance. She had successfully driven off the other miscreants her parents dragged her before. Though she did not wish to live forever in her father's house, neither would she give him what he wanted. This bitter defiance was all that kept her from drowning in a sea of grief.

She rocked herself like a child, dragging a strand of damp hair into her mouth and sucking.

Her mother swept it away and then wrapped an arm about Eleanor to still her, but only succeeded in drawing more attention to her daughter's behavior.

The baron's mouth hung open and Hart stiffened, his arms terminating in balled fists as the two men stared at Eleanor. She blew a bubble of her own spit. Mayberry gasped, pressing a hand to his chest as if mortally offended, and then turned to his host.

"You have no right to offer the hand of a half-wit. My situation is not so desperate as this. Good day, sir."

The man showed himself out.

Hart rounded on Eleanor. Here was the monster she remembered from the Yellowstone, the man she barely recognized as her father. His face glowed scarlet; his mouth twisted into a menacing glower.

Eleanor stood to face him.

"How dare you pull such a stunt?" His words ground out between clenched teeth.

She stared at his indignant expression and scowling countenance, surprised to find herself tired of this game. She wanted to tell him exactly why she would no longer be his puppet. There in the quiet parlor, she gathered the courage to openly defy him.

"How dare you shoot my guide? How dare you burn my work?"

Her mother gasped. "Nora, you can speak!"

Eleanor did not take her eyes from the menacing stranger before her.

"It was a mistake to indulge you. I see that now."

"Rather, it was a mistake to break your promise."

"You will do your duty to this family, missy. I expect—"

"I no longer care what you expect."

Her mother gasped.

"You ungrateful whelp. You do as *I* say."

"No longer. Your actions have broken the ties between us."

"Don't you speak to me of that half-breed savage."

"I prefer not to speak to you at all."

Her mother tugged at her arm, trying desperately to silence her again. Eleanor shook her off.

"Best endow a hospital, Father, for you will leave no issue."

"I'll disown you."

"Then do so. I will leave this house this very day."

"You wouldn't survive out there without me."

"Watch me." She turned to go.

He grabbed Eleanor's arm with such force she cried out as he spun her to him.

"I brought you into this world."

"But you do not own me."

He lifted his hand and Eleanor stared him in the face.

"Go ahead and I shall call the police."

Her mother gasped and her father faltered.

"John. Please. No scandal. Let me speak to her."

He released Eleanor's arm. "Go to your room."

She looked to her mother, now uneasy to leave her alone with him.

"Go on, Nora," urged her mother.

She withdrew and her mother closed the large sliding doors behind her. She stood for a moment beyond the solid mahogany and then turned to climb the marble stairs.

When her mother appeared an hour later she favored her left ankle.

Eleanor set aside her book as suspicions planted themselves in her mind.

"Did he hurt you?"

Her mother waved a dismissive hand. "Don't be ridiculous. I turned my ankle upon the stair."

Eleanor lifted an eyebrow and met her mother's gaze. Charlotte hesitated.

"I am not here to discuss my ankle, but your future." Her mother recovered her air of authority and leveled her best disapproving stare upon her daughter.

Eleanor wondered when her mother had lost her power to manipulate her. Once such a look of disfavor sent her scurrying to do her mother's bidding. Now she only felt sorry for the woman to be married to such a brute.

"I cannot believe you would speak to your father so. This is not the daughter I raised to be the premiere hostess and grand dame of New York society. You could be the pinnacle of wealth and sophistication. Instead we are forced to scrape the very bottom of the barrel to find an eligible husband. I am so angry with you, there are no words for it."

But she only paused to draw a breath and then continued

on, "You wanted this as well. We talked endlessly about your choices in England, comparing estates and titles. Lady Eleanor, remember? A viscountess or even a duchess. I still want those things."

"But I do not."

She stamped her foot and then winced. "This will stop, do you hear me?"

"I hear you. But I will not marry."

Having failed with disapproval, reason and outrage, her mother changed tactics, collapsing into an overstuffed chair and wringing her hands in dismay.

"Am I never to hold a grandchild? Please, Eleanor, cease this stubbornness. This man you mourn is gone and you are not. You have a right to grieve, but do not cast your life away."

"I did not cast it away. Father did."

"They why would you want to stay in his house? If you marry, you will be away from his control. You will have such freedoms."

Eleanor's gaze snapped up. "You know nothing of freedom."

"I know that once you have an heir, you can do as you please. You needn't even share the same house with him. Just appear at a few formal affairs together. It isn't hard."

"Isn't it?" Eleanor leveled a look of pity on her mother.

"Eleanor, you don't understand."

"No mother—I finally do. That is no life for me."

Her mother rose stiffly and lifted an arm, flinching as she did so. "What could be grander than this house? Eleanor, don't be a ninny. Think what this wealth can provide for you. You are our only child. All this and more will be yours one day. All you need do is marry. It is little enough to ask."

Eleanor's mouth hardened into a hard line. To think she once wanted to be just like her mother—full of style and effervescence, the toast of society and a model for all lesser females to emulate. Now she saw cracks in the perfect facade, lines of worry and sorrow rarely shown even to her family.

"That is your life, Mother. Not mine."

"Eleanor, you are just being stubborn. You know what is expected and·still you hold this childish grudge. It does not become you. I am, frankly, ashamed of you."

"I know this will shock you, but I no longer care what you think of me."

Her mother held a hand over her heart as if shot by an arrow. "What about my friends? What shall I tell them? Please don't shame us, Nora." She paused and leveled her gaze upon her daughter, stepping close. "Your life will not be changed and may be very much improved by making the right match. If you will only try, I know you can gain the attention of any number of eligible men."

"By that you mean titled men?"

She fidgeted with the cuff of her dress. "Well, I would prefer that. As you know, I am anxious for you to join London society. But if you insist on a homegrown boy, that might suit."

"If he is from the right family."

"Certainly."

Eleanor folded her arms before her in refusal.

"I only ask you to consider your options, Eleanor."

Chapter 24

Troy had no trouble finding the "cottage" where Lena's family lived. The grand Newport mansion sat off Bellevue Avenue on a huge estate facing the sea. Abandoning his buckskin and bear claws for more conventional attire, he jumped the walls at night and scouted the property. With his hair drawn back and the light of only a few lanterns, he hoped to pass as a servant.

He reached the stables and headed down the long corridor, past the many horses. A familiar splash of white stopped him. Here in a double stall, Scheherazade lifted her graceful neck over the planking and nickered.

In town, he learned that Lena rode each morning and that an English suitor had stopped at a local tavern after leaving the Hart mansion to report that she was mad.

"How is your mistress, girl?" he asked.

In a few hours he would learn for himself. Voices at the far end of the stable sent him ducking into a vacant stall where he waited until the men passed by. The arrival of the stable boy sent him out.

He found a place to rest in the loft of a neighboring barn that gave a fine view of the entrance to the stable. In the hours before daybreak the stalls were cleaned and horses tended.

He waited, anxiously, unable to rest as he searched the windows of the house for a glimpse of his beloved.

Finally, she appeared in the morning mist.

Lena.

Only not Lena.

At first he thought it was the mist that drew all the color from her. Then he recognized the truth. She covered her glorious mane of hair in a gray veil and hat. All her colorful finery had been discarded as if she dressed to match the drab colors of the day.

Troy pursued her to the stables, but she rode out before he reached her. He stole a dapple-gray and bridle, then set out. Misty morning fog softened the edges of the world as he searched the mud for the new tracks of a tiny mare. He found them near the hedgerow and followed the trail.

Finally he saw Lena, shadowy like a ghost, coming across the open field, leaping the hedges on her familiar white mare. He nearly called out, but they were so close to the house. He glanced back to note the mansion he knew stood not two hundred paces behind him, was now blanketed in fog.

The innkeeper's words returned. Her mind was weak. The man's story clashed with memories. He'd never met a woman more single-minded, stubborn or strong willed. He glanced about. She rode straight for him. His heart constricted. He knew the instant she saw him.

Her hands lifted and she drew up on the reins. From this distance she might not be sure. He wore black trousers, a coarse blue shirt and knee-high riding boots. His hair was greased back.

Did she know him?

Her horse danced nervously, relaying his mistress's distress. She gave a sharp tap with her crop and the ghost horse leaped forward. Lena's eyes flashed wild and rounded as she rode at him.

Mist beaded upon her hair, pulled into a severe bun that

lacked the frivolity of the past. The black hat perched upon her head reminded him of a crow.

She charged forward. He readied himself for the collision. Too late, she reined in, sending her horse's front legs bracing against the ground and she skidded to a halt. Her mare bumped his dapple-gray.

Her eyes flashed wild.

"Lena, it's me."

But Lena did not move, except to draw great ragged breaths as if she meant to scream. Did she know him? In a heart-stopping instant, he feared her mind *was* gone, that despite all, he had lost her.

"Lena, do you know me?" He reached for her and she drew back.

She gripped the reins, swaying. "Troy?"

Her face grayed. He dropped from his horse and ran the last two steps, catching her as she fell. He carried her away from the mare. She lay immobile, her color still ghastly pale.

He stroked a stray strand of hair from her forehead, accustoming himself to her changed appearance. It was not so much. He touched the scar across her cheek, remembering Jeb Macey telling of her father's blow with the butt of his saber. She was thinner now. Too thin. She'd suffered, much as he had. Only hers had been worse for she had no hope. She had not known he lived.

She did not revive even when he stroked her face. Fear gripped him as he reached beneath his coat and withdrew his skinning knife, ready to slice through the stark row of gray buttons and the damned constricting corset strings he knew lay beneath.

Just then, her eyelids fluttered and then he gazed down into the unchanged beauty of her blue eyes.

She caught his wrist, staying his hand.

"You promised."

The corner of his mouth twitched as he attempted to give a reassuring smile.

"That damned thing is cutting off your air."

A tear came to her eye. "I knew I'd see you again some-day. I knew. Am I dead then?"

"Dead? You just fainted."

"You...you are really here."

"What?" He paused allowing her to recover. Her eyes rolled white and his insides turned to ice. Could she be mad?

He shook his head. "We're alive, Lena. They didn't shoot me. My friends Black Feather and Jeb Macey, they pretended. The charge was only black powder." He thumped his chest. "You see? No bullet. Just to fool your father."

"What about the saber cut?"

He grimaced. The pain of his healing muscles reminded him daily of the encounter. "That's why I didn't come at once. He broke my ribs and I was weak from bleeding."

She lifted a hand and touched his cheek. Next came a cry of joy as she lunged into his arms.

"Troy!"

"Oh, Lena. How I've missed you."

She wept as he rocked her. He stroked her hair and murmured words of love and promise until her cries ceased. Her fingers gripped him as if she feared someone might separate them again.

Something nudged him. He looked up and Scheherazade blew a great breath of hot air upon him.

Lena lifted her head and laughed.

"She's worried about her mistress," said Troy.

"She had reason to worry." She tried to stand and he helped her to her feet. She wobbled and he studied her face, reach-ing again for his skinning knife. Her hand stilled his.

"It is not the corset. I have not been able to breathe since we parted—until now."

As if to prove her words, she lowered her head to rest her cheek upon his chest and drew a ragged breath.

His heartbeat pounded as he dipped to taste her lips once more.

She relished his touch, needing him as much as the air she breathed. In his arms she came alive once more. He drew back and she blinked up at the face she thought forever lost. Yet here he stood. Eleanor glanced about; the mist shrouded them from view. Here her world was only the horses, the black bark of the cherry tree and Troy.

Too perfect.

In a moment she'd awaken to the desolate landscape of her chamber, her tomb. Her grip tightened, determined not to let him go again.

His arms enfolded her, his hot breath fanned her cheek and the familiar taste of his mouth set every nerve a jangle. He pressed her more closely to his wide chest and the truth of his reality shone like the first rays of sunshine through the mist.

"You've come for me," she whispered and felt him nod his head. She pressed her back to the trunk of the ancient tree.

He pursued her as relentlessly as any of his quarry. She recognized the predatory glint shining determinedly in his eye. "I've missed you."

Tears streaked her cheeks. "I saw them shoot you."

He nodded, remembering. "A bad day that."

"My father ordered you killed." The anger sizzled within her. "He broke our bargain, burned my paintings."

His brow wrinkled. "Jeb told me."

She clenched her jaw, as her nostrils flared with angry breath. "They are trying to force me to wed."

His serious stare seemed to look into her soul. "That's why I've come." His sad smile broke her heart. He gazed up at the branches above as if drawing strength. "I know you've got obligations, Lena. I understand them now. I didn't come to bust up your life. I just wanted to tell you I love you. I should have told you sooner, only I didn't see no way for us."

She sobbed as she fell against his chest. His arms encircled her in a tender embrace.

"A while back you said that a lady sometimes takes a

lover." He cleared his throat. "I'm offering myself to you, Lena. I know you love me and I can't be your husband. So I'll take what I can get."

Lena gasped. "You would do this?"

"If it's the only way to have you."

She pushed past the obstruction in her throat that threatened her words. "You would stay here, give up scouting and trapping, give up your freedom for me?"

His gaze never faltered. "I would."

And she knew it was so. He loved her enough to leave his world to share some part of hers. Her heart thumped against her ribs. Possibilities rose before her.

But she couldn't do it. He was proud and wild. Once she had thought to cage him, to turn him into a lapdog. Nothing could be so cruel.

"No."

His jaw went rigid. "You won't have me then?"

She stroked his cheek. "Not like this. We deserve better."

Now he stepped back, eyes intent. "What about your duty, your promise?"

"My father released me from our bargain when he broke his word and burned my work. And as for duty, mine lies with you and with myself. We deserve what happiness we can find."

"You once said you loved me, Lena. If you'll come away with me, I'd like to ask for your hand in marriage. I brought you this here ring." He took her hand and pressed a black velvet box into her palm.

She hesitated almost afraid to believe this moment was real. Here he stood, back from the grave, alive and asking for her hand. He sunk to his knees before her.

"Open it."

She lifted the lid. Nestled in white satin lay a pale blue faceted stone set in white gold.

"I had it made in New York, by a feller by the name of

Charles Tiffany. He was real interested in that stone." He motioned with his index finger.

"Lovely."

"Recognize it?" he asked.

She stared at the gem again as recollection dawned.

"The blue pebble."

"The blue sapphire."

Memories of the day she'd first seen buffalo stirred in her mind. She had been blue that evening and he he had given her a stone.

"A sapphire?" She stared down at the facets in wonder.

"That's what the feller in New York tells me." He imitated the man's accent and raised the tenor of his voice. "Of the highest quality."

He rose, sliding his hands about her waist. He rested his forehead upon hers. Tears streaked her face.

She choked on the words. "Why do you want to marry me?"

"All my life I've been looking for a place where I belonged. You were right all along, Lena. It ain't a place I was searching for. It was you."

Troy must have read the worry on her face, for he scowled.

"What?" he asked.

"He will disinherit me. I'll not receive a nickel."

He snorted. "Is that all? Let him keep it, the old stodger. I'll care for you, Lena. You don't need his money."

Her smile returned. He didn't want the money. Here stood the only man in her acquaintance who cared nothing for her fortune, but only for herself.

Another thought struck. "What if he follows us?"

"Let him try."

He was the best scout in the West. If anyone could disappear it was Troy Price. She nodded as his confidence filled her.

"Oh, Troy, how I love you."

"Then say you'll marry me."

There was nothing else she wanted in the world. The ice about her heart melted in the heat of his embrace.

"Yes, Mr. Price, I will be honored to be your wife."

He gave a howl like a wolf as he lifted her high into the air and spun her in dizzying circles. Her laughter mixed with his wild joyful call.

At last he set her upon her feet.

They smiled at each other.

Then he seemed to remember something. "I showed your paintings to your Mr. Audubon."

"What? But how could you? My father burned them."

"Not the ones you painted at Fort Union."

She gasped.

"I showed them to him and he says you got real talent. 'Course I don't need his say-so to know that. He offered you a job painting backgrounds for his next book, the one about animals."

She stared up in wonder; her breathing coming in short bursts.

He wagged a finger at her. "Don't you faint. I ain't finished. Audubon wants me to guide his party."

"Truly?"

"Sure does. And while I was waiting for that stone, I also showed your paintings to a magazine publisher, a feller called Benjamin Grove from *Harper's Review*. He'd like you to illustrate some articles on Indians for his magazine. So you got two jobs. You've come a long way for a lady who couldn't tell beaver from weasel a few months ago."

"And you have journeyed far from your Georgia hills as well."

His smile showed some flicker of pride. "Guess we've both got some miles beneath our moccasins. From now on we travel together."

She gazed up at him and to the clear blue sky beyond. The fog had lifted. The dreamy lassitude extinguished in a heartbeat. Her breathing caught. "They must not find you here."

He stood beside her now. "Who?"

She gazed at the house no longer shrouded in mist. Anyone looking out the breakfast room window…good God, it was breakfast time now.

"You have to go."

"Not without you."

She glanced at the house, which now threatened her newly found joy. How many servants looked from those panes of glass? "I'll come to you as soon as I can."

Lena tried to draw away but he captured her wrist.

"When?"

"This evening, after everyone has gone to bed."

"Where?"

"Outside the gates. I'll meet you at the Long Wharf."

"You'll come?"

"Yes, yes, only let me go or it will all be ruined."

He smiled and kissed her brow. "I've so much to tell you."

"Not now. If they find us, I'll never get away."

Lena swung up onto her horse unassisted and after casting one glance back, galloped away. Her heart pounded with the striking hooves.

He lived.

She returned her horse to the stables and entered the house, pausing as her mother called her from the breakfast room. Eleanor's mouth went dry as ash as she crossed the hall and stood in the immense arched doorway of the gilded dining room.

Her mother sat before a plate of strawberries and clotted cream, resting beside a cup of tea. Eleanor cast a glance to the window and her heart sank to see the serving table laden with food. Behind the table, the windows framed the cherry tree in perfect symmetry.

Chapter 25

Her mother waved to the empty seat beside her. "Come join me."

Eleanor hesitated as a creeping uncertainty inched up her spine.

"I am not hungry."

Her mother's voice changed tenor, no longer lilting, it now carried authority. "Sit down, Nora."

Eleanor crossed the room like a condemned prisoner. Had her mother seen? Would she sound the alarm? Eleanor did not know. Her mother protected her and supported her, but she also wanted her wed.

"Who is that man?"

Eleanor's face heated and she stared fixedly at the spotless white linen cloth before her.

"What man?" Her voice cracked. She was a miserable liar. Her ears tingled and she refused to glance up, knowing her eyes would betray her.

"Come, come, my girl. I saw you sitting beneath the cherry tree with a servant. Though I am gratified you are taking a natural interest once more, I must say I am disappointed in your choice. At the very least I will see him dismissed."

Her attention changed from the table to her mother's knowing gaze.

"It's him," she whispered.

Her mother leaned forward and also spoke in a whisper. "Whom?"

"My scout. He survived and has come for me."

Her mother straightened, as shock and concern flashed across her usually reserved face. Finally, her eyes narrowed as if to a threat. "What are you planning to do, run away with him?"

She did not deny it.

Her mother gasped and carefully set her napkin aside. "You will not marry a baron, but will elope with a savage. Have you lost your wits?"

"Mother, I love him."

Charlotte fanned the air in a dismissive gesture. Then leaned toward her daughter, casting a look of deadly seriousness.

"I am all for love. But not at the cost of your reputation. This is pure selfishness and will lead us all to no good."

"Am I not entitled to some measure of happiness?"

"Not at the expense of your family."

"Do not force me to choose, Mother, as you might not like my decision."

Her mother drew an indignant breath.

"Think what you are about, my girl. Your father will most assuredly pursue you. Do you wish the man dead?"

Lena's heart pounded in her throat as certainty froze her heart. Her father would follow, bringing his armies of men and this time he would kill Troy. He had resources beyond even her imagining. Troy believed they could evade him. Could they?

Doubt squeezed her belly.

She set her elbows upon the table, clasped her hands as if in prayer and lowered her head. Her shoulders shuddered with her sobs. Her mother leaned across the space between them.

"Now, there. No tears. I am not going to tell your father. I want what is best for you, after all. And what is best is to marry a titled gentleman and then seek your pleasures elsewhere. There is no reason that you should not continue your affair with this man until you tire of him. But after you fulfill your duties. If he is wise, he will wait."

Lena felt her dreams burning to ashes. Her insides ached. "But I want him for my husband."

Her mother dabbed Eleanor's eyes with a napkin. "Do not be ridiculous. You'd never be allowed in society again. And think of the shame your selfishness will heap upon our heads. We shall be forced to disown you. Do you understand? You will get nothing. Surely, he will understand what you stand to lose."

"He doesn't care about the money."

"Then I shall expect you to do the sensible thing."

"I don't care for it, either."

"One rarely does when they have an abundance."

"You know nothing of abundance, mother. Only money."

"They are one and the same, my darling."

Eleanor pitied her mother. Her world was so small and rigid. She was so convinced that this way was best, she was willing to force her unwilling daughter down the same path even as she sat as a living example that wealth could not buy happiness. Eleanor needed no further evidence. She would follow her heart.

"I will marry Troy."

"That is out of the question."

Eleanor drew away from her mother's embrace. "I know you want what is best for me."

"No more talk now. Have some tea."

The head butler appeared from the servant's door and waited for her mother to note his presence.

"Yes, Matthew?"

"I have notified the patrolmen, Madame. They are on their way."

"Thank you, Matthew. That is all."

Eleanor stared at her mother. "Patrolmen?"

"It's for the best."

Eleanor stared in astonishment. Her parents moved her through life as if she was a chess piece and she was only now becoming aware of their manipulations. She leveled her gaze on her mother, seeing a woman who valued power and propriety more than her daughter's happiness.

"You should thank me. If I catch him, he goes to prison. If your father catches him, he goes to his grave."

Lena leapt up as the desperate truth of her situation settled. If she ran, they would not clear the door before her mother sounded the alarm. They'd never escape. She stared in utter astonishment.

"Did you ever care what was best for me or was it always for your benefit?"

"There is no difference, darling. Come sit. You needn't witness the arrest."

"How I hate this world you foist upon me. Do not speak to me again of what is best for me." She straightened as the painful truth settled over her like a shroud. "I will send Troy away, to save him. But I will never marry."

Lena headed for the door, when her mother called out.

"Wait. You *must* marry."

Her mother rose from her chair, hands clasped tight about the napkin, wrinkling the carefully pressed linen.

She read the fear in her mother's voice and like her mother's daughter she paused to pounce. "Why?"

Her mother wrung her hands. "I cannot say."

"Then we are done."

"Wait. All right. The truth then." Her mother sank into a chair looking suddenly small, defeated. "I only meant to give you what was best."

Lena took a step closer. "This is not best."

Her mother fussed with her long string of pearls, running

them through her fingers like a rosary. Rarely did Eleanor see even this small a break in her mother's air of aloof confidence.

"You must marry abroad, so I can accompany you to England."

Suddenly, Eleanor was afraid. Her mother cast a glance toward the door and then reached for her brooch. With trembling fingers she unfastened the clip and then the row of shell buttons. Ivory fingers drew back the high linen collar to reveal a ghastly purple bruise encircling her neck.

Eleanor stared at the obvious thumbprints in horror as her hand lifted to her own throat.

"He beats me," said her mother.

Eleanor's breath came in jagged little gasps.

"Never where the marks might be seen. On more than one occasion I thought he would kill me."

Denial sprung to Eleanor's lips and then she remembered her mother's limping and the days she took to her bed. She recalled how infrequently her parents were together and how often her mother visited her sister in Boston.

"You see now why I must get away from him. Eleanor, if you marry, I will have a valid reason to leave. I will see to your wedding and then your children. God willing, he will never lay a hand upon me again."

Faced with this revelation, Eleanor faltered. "I—I must speak with Troy. You must come with us."

Her mother refastened her buttons. "And do what? Live in a teepee in the woods? I am the daughter of Merriweather Pace Barrington. I deserve better."

"Then you must divorce him."

Her mother stood with rigid outrage. "I will do no such thing. He shall not send me packing like some upstairs maid. I deserve better for what I have endured. I shall outlive him— I'll not be denied that pleasure."

"But you said he would kill you."

"No scandal will touch this family while I am mistress here."

Eleanor heard the click of his boot heels as the man in question strode in their direction across polished oak. She glanced up at her father.

From the red of his face and the twisted expression on his lips, it was evident he had heard enough of their conversation to discover his wife's betrayal.

His voice growled between gritted teeth as he stalked Charlotte. "Divorce? I'll see you dead first."

She staggered backward as her face paled. She placed herself behind the solid mahogany chair, giving that small measure of distance between them as her husband loomed, fists balled at his sides.

Her father snatched the chair from before his wife. She shrieked and darted away as he hurled the chair at her with all his might. Charlotte threw herself to the hand-hooked carpet as the gilded frame sailed over her head, smashing through the huge, hung windows. Glass exploded in all directions, raining down upon the polished oak flooring.

Charlotte crawled upon the jagged shards. Blood streaked the flooring as her husband lifted a silver serving platter of sausages and hurled them at his wife. The tray clanged off her temple as links scattered upon the glass.

Eleanor tugged at her father's arm in a vain effort to stop him. He lifted a hand and pushed her. She fell backwards over her chair, landing hard upon the carpet.

Two maids ran in from the kitchen and stopped, transfixed at the unfolding scene. A footman appeared and tried to assist Charlotte to her feet only to be punched in the face by her husband.

"Out!" He bellowed, sending maids and footmen scurrying.

He grasped his wife's arm and dragged her to her feet, beginning a violent shaking which sent Charlotte flailing like a rag doll.

Eleanor reached him again, clasping her father's arm with both of hers. He released one hand from his wife and slapped his daughter across the cheek, sending her reeling. Her ears rang as she fell upon the carpet.

He towered over Eleanor, his wife momentarily forgotten.

She scrambled beneath the huge mahogany table, but not so far as to avoid a boot to her hindquarters that sent her sprawling across the center beam. She turned to watch him descend upon his wife, taking time to push his sleeves up from his balled fists.

Eleanor emerged from the other side of the table by the fireplace as the sickening thud of fists striking flesh reached her. Lifting the cold metal of the cast-iron poker, she raced to her mother's defense and swung the weapon. The blow landed across his broad shoulders.

He cried out and staggered aside, but did not fall. His murderous eye turned on Eleanor. Behind her, Charlotte cowered, clutching a bloody cheek.

Eleanor raised the poker before her in a position of defense. Her father paused and then turned to the serving table to select his weapons. As he glanced away, Eleanor tried unsuccessfully to drag her mother to her feet as seconds ticked by and their chance of flight vanished.

Eleanor raised the poker, shielding her mother, and stood to face him. He came holding a carving knife in one hand and a meat fork in the other as if he meant to slice her like a ham.

"I'll cut off your head, Charlotte."

She turned to her husband. "If you kill me, they will hang you, John."

He slashed with the knife and Eleanor's throat went dry. She stared at the spitting madman her father had become.

He slashed again. She lifted the poker and the blade struck, shocking her at the numbing vibration transmitted through her hand and up her arm at the ringing contact.

Her mother found her voice and shouted, "Murder! Help us!"

A crashing sound brought all eyes toward the windows. What Eleanor saw made her heart leap with hope.

Chapter 26

The wooden remains of the window sashing splintered as Troy dove through the gap, rolling to his feet like a crouching cat preparing to spring.

Her father faced this new threat with a roar of recognition.

"You!"

Troy smiled, preparing for battle.

John charged like a wounded bull, stabbing with the vicious carving knife. Troy sidestepped and tipped a platter of poached eggs upon the man as he fell. The slimy mixture spattered John's black coat as he slid on the broken glass. He caught himself on the serving table, releasing the carving fork to regain his equilibrium.

Troy sprang forward as her father threw the large silver carafe. Scalding coffee spewed through the air. Troy shielded his face as the hot liquid struck his head and arms. In that instant, John lunged.

"Troy!" cried Eleanor.

Somehow Troy managed to grasp his foe's wrist as the two swung around in the sweeping dance of battle.

The knife disappeared between them as John lunged and Troy jerked. The men stood, locked in each other's deadly embrace, as Eleanor bit her lip and tasted blood. She rushed forward as Troy stepped back, gripping the wrist holding the knife. With a twist of his arm, her father released the blade. The shining steel stuck, point first, in the polished wood floor vibrating wildly. Eleanor scooped up the blade.

John swung at Troy with his free arm. Troy easily dodged the blow, still gripping his opponent's wrist, then landed one of his own to her father's jaw. The sickening crack made Eleanor wince.

Her father collapsed to the carpet.

Silence. Lena heard the ticking of the clock above the mantel and the pounding of her own heart. Next came a whimper from her mother.

Troy faced the herd of servants now huddled in the swinging door.

Eleanor scrambled to her mother. "Get our physician."

A woman ran from the room. The others stood as wide-eyed as owls.

Troy stepped over his bested opponent and knelt before Charlotte.

"Mother, this is Troy."

Charlotte held her palm pressed to the side of her face as she stared out at them in a daze.

Troy touched her wrist. "Let's have a look."

Her mother moved her hand, revealing her right eye completely swollen shut, the tissue an angry violet.

"I can't see," she whispered.

"Help me get her to the drawing room," said Eleanor.

Troy stooped, sliding a hand behind Charlotte's back, gently lifted her mother into his arms. Lena led the way to the chaise lounge where Troy laid her mother.

"I'll be back," he said, leaving her with a wide-eyed parlor maid.

Eleanor turned to the woman.

"Fetch some chipped ice, Nelly."

The maid bobbed a curtsey and darted away.

Charlotte groaned and pressed her hand over her swelling eye. Troy returned a moment later.

"Tied him to that table the size of a keelboat."

"My father?" she asked.

He nodded. "Still out cold."

Charlotte's voice shook with emotion. "He meant to kill us both. You see now why I never told you."

Eleanor brushed back a strand of her mother's fading blond hair. Her insides pitched like a ship in rough seas. The bedrock upon which her world stood now seemed as insubstantial as sand. She was the daughter of opulent wealth and perfect breeding. Her father was a powerful man and one of the richest men in the country. Her mother was the picture of the social elite. The best of New York society yearned for an invitation from Charlotte Hart.

All a lie.

Here was her real mother, battered and broken, while her father used his power to bully and bruise.

"You should have told me."

A tear trickled from Charlotte's undamaged eye. "I wanted to, so often. But I was so ashamed."

Troy sat silent in a chair beside the settee. Eleanor met his gaze.

"Can she come with us?" she asked.

Without the slightest hesitation, he nodded.

Eleanor gripped her mother's shoulders. "Come away with us. I'll see he never touches you again."

"Where could I go that he could not follow?"

"You shall get a divorce."

Her mother gasped. "Don't speak of that again. I will never do no such thing."

Nelly returned with the ice wrapped in a clean towel. Charlotte winced as she placed the cloth upon her battered face.

"The patrolmen are here at your request, mistress," she said.

Charlotte looked horrified.

"Thank you, Nelly. Ask them to wait in the entrance for us," said Eleanor.

Charlotte waited until Nelly left the room.

"What shall I do? I can't have them see me like this and John is—well, indisposed."

"Got here mighty quick," said Troy.

Eleanor confirmed his obvious suspicion. "They were called to arrest you."

He nodded. "Should have figured."

"Mother, I am leaving with Troy. Before I go I will tell the patrolmen that father attacked me and seek his arrest. You should do the same."

Her mother set her mouth in a stubborn line.

"He'll kill you the next time," said Eleanor.

"The scandal," she whispered.

"Mother, you are a strong woman with wealth of your own. Leave him."

Her mother cried.

"Mother, please."

"I'm afraid."

Eleanor's eyes narrowed. "Of Father or of the scandal?"

"Scandal," whispered Charlotte.

"Mother, you set the standard for all New York society. If you get a divorce, others will, too."

Some of her mother's confidence returned. She was considering it. Then her shoulders slumped and she fell back to the couch. "John would never agree. He will fight me tooth and nail."

"Not if you have him arrested. A good attorney and the threat of a long and scandalous court trial should rather give you the upper hand."

Her mother bit her lower lip.

"Eleanor, I have taught you a thing or two, haven't I?"

She smiled as her stomach twisted at the sight of her mother's bruised face.

"You must press charges. Otherwise you lose your advantage."

Charlotte lifted a hand to her mouth. "Great heavens, what a conundrum. I need my solicitor. Call Mrs. Beardsley and have her send for Kingsley."

Before Eleanor could tug the velvet cord, a knock came at the door. Mrs. Beardsley barely had the doors open when two patrolmen rushed, each clutching a raised baton.

"That's him," cried the younger officer, pointing his club at Troy.

The older patrolman brandished his stick. "You're under arrest for attacking John Hart. Hands behind your back, now."

Troy curled, preparing to defend himself.

Charlotte swung her legs to the floor, regaining her confidence with her authority.

"Just one moment. This man saved my life."

The young patrolman paid her no mind as he circled Troy, who rose like a grizzly to face his attacker.

The second constable turned to Mrs. Hart.

"Your husband says this scoundrel's a burglar who attacked the three of you while you were at breakfast."

"He did not!" cried Eleanor.

John charged into the room, red-faced, his swollen nose now a shocking purple. He panted like a dog through his wide pink mouth. "That's him! What are you waiting for?"

"Mother," cried Eleanor, "tell them what happened."

Charlotte hesitated.

"I've already told them," growled Hart.

The older officer seemed uncertain as he looked from father to daughter. "See here," he said.

The younger man made a lunge with his baton. Troy grasped the weapon and pulled, sending the patrolman sprawling on the carpet empty-handed. Now Troy gripped the club.

The second man charged and Eleanor stuck out her foot, sending him to the carpet as well.

"Arrest him," shouted Hart.

Her father seemed content to bark orders and did not approach Troy himself.

"Mother?" said Eleanor. When she said nothing, Eleanor turned to the housekeeper. "Mrs. Beardsley, you saw what happened."

The housekeeper reddened. "Not all. I can't say for certain what happened."

The woman was a terrible liar, looking to the ceiling as she spoke, and then to her master, who nodded.

Eleanor understood.

"Did he threaten your position if you told the truth?"

One patrolman regained his feet and drew his revolver, leveling the weapon at Troy's heart.

"He didn't do it," insisted Eleanor.

Hart took a menacing step in her direction and she darted behind the second patrolman.

Her father pointed at her mother. "Look at my wife's face."

The man did, scowling at the damning evidence.

"And my nose. Look at my nose! The man could have killed us all." Seeing Troy seemingly subdued by the revolver, Hart took a step in his direction. "You'll hang for this, Price."

Eleanor knelt beside her mother resting a hand upon her knee. "Mother. I am leaving with Troy. You shall be alone with him when these men leave."

Charlotte's uninjured eye widened and she winced.

Her husband came to stand beside the settee, menacing her with his presence. "Charlotte, this is best for all concerned."

The second patrolman aimed his revolver at Troy as well. Eleanor felt herself losing him all over again. She took a step in her love's direction only to be brought to an abrupt halt by her father. He jerked her back and she kicked him in the shin with all her might. He wobbled, but maintained his grip to deliver a clout to the head that set her ears ringing as she dropped to her knees.

Momentarily distracted by her cry, the patrolmen glanced her way. Troy seized the barrels of both revolvers, thrust them to the floor and twisted. One shot sounded. The smell of gunpowder filled the air.

"Enough!" cried Charlotte.

Troy paused as her mother rose from the settee. "This man did nothing more than—"

John swung at his wife as Eleanor threw herself on his arm diverting the blow.

"Liar." Hart shook Eleanor off and lunged at his wife who toppled backward over the settee.

The men abandoned Troy in favor of subduing Hart. The task proved less of a challenge. With one tackle, her father fell to the settee with a patrolman sprawled upon his chest. In a moment the two men had secured his arms.

"Let go. This is my home. I'll have your jobs."

Troy stepped beside the two men.

"See why I tied him up?"

The older patrolman motioned his head in Charlotte's direction. "He did this?"

Troy nodded.

The news so stunned the younger officer that he lost his grip on her father's arm and he had a devil of a time recapturing it.

"Don't make me thump you," said the young man.

"You aren't thumping anyone, Robert," said his senior. "This is John Hart. I'm not arresting John Hart."

Eleanor stiffened. "You most certainly are. He blackened my mother's eye. You witnessed him striking me."

The two men exchanged looks of dread.

The senior man's voice pleaded. "Miss, we can't arrest John Hart."

Eleanor glared. "I will press charges and you are both my witnesses."

"Eleanor," bellowed her father. "You would betray your own flesh and blood?"

"Is that not what you have done to me?" she asked.

He glanced away then his gaze flashed back. "I acted in your best interest."

Eleanor fingered her bruised cheek. "Yours, rather."

"Nora, I forbid it," said Charlotte.

"We need our captain," said the patrolman.

Her husband struggled against the grip of the younger men. "You have no right to hold me."

"We do if she'll bear witness," said one patrolman.

"Hush now," said the other.

"This is outrageous," said Hart.

Troy cocked a pistol. The distinctive click drew the attention of every person in the room.

Chapter 27

Troy leveled the pistol at her father, who instantly ceased his struggles with the patrolmen to face this new threat. Instead of protests and bluster, he trembled. Sweat beaded on his upper lip.

"He means to kill me. You must protect me." He drew back in an awkward attempt to drag the two patrolmen before him while they still clasped his arms.

"Lena, you got a room you can lock up?"

"Several."

"Pick one, 'cause if I have to listen to another word, I'm likely to shoot your pa."

Eleanor lifted a brow at the patrolmen, who exchanged confused looks.

"Gentlemen?" she said and motioned toward the door.

The older one shrugged. "Can't fault us if we're at gunpoint. Lead the way, miss."

She stepped from the room and waited as Troy motioned with the barrel of a revolver for the men to follow. In a few minutes they had secured her father in the wine cellar where he howled like a madman.

Troy took possession of the key and then returned the revolvers to the patrolman. "You two best wait outside for your captain."

The men hurried up the stairs, bumping into each other in their rush to vacate the premises.

"Eleanor!" bellowed her father. "Release me this instant."

She faced him. "No, Father. I think that is just where you belong."

He threw himself against the iron bars he'd installed to keep his thieving servants out of his supplies. The hinges shuddered, but held. She turned away from the sound that sent a chill up her spine. At the top of the stairs she glanced back at the spitting, frothing man that was her father.

"Eleanor!" he shouted. "I forbid you to go with this savage."

Her eyes narrowed as fury erupted from within her.

"The only savage here," she said, "is you."

With that, she lifted her skirts and ascended to the upper floors, leaving her father to throw himself against the iron bars like the animal she now knew him to be.

Chief Constable Martin listened to the servants, Charlotte and Eleanor, before turning to Troy.

"So you admit to striking Mr. Hart?"

"I tried to disarm him but he was against it."

"So you hit him?"

Eleanor rose to her feet, anger making her bristle. "What is the matter with you? We have all told you what happened. If not for Mr. Price, my mother and I might both be dead. He saved us."

"He broke into your house, assaulted Mr. Hart and tied him to the table."

Her mother set aside her cold compress. She motioned to her footman. "Send for Mr. Howard March. Tell him I am in need of his immediate assistance."

Martin paled at the mention of his superior, then seemed to gather his courage and faced her mother. "A prominent man has been attacked in his own home. Someone is to blame."

"Mr. Martin, please recall that it is I who supports the patrolman's benevolent society, not my venerable husband."

Martin's forehead gleamed with perspiration. "I can't arrest Mr. Hart—I'll lose my job."

"Good heavens, I don't want him arrested," said Charlotte. "Only temporarily subdued."

"Mother!" cried Eleanor. "Of course you do."

Charlotte turned to her daughter. "Now you listen to me, my girl. It is bad enough for the servants to gossip. I won't have the whole town knowing my business."

"Well you can't keep the man locked in his own cellar," said Martin.

Charlotte tapped her index finger to her lips as she thought. "How long do I have to file charges?" she asked.

"Usually we just arrest them when we learn about a crime."

"Not in this case. I want you to interview my daughter, Mr. Price and my staff in my presence. Then I want a copy of all reports brought by courier to my sister's residence in Boston. I'll be staying there."

"I can't do that."

"I see. Then you have grown weary of your work as constable? Perhaps you do not need favorable references to pursue this new opportunity?" She touched a finger to her pointed chin, thoughtfully. "We shall wait for Mr. March and see what he makes of it. I'm certain he will concur with me."

The man rubbed his neck as if feeling the noose tighten. Eleanor admired her mother's use of connections. By summoning the Chief Constable of Newport as if he were an upstairs maid, she had achieved her purpose. This underling was well and truly cowed.

"Why don't we just arrest Mr. Price?" said the constable, who no longer sounded at all sure of himself.

"And take my rescuer off to prison? I think not." How her mother managed to look haughty with one eye completely swollen shut was beyond Lena. "I will assume responsibility for this man until you finish your investigation. Should you find need to question him further, contact my solicitor, Mr. Kingsley. Now if you will kindly wait across the hall in the dining room, I shall assemble my staff."

Thus dismissed, the man nonetheless continued to linger a moment, seemed on the verge of further discourse and then reconsidered.

"Yes, Mrs. Hart." His bow held the stiffness of a man ill at ease with his situation.

"Fetch him some tea," her mother said, waving a hand at the footman standing guard by the door. "Then bring 'round Mrs. Beardsley."

When the housekeeper appeared, Charlotte rallied from the settee once more.

"Mrs. Beardsley, please gather all the servants who witnessed the altercation in the dining room. I wish a word."

Beardsley's eyes widened and her face turned a bright shade of pink. "Yes, madam."

"I expect the constable will want to hear the truth this time."

"Yes, madam. It's just that—well, Mr. Hart, he told us that he'd have our jobs if we said a word."

Charlotte's eyes narrowed.

"Tell them that I shall add a silver dollar to their month's wage and guarantee employment to each man and woman who tells Constable Martin the truth."

"Yes, madam."

"I also require a coach prepared. I am leaving for Boston today. Please make the arrangements. I shall not sleep under his roof one more night."

"Yes, Mrs. Hart."

She turned to her daughter. "Gather what you need. You will accompany me."

Eleanor turned to Troy. He stood silent waiting for her.

"No, Mother. I go with him, if he will still have me."

Charlotte cast her withering gaze upon Troy. "Why

wouldn't he? Through you, he'll become richer than Midas. Even without your father's inheritance, which I seriously doubt, you are still my heir and that amounts to a fortune."

"Troy is not interested in my money."

Charlotte laughed, turning her swollen face into a grotesque mask. Then she leveled her one useful eye on Troy.

"You do not deserve her."

He nodded. "True enough. But neither do you."

Charlotte gasped. "How dare you?"

Lena scowled. "Mother."

"He is beneath you."

Troy wisely remained mute.

"Mother, he will be my husband. You can't stop me with threats or bribes," said Eleanor.

She waited while her mother mulled this over.

At last she nodded her understanding. "Are you certain, Nora? Even I will not be able to orchestrate your readmittance into society if you wed this man."

"I don't care about society or their petty rules. I have no more use for them."

Her mother looked doubtful.

"There is more to the world than New York and Newport, Mother."

She scoffed. "Yes—but we shall never see London now."

Lena clasped her mother's hand, feeling the warmth and inhaling the familiar scent of gardenias. "He is my world."

"Oh, Nora. Don't ever give a man your heart. They are such clumsy, thoughtless creatures."

Eleanor looked at Troy, whose eyes twinkled with mischief.

"Goodbye, Mother," said Eleanor and kissed her cheek

Charlotte glared at Troy. "You shan't have a nickel from me, my boy. Do you understand?"

Troy moved to stand beside Eleanor, his hand proprietary upon her lower back.

"Always managed without it. Besides, Lena and me got jobs waiting on the Missouri."

Her mother paled. "Jobs! You cannot mean to force your wife to work."

"I've seen what happens to folks with no work. You and your husband are the laziest, most useless folks on God's green earth. I wouldn't trade a hair on Lena's head for the whole lot of you."

"Harts do not work. It is simply not done."

"She's a painter, a damned good one, plus she'll be a Price soon enough and free of the whole superior lot of you."

"Barbarian."

"I take that for a compliment." He spoke to Eleanor now. "Best be going before they sic the dogs on me."

"I'll just get a few things."

Troy rolled his eyes. "I ain't got all day."

"Nora, you can't mean to go with him now? Come to Boston. Your aunt and I will give you a proper wedding."

Eleanor glanced at Troy who made a face. "Sounds awful." She giggled.

"We will visit before heading west."

Charlotte glared at Troy.

"I'll wait outside, but if you're not out in twenty minutes, I'll kick in the front door." He headed out leaving Charlotte and Eleanor alone.

"You are making a dreadful mistake."

Eleanor sighed and nodded. "I shall hope that my mistakes prove less disastrous than yours."

Charlotte sighed and returned the ice to her eye.

"Will Father follow us?"

Her mother thought for a moment. "I am going to offer your father a bargain. He and I will keep separate residences henceforward. In return I will not press charges. I believe I can convince him to leave you in peace."

"No divorce."

"Certainly not."

"What if he refuses?"

"Oh, he won't. Your father loathes a scandal."

"Will you be all right?"

"Nora, you know my connections. Your father will not wish to jeopardize them. He'll allow it."

"Then why did you stay with him all this time?"

"I didn't really. I stayed here and he worked in New York. We rarely see each other even when we're living in the same house. I don't care who he sees and he allows me the same freedom. It was the perfect match."

Eleanor felt a well of pity for her mother and the life she had chosen.

"In any case, I shall just formalize our understanding. With luck, I'll not see him again."

"The perfect match," said Eleanor.

Her mother suddenly looked small and fragile.

"I'll miss you, mother."

Charlotte hugged her daughter. "I will see that he does not follow. I shall insist that Constable Martin leave him in the cellar until after I vacate the premises and that will take me the rest of the day. I shall not go before I have his name on a signed contract. But, Nora, he shall certainly disown you."

Eleanor kissed her mother's cheek. "Farewell."

"Wait. I did not say *I* would disown you. When you reach New York, send word. I'll see funds released to you. But they shall be in *your* name. If you are to ruin yourself, at least you won't starve."

"Thank you, Mama."

Charlotte lowered her compress to hug her daughter. "I shall miss you, Nora. Write to me soon."

"Yes, Mama."

She left the room, hurrying upstairs to gather the pieces of her old life she could not yet abandon and to don a heavy woolen cloak. She exited the grand entrance holding only a reticule, but trailed by two footmen carrying her bags.

Troy drew his hat from his head. "I don't have a mule here, Lena."

"We don't need them."

She turned to the footmen, who loaded the bags into the waiting carriage and tied Scheherazade to the back. Beside the mare stood a black Arabian gelding. Troy lifted his brow.

"A wedding gift from your bride," she said.

The men withdrew.

He glanced about. "You gonna take a carriage all the way to New York?"

Lena bounced on her toes with excitement. "Certainly not. There is a steamer at 4:00 p.m. today."

The footman held open the door and Eleanor swept inside, settling in as Troy crawled in beside her. The door closed and a moment later the wheels ground on the gravel as they rolled past the great lawn before her parents' palatial summer home. Up until this moment, it had been her home as well.

Uncertainty fluttered within her.

"It's a lot to give up," Troy said.

She stared into his confident eyes.

"I'll love you all my life, Lena. As for the rest, this world is safer than the way we'll make together."

She fingered her throbbing cheek unsure that was true. Certainty swelled anew. She belonged with Troy.

"I shan't miss it." She snuggled against him as they cleared the wrought-iron gates. Now he hesitated.

"I'll never be able to give you anything so grand."

She smiled reassurance to him as she captured his hands.

"You already have. Your love is more grand that all this finery." Her hand swept toward the house. "This is a trap. A lovely gilded cage full of luxury and emptiness. I am the luckiest woman in the world. Soon I'll be Lena Price."

He gave her a dazzling smile and she threw herself into his arms for a kiss filled with promise and longing.

Warm autumn sunshine greeted her like a promise as they rolled down Bellevue Street past the manicured lawns and neatly trimmed hedges.

Freedom filled her lungs.

"What about your paints?" asked Troy.

"I've packed them."

Troy rolled his eyes.

"What?" she asked.

"I'm afraid we'll sink the boat."

She laughed. "Are you insinuating that I do not know how to pack?"

"I seen the folderol you consider essentials, when you don't but need one change of clothes and a proper coat."

She grinned at him. "A woman needs a few more items than that, I'm afraid."

"No—I'm afraid." He gave her a look of mock horror.

She pressed a hand over her heart in a gesture meant to imitate grave offense. "Do you want me to marry you dressed in buckskin?"

"Buck naked would be better."

Her cheeks flamed. "Mr. Price!"

His gaze radiated desire. "I've missed you, Lena."

The heat generated by his words threatened to set her aflame.

"I want to love you again."

"We are not yet wed."

"Pick a church then."

Eleanor pressed a finger to her mole and thought. "I believe the steamboat captain can perform that service."

Eleanor stared down at the simple gray dress and smiled. As a girl she had pictured her wedding day. Her mind had swathed her in ivory silk for a ceremony at Trinity Church in New York surrounded by society's premier citizens. What a relief to never have to face such a charade.

"Perhaps this dress is just right for a bride."

He grinned. "I prefer what's underneath."

She laughed.

They reached the docks of Newport and purchased two tickets for the *Washington*. The steamer already waited there with two huge paddlewheels freshly painted and the dual boilers gleaming copper bright. She arranged a cabin and spoke to the captain, who agreed to marry them as soon as they'd cleared the bay. She found herself nearly desperate to be alone with Troy and waited impatiently for the call to board. As she stood upon the rail, she recalled how Troy had rescued them.

"How did you know to come to our aid?" she asked.

"Figured the chair flying out the window weren't an everyday occurrence 'round here."

She shook her head. "But the window is at least ten feet from the ground and you dived through."

"A trick of the Sioux. They leap on an enemy from horseback. Gives them an advantage."

Eleanor smiled at Troy. "You certainly are a knight to rescue two damsels in distress."

"One particular damsel looked to be wielding a poker with some degree of skill."

She laughed at that. "Well, I am certain my fencing master would be pleased to hear it."

"Lena, do you want to wait to get hitched?"

"For what?"

"For your ma and family. I can wait, if you've a mind to."

She stared up at his earnest face.

"Well, I can't," she said.

He released a breath. "Thank God."

She laughed and he leaned in to kiss her, but she stepped away. "If you kiss me, I'm afraid I shall make quite a fool of myself."

He pressed his lips in a grim line as if in pain and then nodded his agreement.

At last the ropes were thrown clear and the great engines engaged. Soon water streamed off the wheels as the steamer churned into the bay.

A porter arrived.

"Captain is ready for you on the bridge, Miss Hart."

Troy offered his elbow and they followed their guide. Captain Richards bowed to Eleanor and shook Troy's hand. His brown mustache curled up in a smile.

"Quite an honor for me, Miss Hart," he said. "Let's get started then. If you'll just stand over here. I've asked two of my officers to stand as witnesses."

They moved into position and the captain began the ceremony with New England economy.

He finished in record time.

"Bring the bottle," he called to his officer.

A cork popped and champagne flowed into fluted glasses.

Richards passed glasses to Eleanor and Troy and then clasped one himself. "Long life and many children."

After the toast, the captain led them out of the wind, to the bridge to sign the marriage license.

Eleanor wrote her name in elaborate script and then watched Troy hesitate over the document.

"What is it?"

"My signature isn't so grand. I'm afraid to spoil the page."

Eleanor scowled. "If you don't sign, then we are not wed. So write your name so we can—" she stared at the captain "—attend to other matters."

At that reminder Troy bent over the certificate and wrote his name in a quick, tight script.

The captain presented him with the license.

"Best of luck to you both," he said. There was an awkward pause. "Well, we'll see you at dinner then."

"Don't count on it," said Troy, and Eleanor blushed to the roots of her hair.

"Thank you so much, Captain," she managed.

Then Eleanor grasped Troy's hand and walked with a dignity she could barely maintain until they reached the bottom of the stairs. Then she hoisted the room key. Troy snatched it and her hand and then ran her down the narrow halls, past startled passengers. He halted at room eleven.

She swayed, breathless, as Troy turned the key in the lock and threw open the door.

"We are married," she whispered.

He stroked her cheek. "I've been married to you in my heart for months."

She smiled and waited. He motioned his head toward the open door, but she did not move.

"What is it?" he asked.

"You are supposed to carry me across."

With a wicked grin and a wild whoop, he threw her over his shoulder, jarring the wind from her lungs.

She spied a blur of blue carpet as he spun her about and then tossed her upon the mattress. She cried out as she landed with a bounce and had time only to brace herself as he landed beside her.

"Well built," he said and gave her a devilish smile.

Chapter 28

Lena fumbled with the buttons of Troy's coarse woolen shirt, missing how easily his buckskin swept off with but a single tug. He appeared to address the same frustration as he sighed heavily, struggling with the tiny hook and eyes that ran the full length of her bodice.

"Let me," she said.

For the next several moments clothing fell to the floor, thrown in wild disarray. At last she wore only her shift and stockings. The frantic motion ceased and both stood motionless as stone.

He grasped the hem of her shift as his gaze locked to hers. She lifted her arms and he swept the sheath away.

The veil fell and she stood, chin bowed. This gave her an excellent view of his readiness for her. She lifted a hand and stroked the velvet of his stomach and watched him twitch as if her touch brought pain. Her breathing caught as she noted the angry red scar that crossed from his shoulder to hip, the slashing cut from her father's sword.

"I am so sorry." She lifted her gaze to catch his and found his jaw set.

He lifted his hand and swept one finger over the place where she knew the crescent-shaped scar of the sword hilt marked her swollen cheek.

"That's in the past. Leave it there and think of now."

His velvet touch descended to her lip, brushing along the surface and then stroking the mole beneath.

"I'm burning for you, Lena."

How different this felt than their first encounter. The uncertainty was gone along with the sense of impending doom. In all these long months, she thought she'd never hear his voice or feel his touch again. A tear fell from her eye and he trapped it against her cheek with his warm palm.

"I've missed you so," he whispered.

"Your return answers all my prayers."

His kiss burned with tender longing. She clutched his neck and dragged him to her, pressing her nakedness flush against him. The heat and sensual texture of his skin wrenched a moan from deep within her.

The sound seemed to trigger an instant response in him. He had her off her feet and upon the bed in a wink, settling himself upon her. She arched to meet him, as he stroked her breasts, increasing the stabbing need tenfold. Her fingers raked his back, urging him on.

"Not so fast," he whispered.

But she was past waiting. Her need consumed her.

"I cannot wait."

He stared at her as if unsure. What he saw launched him into motion. Roughly he parted her legs and found access, groaning as he discovered the silken moisture he drew from her. Sliding forward he sank himself fully into her passage. There was no pain this time, only a rolling, building pleasure. She grasped his buttock and lifted, fusing them together. He pressed her to the bed and bucked, not sparing her the full measure of his desire.

Each hard stroke hit like the surf upon the sea cliffs, pushing her closer to the pleasure she knew awaited. The speed with which she reached her release startled, leaping upon her like a lion from the grass. A scream of ecstasy merged with his sharp cry of release. They fell replete onto the thick comforter. Her body shuddered as waves of pleasure echoed outward from the place where their bodies still merged.

The lethargy that deadened her limbs pressed her heavily into the covers, as his rasping breath fanned her cheek.

"I've never known the like."

"We are a matched team, like carriage horses."

He gave a laugh. "Never seen a more ill-matched pair."

"That's only on the outside. You have to look deeper to see we are the same."

He squeezed her tight and kissed her, relaying the depth of his joy. He drew back to rest his forehead to hers.

"A perfect match," he said.

She curled with him beneath the covers, content for the first time in her life.

Eleanor entered the sitting room of the brownstone that had been their home since arriving in New York three months ago. Her maid trailed behind her as she noted Mr. Audubon just rising from their meeting. Audubon gave a little bow at her appearance.

"Bring those to the bedroom, Brenda," she said, then turned to meet her guest.

Troy walked Audubon to the door and shook his hand. "I'm sure that Black Feather will be pleased to accompany us."

"Wonderful. Until tomorrow, Mr. Price. I look forward to our journey." Audubon nodded at her. "And to working with you, Mrs. Price."

"Good day, Sir."

She watched him go, knowing that the next time she saw him they would be aboard the steamer *Yellow Stone*, back where it all began.

The door closed and her husband led her to the chair before the hearth. Her husband. How she loved to think of him thus.

He drew her down into his lap. She curled against him like a kitten.

"Where have you been all morning? I woke and you were gone."

"I was at the dressmaker."

He slapped his forehead. "If there is one place in the world you do not need to visit, it's the dressmaker."

She pressed a hand to her hips. "I disagree."

"You'll never wear all the duds your mother sent."

"I needed to order something new."

He looked troubled. "Lena, I can't buy you what you're accustomed to. You have to understand and do with less."

She stood and called for the maid. "Bring the large box, Bridget."

The woman appeared a moment later.

"Take it out, Brenda."

The maid lifted the dress clear and held it for his inspection.

Troy stood and studied the garment then tugged at the waist. "It's too big. You know I hate them corsets, but this will hang on you like a sack."

She giggled. The maid blushed and Troy stared from one to the other. "Put it away, Brenda."

The maid clasped the dress and hurried out.

Eleanor grasped her husband's face in her hands, drawing his attention away from the dress. "Troy, I am with child. We are to be parents."

His eyes rounded as he drew in a great gasp. Then he clasped her shoulders. "You sure?"

She nodded.

He swept her off her feet, whirling her about the room. Suddenly remembering himself, he froze and eased her down to the floor as gently as if he carried an egg. His hand settled upon her waist as his concerned gaze searched for changes.

She gave him a disgruntled look. "I am not *that* fragile."

"You've always looked it." His hands slid to her hips.

"Well, I am not and neither are you. Any man who can face a herd of stampeding buffalo certainly should not blanch at becoming a father."

He rubbed his neck in a familiar gesture of worry. "It ain't the same. Out there I have my rifle and my right arm. But this…" Some dark thought struck and his hand stilled. "I don't want anything to happen to you."

"Dear husband, something has already happened to me. And as a result, I am to be a mother and you a father."

He rested his forehead upon hers and pulled her close. His hands stilled when they reached her lower back. He pulled away, scowling down fiercely at her. "I want you out of that damned corset!"

Her laughter brought a smile to his lips.

"Yes, darling. You will finally have me out of my corsets."

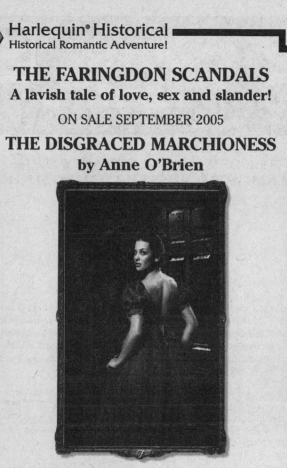

A BRAND-NEW BOOK IN
THE DE WARENNE DYNASTY SERIES
BY *NEW YORK TIMES* BESTSELLING AUTHOR

BRENDA JOYCE

On the evening of her first masquerade, shy Elizabeth Anne
Fitzgerald is stunned by Tyrell de Warenne's whispered suggestion
of a midnight rendezvous in the gardens. Lizzie has secretly
worshiped the unattainable lord for years. When fortune
takes a maddening turn, she is prevented from meeting Tyrell.
But Lizzie has not seen the last of him....

Tyrell de Warenne is shocked when, two years later, Lizzie
arrives on his doorstep with a child she claims is his. He
remembers her well—and knows that he could not possibly
be the father. Is Elizabeth Anne Fitzgerald a woman of
experience, or the gentle innocent she seems?

The MASQUERADE

"A powerhouse of emotion and sensuality."—*Romantic Times*

*Available the first week of September 2005
wherever paperbacks are sold!*

www.MIRABooks.com

MBJ2209